Praise for J.L. Bourne's
page-turning novels of
the zombie apocalypse

DAY BY DAY
ARMAGEDDON

"There is zombie fiction and then there is crawl-out-of-the-grave-and-drag-you-to-hell zombie fiction. *Day by Day Armageddon* is hands-down the best zombie book I have ever read. *Dawn of the Dead* meets *28 Days Later* doesn't even come close to describing how fantastic this thriller is. It is so real, so terrifying, and so well written that I slept with not one but two loaded Glocks under my pillow for weeks afterward. J.L. Bourne is the new king of hardcore zombie action!"

> —Brad Thor, #1 *New York Times* bestselling author

"A dramatic spin on the zombie story. It has depth, a heart, and compelling characters."

> —Jonathan Maberry, Bram Stoker Award–winning author of
> *Patient Zero*

Also by J.L. Bourne

Tomorrow War

Day by Day Armageddon: Shattered Hourglass

Day by Day Armageddon: Beyond Exile

Day by Day Armageddon

Day by Day Armageddon

Ghost Run

J.L. Bourne

G

GALLERY BOOKS

New York   London   Toronto   Sydney   New Delhi

Gallery Books
An Imprint of Simon & Schuster, Inc.
1230 Avenue of the Americas
New York, NY 10020

First Gallery Books trade paperback edition July 2016

GALLERY BOOKS and colophon are registered trademarks of Simon & Schuster, Inc.

For information about special discounts for bulk purchases, please contact Simon & Schuster Special Sales at 1-866-506-1949 or business@simonandschuster.com.

The Simon & Schuster Speakers Bureau can bring authors to your live event. For more information or to book an event, contact the Simon & Schuster Speakers Bureau at 1-866-248-3049 or visit our website at www.simonspeakers.com.

Interior design by Davina Mock-Maniscalco

Manufactured in the United States of America

10 9 8 7 6 5 4 3 2 1

Library of Congress Cataloging-in-Publication Data
Names: Bourne, J.L., author.
Title: Ghost run / J.L. Bourne.
Description: First Gallery Books trade paperback edition. | New York : Gallery Books, 2016. | Series: Day by day armageddon ; 4
Identifiers: LCCN 2016006455
Subjects: LCSH: Zombies—Fiction. | Armageddon—Fiction. | BISAC: FICTION / Horror. | GSAFD: Horror fiction.
Classification: LCC PS3602.O89274 G48 2016 | DDC 813/.6—dc23
LC record available at http://lccn.loc.gov/2016006455

ISBN 978-1-5011-1669-8
ISBN 978-1-5011-1671-1 (ebook)

*This novel is dedicated to my mother and father,
who have left this earth for other planes.*

*For those that still have theirs,
put down this book, pick up your phone,
and tell them how much you love them, right now.*

I'll wait.

Author's Note

If you made it this far, you have likely spent some time in my post-apocalyptic world through the pages of the first three Day by Day Armageddon novels. Foremost, I'd like to thank you—my dedicated readers—for punching yet another ticket on the train with nonstop service through the bleak landscapes of undead Armageddon. From the days of the black cover to now, you've been there for me, and for that, I remain humbled.

Although the series is best enjoyed chronologically, if you are just beginning the Day by Day Armageddon saga, allow me to bring you up to speed.

The three-minute version:

The first volume of the Day by Day Armageddon series took us deep into the mind of a military officer and survivor as he made a New Year's resolution to start keeping a journal. The man kept that promise, chronicling daily the fall of humanity. We see him transition from the life that you and I live to the prospect of fighting for his very survival against the overwhelming hordes of the undead. We see him bleed, we see him make mistakes, we witness him evolve.

While enduring numerous trials and travails in the first novel, the protagonist and his neighbor John escape the government-sanctioned nuclear annihilation of San Antonio, Texas. They make their way to temporary safety on board a boat dock on the gulf shores of Texas, and soon after receive a weak radio transmission. A family of survivors—a man named William, his wife, Janet, and their young daughter, Laura, all that remain of their former community—take shelter in their attic while untold numbers of the undead search for them below. After a miraculous rescue, the family joins forces with our protagonist to stay alive. As they scout the outlying areas for supplies, they encounter a woman named Tara, trapped and near death in an abandoned car surrounded by the undead. After her rescue, Tara begins to bond with our protagonist, forming a relationship that eventually leads to them falling in love.

The survivors eventually find themselves sheltering inside an abandoned strategic missile facility known by the long-deceased former occupants as Hotel 23. But their union may not be enough in this new world, an unforgiving post-apocalyptic place in which a simple infected cut, not to mention the millions of undead, can easily kill them.

The situation brought out the worst in some . . .

Without warning, a band of brigands, seeing targets of opportunity, mercilessly began an assault on Hotel 23, intending to murder the survivors for the shelter and take the supplies inside. Narrowly pushed back, the survivors were able to hold Hotel 23 for the time being.

In the second installment, *Day by Day Armageddon: Beyond Exile*, our protagonist, Kil, connects with the remnants of military ground forces in Texas. As the last military officer on the mainland known to be alive, he soon finds himself in command. He establishes communications with the acting Chief of Naval Operations on board a working nuclear aircraft carrier on station in the Gulf of Mexico.

Kil also discovers a handwritten letter telling of a family—the Davises—hiding out at an outlying airport within prop aircraft range of Hotel 23. The rescue mission results in the extraction of the Davis family—a young boy named Danny and his very capable civilian pilot grandmother, Dean.

After being allotted a functioning scout helicopter from the carrier battle group, our protagonist and his men begin searching for resources in the areas north of Hotel 23. Halfway through *Beyond Exile*, Kil suffers a catastrophic helicopter crash hundreds of miles north of the facility. Severely injured, he is the lone survivor.

Running dangerously low on provisions, he manages to trek south. He soon encounters Remote Six, a shadowy group with unknown motives, hell-bent on getting him back to Hotel 23. Later, he stumbles upon an Afghani sniper named Saien. Little is known about Saien's background, and his demeanor only adds to the mystery. At the start, neither fully trusts one another, but Saien and our protagonist work together and eventually return to Hotel 23 under the watchful eyes of Remote Six.

Remote Six orders our protagonist to launch the remaining nuclear warhead on the aircraft carrier. The order is ignored and a high-tech retaliation against Hotel 23 ensues. A sonic javelin weapon known as Project Hurricane is dropped by Remote Six, attracting legions of undead creatures to the region.

The sonic weapon is eventually destroyed, but it's too late.

A mile-high dust cloud, generated by the approaching undead mega-horde, signals the need for an emergency evacuation. A harrowing battle ensues to the Gulf of Mexico, where the aircraft carrier USS *George Washington* waits to take on any and all survivors.

Shortly after our protagonist's arrival on board the carrier, orders from the highest level are issued—a directive to rendezvous with the fast attack submarine USS *Virginia*, standing by in western Panamanian waters.

In the third novel, *Shattered Hourglass*, Kil is dispatched to China with Task Force Hourglass to investigate the source of the undead anomaly. Task Force Phoenix, headed by a special operator called Doc, is dispatched to Hotel 23 to secure its remaining nuclear payload. Some of the secrets of Remote Six are revealed shortly before its annihilation at the decision of Task Force Phoenix.

The USS *George Washington* is disabled by the undead just before running aground in the Florida Keys. Meanwhile, Hourglass makes an incredible discovery in China, something that could put humanity back on the scoreboard against the overwhelming numbers of the undead. Upon Kil's emotional reunion with his pregnant wife, Tara, he's told that Task Force Phoenix has gone dark.

Humanity begins to rebuild itself around the two fully functional nuclear reactors housed inside the beached aircraft carrier, but complacency and creature comfort was something in which Kil had little interest. Explorers never stop.

So, then, loyal readers, welcome back.

Put on your gas masks and radiation suits, charge your Geiger counters, load your carbines, and turn the page.

Be ready, for the undead are near.

Landfall

Day 1

The radiation suit pressed against my perspiring skin and my breath was loud through the gas mask. I was two hundred miles from any living human, deep inside the New Orleans exclusion zone. No one knew at the time it happened, but after the government nuked New Orleans, the Waterford Nuclear Generating Station melted down, further contaminating the area. Although my Geiger read above acceptable radiation limits, it wasn't by much, and I was being a bit cautious. My sailboat, the *Solitude*, was anchored out a hundred meters from shore, and about a mile from where I stood.

In front of me was something very interesting. Very unexpected. Pre-undead technology hidden away in some bunker that'd never see the light of day if the dead didn't start walking. A large balloon secured with a thin cable marked the spot like a dropped pin on a smartphone app; I'll come back to that.

I'd stumbled upon a radio distress ping one week ago while out fishing with John. We were a day's sail from our stronghold in the Keys. I didn't say anything to him, as I didn't want him to know I'd been scanning the old Remote Six frequencies. Just in case. People tend to get nervous if they think murderous psychopaths are still around to lob sound decoys like undead dinner bells or nuclear weapons at them. Remote Six tried to kill me a while back, but a group of men sacrificed their lives for a chance to save the Keys and our way of life.

I still chose not to share any of this with John even as *Solitude* made best wind back home. Not for any particular reason, if only that John's advice was generally infallible and I was afraid to hear his take on it. I'd already made up my mind and didn't want common sense to get in the way. After off-loading our haul of fish, crabs, and other scavenged items, I sailed the short distance to the marina. Jan, Tara, and our baby, Bug, were waiting for me and John on the pier as we motored in and tied up. Although Jan had lost half of what she lived for when Will died, she was slowly recovering. She and John were getting along nicely. I mean, it'd been months. Everyone wanted her to be happy. It seemed like Jan thought we'd judge her for moving on when the opposite was true.

It should be noted that it's been a while since I've written anything . . . well, besides a few measurements scratched in chalk on the hull of *Solitude*. As much as I'd protested, my journals were all confiscated after the Hourglass incident; they were sent off somewhere north on the mainland to be scanned and studied along with *almost* everything else we'd found over there.

I honestly thought I'd want to settle down after Hourglass; I envisioned that on board *Solitude* would be the place where Tara and I would live our lives and raise our family. While aboard, we were our own island. We made our own freshwater and generated our own wind and solar power. The undead still ruled the land beyond in all directions, but *Solitude* was under my command. Those miserable creatures washed ashore from time to time, wreaking havoc on our growing shantytown, attracted by the lights and noises that nuclear power provided. Island life wasn't safer than mainland living, mind you, just a bit less stressful. The aged and the sick still died and reanimated, and they still attempted to rip you apart.

Despite the terrors of living on solid land, Tara, urged by the birth of our baby, insisted that we move ashore. After long deliberation, I relented. She was right: Family life aboard a sailboat was cozy, to say the least. About a month ago, we picked out a vacant home on the beach near John and Jan, well inside the patrolled perimeter. Like everyone else, I was extremely concerned with security. I changed out the door on the baby's room from the hollow residential type to a steel door. Her crib was a modified metal dog kennel, so if the undead happened to breach her room, they'd still have to deal with a heavy cage to get to her.

This was the new normal. We were going extinct, and it was up to the last of us to at least slow it down.

After spending a week ashore, I convinced Tara that we needed more supplies for the approaching hurricane season. After all, as a new father, I was concerned that we might not have enough to see us through the next few months. I needed to get out there and bring home our livelihood.

At least, that was the main reason I told myself I was leaving.

The owner of the boat in the slip across the way didn't say a word when he saw me toting my carbine, radiation suit, and gas mask aboard *Solitude*. I had enough canned food for a couple of weeks and the boat's water desalinator was working just fine. The boat had half a tank of propane in reserve, but I could get all of that I ever wanted on the mainland. Millions of suburban back-yards full of barbecue grill propane tanks, ripe for the picking. Signals from the mainland have gone dark with only intermittent HAM chatter. Whatever facility used to talk to us stopped, and no one knew what that really meant.

I didn't get much sleep sailing single-handed northwest into the waters of the Gulf of Mexico. I had to do most of the piloting and all of the navigation myself. Only during the longer legs of the journey through deep water could I risk falling asleep. Even then, only in short intervals with the radar proximity alarm set. Engineers back at the Keys were working on a new navigation system using the old loran standard, but it was still a ways away from being operational for sail navigation and flying. Most of the GPS satellites were off-line, some having burned back into the at-mosphere from lack of ground station intervention. The Garmin chart plotter eerily indicated a GPS signal strength of zero.

The closer I came to landfall, the stronger the distress signal became. Using rudimentary methods, I scanned the horizon with the whip antenna on my handheld radio. Adjusting gain and mon-itoring the signal meter and sound, I began refining my course and direction to pinpoint its location. I'd draw signal lines of bearing on the marine charts stored aboard *Solitude*. These lines would form intersections and give me a basic triangulation. Drawing RF lines of bearing on a chart worked best the faster you were moving, and I wouldn't be moving this fast ashore. Might as well take advantage of it.

After circling an area of interest encompassing about ten city blocks, I folded the chart and stuffed it into my pack. When land appeared through the haze at my bow, the Geiger alerted me that it was nearing time to don the familiar yellow suit and mask.

It didn't take long after anchoring out and paddling to shore before I had my first encounter with the undead.

I'd tied my kayak to the docks and tossed my pack and carbine onto the sun-bleached boards. I always kept a reserve of water, ammo, and food in the watertight compartment on my dinghy. It wouldn't be the first time I had to run for the water with a dry, steaming carbine hanging off my back after fighting off an army of those miserable things. Reluctantly, I climbed the dock support pole and planted my two rubber exposure suit boots on the boards, careful to avoid the rusty nail heads that jutted from them.

My mask had just a bit of condensation, nothing too severe. I could hear my breath as it sucked deadly, irradiated air from the outside through the filter. I shouldered my pack and slung my suppressed carbine across my chest. I was on my second suppressor, a SiCo Saker. My original can wore the hell out on me at about the same time as my carbine gas tube melted during a mainland excursion like this. I had to trade some serious loot for the Saker, as a quality can is a goddamned necessity out here in the badlands. Worth its weight in uranium.

I slowly made my way up the docks toward land, feeling the eyes upon me. I saw movement on the right through my mask, but dismissed it as a piece of unsecured sail flapping through its ripped blue cover. I passed by without giving a thought until feeling the vibration through the thick rubber outsoles of my suit. The heavy footsteps on the dock. I didn't risk a glance before sprinting away, attempting to open enough distance to defend myself. My suit crinkled and scratched against my body as I ran. Nearly to shore, I tripped on a coil of rotting line and then a cleat, certain that the thing was nearly on me.

I swung my carbine around and turned to face my pursuer.

The dock was empty.

I'd nearly shot at a ghost, a sliver of my mind caught in the dimension just ahead or behind this one.

Breathing heavily, I picked myself up from the dock and set foot on the mainland for the first time since I scouted southern Florida on a quest for NICU equipment. People (including myself) were still having babies in the Keys, but not nearly enough. Wearing out my silencer was worth it after watching those newborns breathe via very hard-to-come-by mechanical ventilators brought in despite the dangers of the mainland hordes.

After hitting the shoreline, I stayed low and pulled out my radio for another DF reading. I was looking for the distress ping north by northwest.

A couple hundred meters inland was a two-story bistro overlooking the bay, with a roof access ladder on the side.

A vantage point.

The undead usually walk right off the roofs, so I knew it should be semi-secure up there. I pulled my magazine and visually checked. Black polymer–tipped 300 Blackout subsonics. Giving the can a twist and accompanying it with a series of clicks, I made sure the device was secure on the end of my weapon before scanning my route to the dumpster and the ladder next to it.

The undead were in the streets, but not mobile. They simply stood there, slightly hunched over, movement barely perceptible. They swayed slightly, as if dancing to a tune playing via some undead synapse in a primordial region of their rotting brains.

The good thing about a new radiation suit: I wouldn't die from breathing radioactive particles or skin exposure.

The bad: Until you broke it in, it was like wearing a giant empty potato chip bag.

I moved slowly to the dumpster in a crouched position. My suit crinkled the entire time, causing one of the nearby creatures—shirtless, with a gold chain—to spasm and crane its head sideways at me. It raised an arm, gesturing in my direction. Before it could muster a groan, I leveled my suppressed carbine, placed the red dot at the top of its dome, and squeezed.

Pop.

The thing fell, kicking up radioactive dust as it hit the ground in a tragic pose.

Subsonic 300 Blackout was the shit for undead wet work inside of a couple hundred meters. Outside of that? Run.

Miraculously, my 120-decibel shot only jolted two more of them from sleep. I dropped them to the deck and noticed that the distant creatures, a block in all directions, stayed in stasis, or whatever you choose to call what they were doing.

If I had been forced to shoot unsuppressed on this street, I'd have had the wrath of hell coming down on me in minutes. That's why things like silencers are worth a king's ransom on the mainland.

I kept my knees locked and moved with a stilt-like gait to the dumpster, attempting to lessen the noise of my suit. I quietly rolled the large metal box far enough to get me to the access ladder and then took off my pack so that I could fit inside the ladder cage. Ascending, I heard a muffled metallic sound coming from below and felt a rough tug on my pack line.

I pulled free and kept climbing; my pack swung a couple feet below, secured to my web belt. Reaching the top, I turned to tug my pack the rest of the way and looked down the ladder cage tunnel to the ground.

She, *it* . . . was almost beautiful.

It looked up at me as if gazing at a full moon. For a long moment, it did nothing. It stood about six feet tall, blond hair in a ponytail, jean shorts, and a T-shirt. It was barefoot, but, based on the V-shaped stains on its foot, I could tell it had been wearing flip-flops when it died, or maybe sandals. Its solid white eyes followed my movement from one side of the ladder to the other.

I took the Geiger from my pack and tied some line to it. Turning the volume up all the way, I lowered it down the ladder, closer to the creature below. As it cleared the metal shielding of the ladder cage, my suspicion was confirmed. The Geiger went crazy with static: The creature was putting off high levels of radiation. I lowered the Geiger even closer to it to get a better reading.

It reached for the device.

I yanked the string, pulling the Geiger away like a cat's toy. Angered, the irradiated corpse actually climbed onto the dumpster and began to slowly ascend the ladder.

I watched, nearly frozen in terror.

The creature bared its jagged teeth and hissed as it neared. I shot it in the head and watched it pinball down the lower half of the ladder. The noise attracted two more to the area, but, based on their level of decomposition, they didn't appear to be irradiated and didn't seem to know I was on the roof.

Using binoculars to read street signs and referencing the electronic maps on the tablet I kept in my pack, it looked like I was in eastern Perdido Key, near Pensacola. I confirmed this when I matched the paper charts and saw the name of the marina on the map, the same one where my kayak was moored not far from the rooftop.

I powered down the tablet and plugged in the solar charger. The panels attached to the exterior of my pack served to maintain the batteries for my night optical device, tablet, comms, Geiger, and flashlights. After taking a radiation reading, I took off my hood and mask and placed an N95 mask snugly over my nose and mouth and some goggles over my eyes. I took this time to catch my breath and let the condensation on the inside of my gas mask evaporate. The radiation levels were relatively safe here on the top of the bistro.

After eating two cans of Vienna sausages, I did more reconnaissance from the rooftop in all directions. I could see the small radar dome and wind vane on the apex of *Solitude*'s mast to the south. Across the street to the north, a dilapidated bank—near collapse, actually. Chunks of its brick walls and every pane of glass had been blown outward long ago, along with a large circular vault door that lay halfway on the sidewalk. The bank's blast damage was old but told a story. Mutilated undead bodies still writhed in the brick rubble below like the dying reflexes of smashed spider legs.

A bright blue duffel bag sat in stark contrast on the street near the massive rusting vault door. Some poor bastard actually thought money would get them through or help them in some way. Even in the early days, the time when John and I had first met, money was the last thing on my mind.

According to my transceiver and charts, the distress signal wasn't far from my position. Still north by northwest. Stationary. I had approximately two miles of suburban traveling to do and it was getting dark fast. My night optical device, or NOD, would allow me to see in the dark, but not very far and not with a very wide field of view. Jan was our resident super-nurse, and according to her and the rest of her doctor cadre, those creatures had some sort of close-range thermal vision adaptation. Knowing this, moving at night among the enhanced irradiated undead was not at the top of my list of fun things to do.

I could risk heading back to *Solitude* for safety, but that was nearly three hundred meters away.

Making my decision, I descended the ladder far enough to kick the dumpster out from under it and went back up to make camp for the night.

The moldy wooden pallets leaning against the bistro's air circulator made good fuel for a small stealth fire. This was sunny Florida, but hypothermia never seemed to care. By the glowing pallet wood light, I checked and rechecked my kit for tomorrow's trek.

Between the pops of burning wood, I could hear the undead in the streets below. I'd made a little too much noise with the suppressed shots I'd taken. The undead's throaty moans and clumsy movement made unholy noises that cut through sanity if one let their mental guard down too long. Would I rather be in Tara's arms, hearing the breath of my newborn nearby right now?

Yes.

But there are some out here like me who will never feel at "rest" until they're hugging a ventilation pipe on a roof somewhere in the badlands. Like those shambling creatures on the ground below, part of me had died through all this. I'd left a piece of myself out here somewhere in the ether, between what was then and what surrounds everyone now.

Rooftop Diplomacy

Day 2

I awoke before daybreak to the sounds of distant tide and the wind. No aircraft, cars, or any other sounds made by man. Like Pripyat before, this was a dead place. I put on my mask and hood and made ready to descend into whatever mayhem awaited below.

I lowered my pack to the ground and then climbed down with my pistol in my right hand. Reaching the deck, I switched back to my M4 and checked it. Comforted by the yellow tint of brass inside the chamber, I started moving to the RF-geolocated area marked on my chart.

I had nearly two hundred rounds of subsonic ammunition on me, and a mag or so of supersonic. Black-tipped quiet stuff on the left side of my vest, red-tipped loud stuff on the right. Obviously, I wanted to stay below the sound barrier as long as possible, but if things went sideways, I'd switch to supers.

I moved along the buildings, careful to avoid the streets and alleyways infested with undead. Thankfully, I wasn't near a major city, and was close to water. It was winter back when the first creatures walked, so this beach resort area didn't seem too crowded.

But still, just enough action to keep things interesting.

After avoiding two different busy streets, I took a turn down an alley with only two creatures stumbling around a heap of trash. I hit them both from ten meters and took the time to recover the spent brass. As I did so, the corner where I just came from started to fill with undead.

They gave chase.

I ran down the alley, away from the approaching mob . . . and when I spilled out into the street, I was immediately surrounded.

9

My only option was to enter the large brick building right in front of me. Reaching the glass-paned door, I turned the knob.

Locked.

I bought a few seconds, taking three shots at the closest rotting creatures. Enough time to smash a pane of glass and unlock the bolt. Barreling inside the dark building, I slammed the door and reengaged the lock. Frantically, I piled up as much shit as I could in front of the door but knew it wouldn't hold forever. There were at least two dozen of them out there now interested in me, the appetizer in the yellow suit that had just made a lot of noise right in front of them.

With no time to dig my NOD out of my pack, I flipped on my weapon-mounted light, spilling five hundred lumens of searing brightness into the dark room. Behind me, the undead broke glass and splintered wood, forcing me ahead into a gloomy passageway. To my right, through a series of boarded windows, I peered through the slits and saw something run past outside. Panicking, I sprinted for the boarded-over glass doors on the other side of the building. My heart sank when I saw the chain and padlock holding them securely together. It didn't matter; one of those things was already tearing at the boards on the other side. I gave up on the chained doors, made for the stairs, and began to climb. Somewhere above me, a corpse that was already inside fell over, hitting the handrail behind me. It lay there, crippled from the drop, but still reached for my legs. I ignored it and kept climbing to the sounds of shattering glass and splintering wood on the ground level below.

At the top of the stairs was a red ladder situated against a wall behind an old desk. I climbed for my life, thinking of that airfield tower from what seemed like decades ago. I didn't have a parachute this time.

I could hear the undead now coming up the stairs. Some steps were far more rapid than others.

Irradiated.

I was on the ladder, twelve feet in the air, the light from my carbine illuminating the brass padlock securing roof access. I swung the light around as the first creature appeared at the top of the stairs and began to charge. Its lips and eyelids were gone, unblinking eyes locking onto me like an alcoholic to a bottle of whiskey. In an act of desperation, I put my carbine up to the lock, touching the standoff end cap on my suppressor to the lock clasp. I was risking death from ricochet or, worse, falling into the arms of the radioactive demon now climbing the ladder after me. I squeezed the trigger, missing the lock but punching a hole through the hatch. A single beam of .30-caliber light shone through the steel. Feeling the iron grasp of a dead hand on my steel-toed boot, I squeezed the trigger again. The lock flew off; a tiny piece of steel struck me in the forehead, right between my mask and hood, splattering a few droplets of blood onto my mask and down into the fray below.

The undead went berserk.

I jammed my boot down blindly, striking bone and teeth, loosening the creature's bear-trap grip on my foot. Without looking, I threw myself upward, hitting the hatch with the back of my head and spilling light into the darkness below. Resembling strange deep-sea plant life, an ocean of hands reached up in unison to somehow will me back down the ladder and into their arms. One of them emerged from the array of limbs, flailing the lesser creatures out of its way. It looked up at me with its jaw hanging slack and growled before it began to climb.

I took the shot down the hole, sending the thing back into the waving sea of hands.

I slammed the hatch, hoping nothing else would come for me out of the darkness of the building. I was several stories up and surrounded by buildings of various height. The Geiger was still chattering away; the mask had to stay on. Condensation covered the inside; blood speckled the outside, degrading my view. The wind must be blowing from what was left of New Orleans.

I checked my chart and took another radio reading. The signal intensity was so high now that I could no longer estimate distance to signal. Hearing the hatch rattle behind me, I put my kit away and slung my rifle across my back. The building next to this one was only a few feet away and one story shorter, so I took a running leap, rolling and ending up on my back in a puddle of rainwater. I checked the perimeter atop this new building, noting that all roof accesses had been secured via locked ladder cages.

Fifty yards away, on the building from where I'd just jumped, was a silhouette outlined by the bright morning sun. It stood there like a gargoyle, arms slack, staring in my direction over the gap between us.

Chillingly, it didn't walk off the edge.

Goddamn radiation. Scientists had no way of knowing its effect on the undead before the cities were nuked off the map.

Ignoring the creature, I took the chart from my pack and began to get my bearings relative to the signal source.

Looked like another two blocks or so.

After folding the map, I grabbed my weapon from my back, and turned to take out the corpse. It was gone.

Using a two-by-eight board leaning against a vent, I was able to traverse to the next building. As I carefully walked the plank, I saw them below, standing in undead hibernation. I was safely on the other side before I allowed myself to imagine the board snapping underneath, dropping me onto the sleeping dead. Best not to think that way.

My roof hopping was finished, though. The adjacent buildings were too far away, across the road. After verifying the coast was clear, I climbed down a metal conduit pipe on the north side of the building, listening to the crinkle of the potato chip bag I was wearing.

Staying low, I moved to the next spot of cover, an abandoned ambulance. My Geiger began to chatter. The metal ambulance was soaked with radiation. Crouched next to the metal monster, I felt it rock slightly.

Something dead was trapped inside. Keep moving. Can't stop here.

I made for the Perdido Spirits store across the street and was halfway there when I noticed something strange. Something very unexpected.

Checkers

Day 2

A balloon, tethered by a small cable, floated in the middle of the street. An unidentified body lay sprawled out beneath it, between me and the liquor store. The corpse wore military clothing with a camo pattern I'd never seen. Some sort of spiderweb and hexagonal design. An M9 was jabbed into its mouth and a good portion of the back of its head was missing. Although a gas mask was still in the clutches of its left hand, the corpse wasn't wearing a radiation suit.

The bloodstained leg on its fatigue pants told the rest of the story. The soldier(?), or paramilitary operator, had been bitten. I think it was a man; tough to tell after sitting in the Florida sun for who knows how long. He must have swallowed a bullet after knowing all was lost. I'm surprised his body was still relatively in one piece, considering the varmints running unchecked out here in the badlands.

A large black box was tucked into his body's load-bearing vest, with an antenna jutting out across its cheek and up the tether to the balloon hovering above.

The distress signal radio source.

A pair of wires led from the radio in the corpse's vest to a rectangular-shaped object about ten feet away. The soldier's bag was draped over this unusual equipment. It looked like a large motorcycle saddlebag, heavy and adorned with small flexible solar panels covered in mildew and dust. I unplugged the electrical lead attached from the radio to the saddlebag and moved it to the deserted alley adjacent to the liquor store.

After making sure I had two ways out of the alley, I began to rummage through the bag. The gray digital camo fabric was stiff and sun-faded from exposure. Expectedly, food and water stores were near the top. I'd need to Geiger those later before even thinking of consuming them.

Under the food stores was a tablet, likely what the electrical wires were feeding. Under that were a few odds and ends you'd expect to find at the bottom of a survivor's bag: cordage, folding knife, car slim jim, picks made from hacksaw blades, and a box of 5.56 ammo that was useless to me and my Blackout carbine.

I straddled the bag over a nearby concrete barrier and went back to the street to search the soldier's corpse. Thankful that I was wearing a suit and mask, I grasped the decomposing body under its arms and peeled it from the concrete. Realizing it was still attached via cable to the floating antenna, I disconnected the corpse from the carabiner. The antenna balloon floated slowly at first until it broke the tops of the buildings. I could hear the balloon drag the attached metal cable across a nearby roof and then it was gone.

I was pulling the corpse into the alley when something astonishing occurred.

Through the acoustics of my hood and mask, I heard the muffled sound of quiet servo motors spinning online. Looking over my shoulder, I could see that the rectangular power source was now covered in debris, had four legs, and was standing.

Months of dust and built-up grime dropped from its frame and joints as it began to run what I assumed was some kind of diagnostics program. Fearing the machine's low noise might bring the dead, I continued to quickly drag the body into the alley.

Once the mechanical quadruped's head retracted from its body, I saw what looked like a small but fast-rotating mirror where its eyes might be. The thing was the size of a rottweiler. Its recumbent legs flexed and it began walking in my direction. The eerie sound of the machine's metallic and carbon-fiber legs clicking on the concrete made me want to reach for my carbine and waste it.

With the soldier's corpse positioned, I stepped back and allowed the machine to do whatever it had been programmed for. The machine walked to within ten feet of the corpse and stood there for a moment before the motors quietly spun down and the head folded back inside the body. After this, the legs bent and the machine slowly dropped like a mechanic's hydraulic lift, back to its compact rectangle state of dormancy. Hearing movement in the street, I quickly grabbed the saddlebag and dragged the soldier's corpse into the alley behind the liquor store. Once again the machine spun to life and walked over to within ten feet, stopped, and sat back down.

I checked the corpse for valuables. A fixed-blade knife, a large-face wristwatch with multicolored buttons, and body armor. The armor would stay here, as it was infused with months of putrid decomposing corpse by-product. I placed the knife in the saddlebag and put the watch in my suit's cargo pocket. Satisfied with the salvage, I yearned for the safety of my boat while pondering my current predicament.

The dead soldier was broadcasting on a Remote Six frequency. His organization had been wiped off the map, probably at around the same time this guy put a bullet in his head, but of course there was no way to know for sure. What was his mission? What was the purpose of this doglike machine? And what was making the machine follow him?

I marked the location of the corpse and odd mechanical quadruped for possible future investigation. The sounds coming from the street on the other side of the liquor store had decreased my curiosity about the present salvage.

There was undead nearby.

I slung the saddlebag over my shoulder and began to leave. The sound of electrical and hydraulic motors spinning up behind me got my attention. I turned and saw that the machine began to follow . . .

. . . me.

At first, it was a slow walk. As I sped up, it did the same. At full run, it too began to run, quickly catching up and pacing me within ten feet. I remembered seeing these things on internet videos and news articles before the undead came. A lab in the northeast was working on robotic battlefield assistants that walked like animals.

Moving swiftly through the alleyways behind the main thoroughfares, the machine nimbly and loyally followed. I climbed an embankment leading to a cemetery; it had no trouble following. I weaved inefficiently between the tombstones, and it chose a more efficient route. The extra weight I carried was starting to tire me out, so I placed the scavenged saddlebag back onto the mechanical quadruped, securing it to the machine's chassis. It then followed unfazed, moving just as well with the saddlebag as before.

The machine was covered in battle scars. The bullet-damaged chassis and scratched carbon fiber told me it had been through hell and back. The machine had a checkerboard paint pattern on its breastplate, also blemished by unknown months of following that unknown soldier around the badlands.

I stopped and regrouped in the middle of the cemetery. *Solitude* was about a mile away. The machine seemed like a solution without a real problem. I didn't want a needy pack mule. It wasn't really that loud, but it still made enough noise to make me somewhat nervous near the undead. The second it became a problem would be the moment I'd pump it full of rounds and leave it sparking in the street.

Satisfied with my navigation plan back to the boat, I stayed low and egressed the overgrown cemetery, passing faded artificial gray stone flora. I could see a group of five or six undead standing along my route at the edge of the cemetery. I couldn't go around them. Either direction would put me deeper into a cluster of buildings overrun by corpses. No roof access from here, either.

I lay prone in the tall grass, the undead in my red dot sights. Confident I had enough ammo to blow if things went too kinetic, I started taking out the roadblock ahead. After my first shot, the machine stood up and started trotting out into the open concrete ahead of me.

It was running to the undead.

The creatures were temporarily drawn by the movement and began to shamble to the walking machine. I picked them off one by one while the robot distracted them. After the last creature was dropped, the robot turned 180 degrees and then began to walk slowly back to my position. Within ten feet, its head retracted into its body and it slowly settled to the ground. Its legs folded up into a compact but battle-evident chassis. I sat there in awe of the automated creation, not understanding why it was following me until I remembered.

The watch in my pocket. Of course.

My gloved hand fumbled trying to grasp the Velcro strap. Finally retrieving it, I noticed that it wasn't really a watch at all but some sort of wearable computer—a beacon, perhaps. I placed it on my wrist, careful to avoid pressing the four buttons clearly visible on the face. No telling if my futzing with it would cause an immediate shutdown, put it in berserker mode, or result in some other undesired behavior.

More noise behind me.

I stood and took a shot at the irradiated creature bearing down on my position. I missed. The robot dog machine came to life and again trotted to my target area, confusing the creature. It was clear to me at this point how it received the bullet damage to its chassis—it was programmed to protect its master.

I took another shot as the creature began to sidestep the machine and refocus on its intended meal. Taking the top of its head off, the creature fell onto the machine, shoving it sideways. Its leg servos whirred, instantly compensating for the assault. It made its way back to me and once again commenced what I presumed was its power-saving protocol.

My suppressed carbine was probably three times as loud as the machine. The shots I fired would resound down the streets and alleyways, attracting more undead. As I exited the tall grass for the street, the sound-stimulated creatures noticed me and began to moan in unison, causing an instant chain reaction. Now mobs of them began to pour out of the shops and nearby structures. The sounds of broken glass filled the street. Once again I was forced up, into the decaying brick buildings; I was a modern caveman fleeing the saber-toothed tigers of my time, using height once again to primate advantage.

Leveraging a drainage pipe from the cemetery I hadn't noticed as it was partially hidden behind a good-sized two-story building, I began my climb to the top. Nearing the roof, the machine closed the distance until it was adjacent to the drainpipe and then it just remained there. Its rapidly rotating visual sensors seemed fixated on me now standing atop the building. I looked down at the thing, wondering what it would do when I walked out of its field of view.

The roof was thankfully clear of undead. My mask was partially fogged over from all the exertion. I stood there catching my breath. Checking the Geiger, I removed my gas mask for a few moments of reprieve. A quick scan with my binoculars allowed me to confirm I was moving in the right direction. I could see *Solitude*'s mast swaying slowly in the distance. I took this time to eat some canned food and drink all the remaining water in my pack. I had more on the robot and my emergency stash on board the dinghy.

I could now clearly see the details of the color-coded buttons on the beacon watch. The symbology was similar to a key fob. Arranged in the four quadrants on the watch face, like a miniature Simon game, were a protected red horn button, a blue stay button, and a green follow button. There was also a fourth yellow button but there was no indication as to its function. Checking the edge of the roof once again, I could see the robot still standing at the base of the drainage pipe. The undead that pursued from the cemetery had rounded the opposite side and were streaming into a different street—for now.

I pressed the blue stay button.

The machine's head folded back into its body and it lowered to the ground.

I pressed the green follow button.

As expected, the machine came back to life; however, this time it trotted off around the corner of the building and out of sight.

I ran to the other side of the roof to watch. It circled the front doors of the building and seemed to scan the access points before moving around the next corner. It circumnavigated the building, zigzagging past small groups of undead. The creatures didn't pay it much attention after dismissing it as something they couldn't eat.

The machine stopped where it began, at the drainage pipe, its sensor again fixated on me.

That's when I got an idea.

I hit the green follow button once more. As the machine began to run clockwise again around the building, I pressed the recessed red horn button. A high-pitched piercing sound shot out of a speaker on the machine. Like an ambulance passing, the Doppler effect made the noise change in pitch as it rounded the corner. The mobs of undead that were streaming down the street changed course and began pursuing the machine around the building.

I quickly put my gas mask and hood back over my head and

rushed down the pipe before the machine could finish its revolution. I then sprinted toward *Solitude* as fast as the suit would allow.

Behind me, I could hear the whine of the machine's siren getting louder as it began to gain on me. I fumbled for the red button and pressed it hard. The sound remained for a few seconds before stopping, but it was too late. I could hear the clickety-clack of the machine's feet on the concrete nearby. It had already caught up, and was bringing at least a hundred undead along with it.

The Landfall Marina was only a hundred yards ahead. I ran past the bistro, but as I cleared the corner, something jumped out and tackled me, throwing me to the dirt.

It was the one from the roof.

The creature bit into the thick rubber suit at my leg. Certain I was dead meat, I pulled the ice pick I kept taped to my boot and jammed it repeatedly into its skull.

The horde was nearly upon me. As I stabbed, I could hear the machine building speed, and it then hit the attacking creature with the force of a linebacker. My ice pick, still lodged in its skull, was stripped from my hand. The corpse flew six feet, smacking into the corner of the brick building. I grabbed the D ring on the machine and it began to drag me away from the mass of creatures. I pulled myself up and fled to the marina.

My suit wasn't punctured by the creature's bite, but I could feel the residual pain from the pinch of its jaws. My gun was at the ready. My legs pumped and my upper body turned, firing into the mass of ravenous creatures. Maybe one or two of my rounds hit, but I doubt it. I was downwind from them; somehow the powerful smell had made it through the filters of my gas mask.

I was so full of adrenaline and wracked with fight-or-flight tunnel vision, I didn't realize I was on the dock until I felt the difference in my step. My body was moving instinctively to *Solitude*. I couldn't have stayed to face the mob if I wanted to. I ran, unknowing where exactly the machine was at this point. The docks were now thick with creatures, some falling into the water as the entire horde attempted to enter the marina at once. I wasn't going to die worrying about a four-legged machine, so I just kept running.

Checking over my shoulder one last time before my final sprint to the dinghy, my blood went cold.

Three irradiated undead had broken through the crowd and were making a beeline for me, fast.

I didn't take the time to untie the dinghy. Pulling the Halo knife from my belt, I flicked it open and sliced through the mooring line. With the runners nearly on me, I half jumped, half fell into the dinghy, careful not to stab myself with the open knife. The momentum pushed the kayak farther out, away from the docks. I was partially in the water, hearing the splashes of all the bodies falling in around me. Some of them flailed about like drowning swimmers; others sank to the murky depths, waiting to tug on your feet like in a bad horror movie. The three irradiated runners stood on the dock, gnashing their teeth and clenching their bony hands. They'd easily have ripped me to pieces if I hadn't left in time; I'd likely be bleeding out on the bleached wood, entrails dipping into the water, bringing all sorts of sea life to the shadows under the docks.

I paddled a few feet farther away, just in case those suckers would jump.

After arranging my gear, I checked the radiation levels: a bit high because of all the activity on the docks, so I was forced to remain masked, despite the mild claustrophobia setting in. More of the creatures fell into the water, either splashing or sinking. With the herd thinned by gravity somewhat, I searched for the quadruped machine. I could barely make out something down the docks. The undead were being knocked aside. I pulled my gun on the three irradiated creatures and spread their brains out into the bay, two of them falling lifelessly into the drink and the third lying crumpled on the dock.

I could make out the painted checkered pattern on the machine's "chest" as it neared the end of the dock. And it wasn't actually trying to push the undead into the water but merely counterbalancing being relentlessly nudged by them.

It reached the frayed rope where I cut my dinghy loose and just stood there, staring at me with its rapid rotating mirror-like visual sensor. There were too many undead still on the dock—I didn't think the machine could jump down into the kayak and doubted that the salt water would be very good for it. From my estimation, the thing weighed well over a hundred pounds. But I still wanted what I had in the saddlebag; doom on the machine.

I pressed the blue stay button on the beacon device and watched its head retract and its chassis lower to the docks with a dull thump. With the marina infested and the surrounding waters churning with undead, I decided to forgo retrieving the saddlebag for now and head back to *Solitude*.

Back on board, I moored the kayak to the aft end of *Solitude* and began to strip down. My body was filthy from hours in the plastic radiation suit. Down to my skivvies and gas mask, I tossed the contaminated suit into the water. Using a bar of soap and the boat's potable water, I took a quick but glorious shower on the fantail. I could hear the propane kick on when I turned the shower nozzle, instantly heating the water right before it exited the showerhead.

After checking the radiation readings, I tossed my mask below-decks and put on some clean clothes and a paper N95 mask, along with the decontaminated beacon watch. At this distance, it was impossible to make out the machine, but I could see undead still milling about on the docks. With plenty of daylight remaining, I fully decontaminated and stowed my kit, and decided to rack out for a couple of hours.

My alarm went off at 3:00 P.M. I sat in my rack for a few minutes before swinging my legs over and lacing up my boots. I poured some water into my metal coffee cup and brought it to near scalding on the propane stove before adding the instant coffee. I hoped that my supply would never run out, but knew it was an eventuality. Someday there would be a world without coffee, albeit instant. It was raining lightly, disturbing the murky green Gulf Coast water.

Checking the Geiger, I felt okay about not wearing the full-on gas mask. The N95 would be more than enough, especially with the light rain keeping any radioactive dust settled.

The docks were calm now; I could only see a handful of creatures through my binoculars. I secured the dinghy and started *Solitude*'s diesel engine. With a flick of a switch, her windlass began hauling the anchor from the depths, back into the sunlight.

I wouldn't attempt to single-hand a boat any larger than *Solitude*, and even then it wasn't easy. I brought her around and made my way back to the marina, keeping a careful eye on the Geiger and the waters ahead.

As I neared the dock, *Solitude*'s bow parted undead bodies like an Arctic icebreaker. Passing by, I saw they were being nibbled apart by fish; some had massive bite marks.

Sharks.

I throttled down and got the line ready. The engine noise was beginning to draw attention. With my boat in idle, I slipped the line over the cleat, letting the aft end drift. I ran up the bow and jumped off the metal rail onto the dock.

The rain was beginning to come down hard. I couldn't see too far beyond the marina. The wood creaked from half a dozen corpses advancing, arms out. One of them tripped over the uneven boards, face-planting. I couldn't help but laugh out loud. I shot its entourage and then removed the saddlebag from the dormant machine.

Human beings aren't always rational. I had every intention to jump back on board *Solitude* and just leave, but I had to ask myself, *Why did you bring* Solitude *in the first place if all you wanted was the saddlebag? You could have just paddled the dinghy* . . .

I pulled the mooring line, bringing the boat's bow closer to me. More undead entered my fishbowl of available vision as the rain pounded down onto the docks. There were too many. I generally liked to opt out of situations that required mag dumps to survive.

With the boat in position, I pressed the green follow button on my wrist. The machine stood facing me, its checkered paint on its gray titanium-clad chest contrasted sharply against the advancing horde behind it. I knew the machine wasn't intelligent, but it looked at me with its head cocked sideways as if asking, *What now?*

I grabbed it by its chassis and carefully led it onto the bow of *Solitude*, stepping back on board myself. With the undead only a few feet up the dock, I untied the mooring line and secured it to the machine, creating a short leash. As I tied the line, I watched it gracefully balancing for the gentle roll of *Solitude*. Finishing the knot, the machine's swift head movement startled me right before I heard a loud thump from behind. I felt an icy grip on my calf just before being yanked to the deck, hard.

Stars filled my eyes for a few moments. As my vision returned, I saw the irradiated creature was nearly over the metal guardrail, having jumped back from the docks. My gun was slung across my back, so I pulled the Glock on my hip and took the shot. Although I was acclimated to and expected a suppressed report, I nearly dropped the weapon after the ear-piercing blast rang out, splitting the creature's skull. Using my gaff hook, I pushed the corpse back over the railing and into the deep.

I was nearly deaf, ears ringing, which is what made the next sound so disturbing. Booming moans and screeches were echoing back in response to the shot.

I brought *Solitude* about and headed south, away from the advancing army of undead. Too many irradiated undead in this area to be worth a return visit.

The rain fell hard, and the machine stood there on the deck, watching its new master with unblinking eyes.

Pirates

Day 2

The bow is slowly pitching in a soothing rhythm. *Solitude*'s sails are steadily pulling me east along the Gulf Coast, out of the radiation zone. My kit has been fully decontaminated and the machine I've now dubbed as "Checkers" remains in dormant mode on the bow, covered with a tarp to keep the salt spray off. It's the only thing on board *Solitude* still giving off radiation. Even after a thorough cleaning, I'm still getting some static from the Geiger . . . not a lot, but enough to make me keep it stowed topside in the elements instead of bringing it down to my sleeping quarters.

Visibility remains poor, which is why I'm keeping the Gulf Coast in sight off my left shoulder as *Solitude* presses on at a blazing five knots. Her hull needs a good scraping, but after all the corpses I saw fall into the water, I don't think I'll be putting on the scuba gear anytime soon. Even sitting in the captain's chair back aft, the wind sometimes throws cold salt water my way, drenching my T-shirt, jeans, and flip-flops. My M4 remains in its scabbard adjacent the helm in the event I encounter something far more wicked than the undead.

Pirates were a thing here now.

It wasn't that far back, maybe two months ago, shortly after my trip to China. I was east of here, off the coast of Panama City. I'd just made it back from the mainland to retrieve all the canned baby formula I could find for Bug. An entire shopping cart full, to be more precise. I was stacking cases into the inflatable raft tied behind my dinghy. As I made my way back to *Solitude*, gunfire erupted from another marina about five hundred meters away. The downside to my subsonic ammo was that it wasn't particularly effective beyond two hundred meters.

That rule I had about running away from anything farther than that didn't apply when the enemy was shooting at you in open water with a thousand-meter weapon.

The rounds hit near, skipping across the water, thudding against *Solitude*'s steel hull. With my sailboat between the shooter and me, I jumped from the dinghy onto the aft end, letting my haul drift. I got low to the deck and retrieved the 240 from my cabin, quickly mounting it to the pre-positioned bracket installed near the bow. With sniper rounds hitting my boat, I opened up with the belt-fed machine gun. I could see the sand and rocks explode and the abandoned boats splinter. I hit a propane tank on one of the derelict vessels, blowing out windows and sending a huge fireball into the sky. With no way of knowing where the shooter might be, I blew through an entire ammo can full of linked 7.62 in no time.

With the SAW out of rounds and the barrel smoking from the evaporating grease I keep on the gun to ward off rust, I sat there with my ears ringing in pain. I wondered for a moment what crazy motherfucker would be dumb enough to start a firefight from the shores of Panama City with a million undead on three sides.

The kind with a getaway plan.

A half-million-dollar red speedboat shot out of the marina and began tearing ass in my direction. My ears were wrecked from the 240; I didn't even hear it start its engine. I fumbled for another ammo can and began to load the SAW, burning my forearm on the barrel in the process. Cursing, I racked the machine gun.

The speedboat was nearly on top of me.

I squeezed the trigger, pumping rounds into the shiny chrome engine cowlings and beautiful red paint. Sparks flew and fuel began to spray all over the place, coating the water with the rainbow residue of dead dinosaurs. The boat sputtered, backfired, and caught fire, but the two pirates weren't finished. Dressed in body armor and armed with rifles and spiked baseball bats, one of them lobbed something in my direction that bounced off the hull and into the water.

Grenade.

I had a choice: I could either jump overboard opposite the grenade or keep firing.

I Swiss-cheesed the speedboat drivers, blasting bone, muscle,

Kevlar, and body parts into the gulf. Midway through the burst of gunfire, the grenade went off with a thud, sending an underwhelming amount of water into the air.

I sat there on the bow with the smoking 240, looking out over the water at the carnage. The luxury speedboat was wrecked, riddled with Bonnie-and-Clyde-level bullet holes. The bodies were torn to pieces, faces unrecognizable with most of their heads gone.

The water near the would-be pirates' speedboat was churning with activity. I watched a bull shark partially surface, taking a hunk of red meat down below. After a minute, the boat was fully engulfed in flames. Thankfully the wind took the smell of burning flesh away from *Solitude*.

Over the side, I saw half a dozen fish stunned on the surface. I netted them and put them in the cooler for later, when my appetite would return.

I vowed to never tell Tara about this, about how close I was to never coming back, all for baby formula.

Yes, there are much worse things than the undead.

Windtalker

Day 3

I was at the helm most of the night, fighting swells. At about 0330 this morning, the storm passed, leaving *Solitude* dead in the water. I was too far away from home port to waste diesel, so I doused the sails and activated the radar proximity alarm. *Solitude* began to drift at the whim of the gulf current.

I went to sleep at about 0430, confident that the Furuno radar would wake me if I drifted too close to anything. I closed my eyes and dozed off, bundled in scratchy wool blankets. Despite the palm tree postcards alluding otherwise, sailboats do get cold at night.

I woke suddenly to the piercing sound of the radar proximity alarm. I splashed my face with water and made way topside, my arm shielding my face from the bright midday sun.

From the deck, I could see the source of the radar alarm. *Solitude* had drifted to within two miles of the mainland. The air remained calm, so I decided to turn off the Furuno and drop anchor for a while. As *Solitude* settled in her anchorage, I realized I hadn't turned on the boat's onboard radio since I'd used it to find the distress signal. I flipped on the DC power to the radio, instantly recognizing the Remote Six frequency on the digital display.

Morse code began erupting from the boat's tinny mono speaker.

Instinctively, I grabbed a nearby roll of paper towels and the Sharpie pen from my chart box. I hadn't copied Morse in more than a year, since back when I found John in San Antonio before the nuke wiped out the city.

The signal was very weak. Listening, I thought to myself, *Why didn't I hear this before today?*

The soldier. The one with Checkers. His beacon must have been putting out enough juice to overpower the Morse code being transmitted over the same frequency. The radio could have been emitting for months and the vantage point of the floating balloon antenna likely canceled out anything on the same frequency. The handheld radio from my pack couldn't receive the faint transmission; only the boat's powerful transceiver and more capable antenna suite was able to pick it out of the RF noise. Judging by the reading and assuming the same effective power as the soldier's radio, the transmission was coming from somewhere far inland . . . but there was no real way to know for certain.

I began to feverishly copy the code, realizing I'd caught the tail end of what hopefully would be a looping and continuous transmission. Most of the broadcast was static.

Between the heavy white noise, I managed to decode words that hit me like a slap to the face.

. . . P H O E N I X . . . C U R E . . . S O U T H . . . A T L A N T A . . .

I lay there on the chart table, trying to listen through the static, unable to make out anything else that made any sense. I was just too far away from the transmission source. I attempted to radio back to the Keys, to let them know what I'd found. Nothing. I was too far north.

My choice was simple: sail a few days south to make the call and potentially lose the signal, or investigate the signal and attempt to make contact. They both had their merits, the former being that I could bring John or Saien. However, that round trip would mean a week of weary sailing down to the Keys and back to where *Solitude* was now. Going to Atlanta seemed out of the question. Maybe I'd just travel inland far enough to find a tall building so that I could get a better copy on the signal.

Just a few miles inland.

Not too far.

Thinking of what to do next, I remembered the machine's gray saddlebag. Still dead in the water while I waited on the wind to return, I dumped the bag, letting its contents thump on the chart table.

I'd nearly forgotten about the tablet. I powered it on, and a splash screen appeared, depicting a four-legged robot just like the one on my boat dragging a wounded soldier out of harm's way. Below that image was a basic prompt:

Ramirez Login
or
New GARMR Login

I went topside to make sure the machine was still folded up and under the tarp.

I then reluctantly selected: *New Login.*

During the software loading sequence I watched the term *Ground Assault, Reconnaissance, & Mobilization Robot (G.A.R.M.R.)* appear on the screen ahead of the user interface. The prompt asked for my fingerprint and I complied, several times from different angles on the home button as instructed. It then asked for a photo of my face. I half expected the tablet's camera to activate for the photo, but it didn't.

There was a rustling sound from behind me. The tarp was moving. Remembering that the machine was secured to the railing with mooring line, I walked over to it.

Powering up, it stood, shedding the tarp as it began to slowly inch closer to me. Stopping at the end of its rope, it craned its head and stood staring at my face with its creepy rotating sensor. Without warning, it folded back up and sank to the deck of the boat. A high-resolution image of my face appeared on the tablet in my hands with digital measurements between the prominent features of my face. The tablet then asked me to say a series of phrases and every letter of the alphabet in long and short syllables. After this, the tablet requested how I'd like to orally identify the GARMR.

"Checkers," I responded.

A green check mark on the new log-in progress bar indicated I'd completed the process. A tutorial video began to play on the tablet, showing the GARMR negotiating complex obstacles while being loaded down with cargo. The GARMR appeared to easily climb hills that I'd have trouble with. In the video, it was sent across a frozen parking lot while being kicked and shot at with beanbag guns. It absorbed every hit, counterbalanced, and kept moving.

The next part of the intro was a GARMR construction overview. People in lab coats held gray bars of what looked like titanium as the screen cut to a carbon fiber molding bay.

Then things got a little more interesting.

The presentation faded to CGI of a probe flying through deep space at unimaginable speeds. The graphic zoomed in on a part of the spacecraft called an RTG, IDed as a radioisotope thermoelectric generator. Then animation moved the RTG from the probe into an overlay of a moving GARMR, indicating its location mounted underneath the body of the robotic unit.

This sucker was nuclear.

The video went on to state that the GARMR utilized a highly advanced RTG for its primary power supply, but supplemented it via efficient solar panels, which I had currently laid out on my chart table. The screen then indicated the electrical signal flow from the RTG and solar panels into a series of capacitors for energy storage. When depleted, it took the GARMR unit two hours to recharge the capacitors via RTG. The unit had a range of twenty miles per day, fully loaded. When depleted, it would simply go dormant, allowing its nuclear battery to charge its conventional battery banks. Finally, a series of short segments outlining self-healing joints, tackling maneuvers, night vision capability, and common oral commands ended the GARMR introduction.

After watching the entire presentation, I was taken to a new tutorial on setting up the Simon watch worn by the dead soldier. All four color-coded buttons were programmable. There was an embedded microphone in the center of the watch for voice commands out of the GARMR's organic hearing range. All I had to do was drag-and-drop the command I wanted onto the graphical representation of the Simon, hit *Save*, and the watch was programmed via the data link between the tablet, watch, and GARMR.

I didn't change the original Simon button functions but did add yellow-button functionality as *Scout*.

Hitting the yellow button would now send the GARMR a quarter mile in the compass direction of my choosing, giving me the ability to slew its camera via the tablet. Direction could be relayed via voice, tablet, or by simply pointing where I wanted the GARMR to go. Upon reaching the end of its scouting algorithm, it would return to me unless otherwise instructed via tablet or Simon.

The GARMR could even be told to go anywhere on the map of the United States I chose, but a caveat came with that option:

Dispatching GARMR on long-range reconnaissance missions may result in loss or damage of the asset. GARMR functions most efficiently as a battlefield human assistant.

GARMR's RTG power source concerned me, especially considering the warning I now read telling the user not to remain within one meter of GARMR for extended periods of time and the mention of an RTG self-destruct protocol. That could make things very interesting.

I waved the Geiger over the machine and heard the faint clicking, indicating low-level radioactivity. Far from lethal and not even comparable to the rubber boots I tossed in the water after leaving the docks. Even so, I'd be keeping my distance—that is, if I didn't decide to simply dump the seventy-kilogram GARMR overboard and let the salt water take care of it.

It goes without saying that Tara would literally shit a brick if she knew what I was thinking right now.

Sand Island

Day 4

The wind finally returned this morning.

I awoke to *Solitude* shifting at anchorage. After boiling water for coffee and having some canned beans and fruit for breakfast, I pulled anchor and set sail for the nearby island. It was hard to even call it that, as I could see the entire length of it from the helm. At maybe a mile long, it was void of trees, but had some grass and high dunes that could conceal trouble.

I was able to drop anchor a hundred yards out. My depth finder indicated that the bottom was twenty feet, a safe clearance for the keel. Running hard aground out here would mean certain death; the only place to go would be the mainland. Using *Solitude*'s boom, I was able to rig a block and tackle to get the dormant GARMR on board my dinghy. It was ugly, but it worked.

Having the whole night to read up on the machine, I was now fairly familiar with its capabilities. The GARMR was heavy, weighing down my boat to the point that leaning too far in either direction would bring on water.

The sound of the dinghy sliding across the sand reminded me how few times I made landfall this way. I'd almost always tie up to a dock or other deep object. I felt vulnerable in the shallows, where the dead had no fear of going.

I jumped out of the dinghy into the shallow Gulf water wearing my T-shirt, shorts, and sandals and with the M4 across my back, careful not to let the Simon watch on my wrist get wet. I grabbed the dinghy's bowline and began dragging it onto the beach. Using some driftwood, I made a sand anchor, ensuring my ride would stay where it was.

I put on a pair of heavy leather gloves and started unloading the boat. The GARMR was first. It was a two-man lift, so I wasn't surprised when I nearly dropped it into the water. It was warm to the touch, something I hadn't noticed before when I was shoving it on board *Solitude*. With a lot of effort, I finally got the heavy machine onto the beach and then grabbed my pack from the boat.

I climbed up the grassy dune to the center of the island to get a better look. I couldn't see too far because of the way the dunes were shaped.

I pressed the follow button on the Simon.

With predictable reliability, the machine rose from the damp sand.

Walking down the beach, I was suddenly stricken by the feeling of loneliness. It went on for a mile in front of me with nothing to interrupt the white sand ahead but intermittent pieces of driftwood. I could hear the GARMR behind me to my right. It seemed to be carefully avoiding the water. I checked the tablet and touched the video icon. I could see myself walking in front of the GARMR. I looked down at the high-definition screen and watched the GARMR's vision. I hit the IR button and the whole screen went black-and-white. I was able to alternate between the two for hot/cold colors. The GARMR software placed small green boxes over the wave movement it detected just offshore. This intrigued me.

My head was down in the tablet, when one of the pieces of driftwood stood up and started walking down the beach toward me.

In the split second before I looked up, I saw a red box appear over the movement.

Hostile.

The GARMR trotted out ahead to the undead creature. I hung back to see how it performed in the sand. I was a good fifty yards away from the thing, so I checked my surroundings before looking at the tablet feed again. I was very impressed by how stable the video was, considering the GARMR was nearly running to the creature.

I zoomed the camera in to its rotting frame. Crabs were attached to its leg muscles, still eating while it walked toward me, completely ignoring the GARMR. It was nude and most of its skin was missing below the waistline.

The GARMR positioned itself in front of the creature, forcing it to walk around. When it did, the machine put itself in front of the corpse again. I didn't want to waste any more time or risk the GARMR falling into the water, so a head shot to the corpse completed the exercise.

I pressed the yellow button and pointed down the beach. The GARMR did as instructed and began its scouting mission.

I watched on the tablet, gobbling through a package of freeze-dried pineapple. Sure would be nice to be sipping on an umbrella drink with Jimmy Buffett singing nearby.

The GARMR went along the beach fairly quickly before hitting its programmed return distance.

I put the tablet into my pack and crossed over the dunes to the leeward side of the island. Through the binoculars, I could see the buildings across the water on the mainland. One of them was a white ten-story office building. A fire had broken out at some point, leaving a great black streak from its seventh floor to the ceiling. I could barely make out at least half a dozen corpses standing on the roof.

The faint sound of electrical motors revealed the GARMR's return. Without looking, I could hear its standby routine; first a folding click and then the sound of settling servos. Fish jumped in the surf and I could see their glimmering scales.

I gazed out over the water to the mainland and began thinking of what to do.

If not for Task Force Phoenix, I might not even be here. I might never have felt Tara's embrace or held our new baby. I knew that this was a terrible idea, something that should never be attempted by any lone person, or even a hundred. If I didn't at least try to pick up their signal, I'd return a coward. After all, Phoenix might still be out there somewhere, alive. The Warthogs that scouted Hotel 23 after the nuke launch found signs that the team had escaped, moving east.

I was east, too.

I returned to the beach and began to search. After walking down the warm white sands until nearly at the end of the island, I found what I'd been looking for: a long, slender, and straight length of bamboo that could soon become a spear.

I sliced a fine point into the wood with my pocketknife. After building a small fire in a sand pit, I hardened the spear tip and headed for the dinghy.

The fish were jumping. The GARMR followed me to the water's edge and stood there with its small robotic head cocked sideways as I climbed into the dinghy. I paddled slowly alongside the island, thankful for the polarized sunglass I was wearing.

Paddle, drift, paddle, drift was the routine.

After a few cycles of this, I found what I'd come for. I wasn't always good at this, but much of the fresh meat on the Keys came from fishing. Cattle were rare, having been killed off on the mainland by the undead. I'll never forget the time that pontoon boat made it back to the Keys on fumes, a cow strapped to its flat deck. The captain had been out scavenging and found her, still alive, on a large field surrounded by a chain-link fence, complete with a pond and a massive open barn that looked like it had once been full of hay. That captain became a very rich man that day.

The flounder swam just below the surface to my right. Suppressing a sneeze, I watched it and slowly positioned my spear to strike. Knowing that the fish wasn't where it appeared to be from the refraction, I compensated; this was a skill taught by hunger. I jammed the spear into the water and hooked. The foot-long flounder came up out of the water, flailing. I'd stuck it cleanly through the gills and out the other side. After sweeping it with the Geiger, I tossed it into the well and paddled slowly back to the rising smoke up the beach, hoping to see another meal.

No such luck.

Back at the beach, I cleaned the fish on the bow of my dinghy and cooked it over the small fire along with the can of green beans I'd brought from *Solitude.* If someone were to ask me a couple years ago if I could survive long-term without a grocery store, plumbing, or electricity, I'd have called them crazy.

The fish was outstanding and the view was unforgettable if you could push certain facts out of your mind, one being that the mainland was thick with walking corpses. There was a lot of daylight left, so I decided to take advantage of the clear blue water and bathe using the bar of lye soap I'd traded for with five rounds of .22LR. I didn't really need it; I had boxes full of real store-bought stuff put back for a rainy day.

Bug's retirement fund.

I don't like writing about her or Tara too much when I'm out here. My mind starts going places and I lose focus. That will surely kill you if you let it go too far.

Clean and dry, I packed my things and clumsily loaded the tested GARMR back onto the dinghy. The unusual warmth reminded me of the GARMR's power source. It worried me a little, but another quick scan with the Geiger put my concerns at ease. I paddled toward *Solitude* as she drifted slowly around her anchorage. Stowing the GARMR back on the bow, I now knew what had to be done.

Beachhead

Day 4

Sailing east, I meticulously studied my charts; I'd do everything I could to shave any ground distance. I planned to make landfall south of Tallahassee and trek inward, looking for the tallest structure left standing. The Morse code is still transmitting, although just as faint as before.

The moon was absent when I tied *Solitude* to the aluminum docks. When given the choice, I preferred wood; it was a lot quieter underfoot. The Geiger checked good, so I wore my NOD. It was impossible to use over a gas mask. In the early days of all this, I only moved at night; that was until I was briefed on the short-range thermal vision side effects of the anomaly. Traveling at night was out of the question in the irradiated areas in and around New Orleans, as the contaminated creatures were fast and noticeably more cunning.

The familiar green glow of the NOD comforted me even though my field of vision was severely restricted. Someday, probably a few years from now, this once expensive piece of technology would die along with the last remaining lithium batteries out there, never to power on again.

But until that time came, I owned the night.

Before leaving, I topped off my gun and lubed it with a few drops of synthetic motor oil I kept on board for weapon maintenance. Running a dry M4 could lead to serious issues out here; I kept a small bottle of the oil in my pack for those miserable times my gun needed to take an unplanned saltwater swim with me. Turning to the machine on the bow, I took one last look at the tablet through my nonassisted eye.

"Checkers, power on," I commanded.

GARMR's electrically actuated joints whirred into action. I watched it curiously through night vision while its legs kept balance on *Solitude*'s gently rocking bow. It looked almost natural . . . almost.

Scanning through the tablet video feed, I switched to IR. GARMR's night vision illuminator was much more capable than mine. I used the virtual direction pad, slewing the machine's head down the vast expanse of the docks to get a better look at the shore. They were out there.

Leery of an RTG leak, I checked the machine for abnormal readings. Satisfied by the Geiger output, I could feel the heat again emanating from the machine as I led it to the port side of *Solitude*. The GARMR's titanium and steel hooves were shoed in some sort of honeycomb-pattern impact-resistant polymer, but they still made noise like football cleats on metal bleachers. As the GARMR boarded the docks, the sound rang out like great dinner bells.

Panicked, I reached for the carbine on my back, but it wasn't there; I'd left it by the helm.

Shit, stupid me. Another screw-up like that could have me ripped to pieces. And the night is still young.

"Checkers, stay!" I hissed.

The machine began to retract its legs and drop to the metal dock. I walked backward to the helm, waiting for hell's gate to open and for a hundred irradiated dead to come barreling my way. I lowered the brightness on my red dot to its lowest setting and peered through with the NOD.

Oh yes, they were coming.

Based on my sight picture, they were a hundred yards down the docks. I watched as they advanced, hearing the distant sound of dock metal shifting from the weight of a platoon of marching corpses. A loud splash broke the near silence, prompting me to put my carbine in full auto. A few seconds of controlled breathing helped me back off that bad idea and move the selector switch back to semi-.

The creatures were fifty yards out when I made the decision to send the GARMR.

After pressing the scout button on the Simon watch, the machine stood and looked over at me with its head cocked sideways like before. I pointed down the docks and before I could think, it was trotting in the direction of the advancing undead.

I watched it through the tablet video feed. Dauntless, it didn't even slow as it selected the best space between corpses to enter the mob. The screen was thick with undead; I couldn't see anything but tattered clothing and rotting flesh.

After three distinct splashes, the GARMR broke through to the other side of the mob and continued its scouting mission into the green beyond.

The macabre platoon turned and followed it, creaking metal on the dock as they all slogged after the GARMR.

With the docks now clear, I tossed my heavy pack on deck, reminding myself to share some of the load with the machine the next time we met up. Anything over forty-five pounds was a huge pain in the balls to carry over a prolonged period, and my pack felt closer to sixty. The magnified light of the cosmos reflected off the narrow aluminum planks. I adjusted my intensifier and kept moving toward land, comforted for the moment that nothing could come at me from the side. When my boots pressed into the overgrown grass, though, it was game on, their rules. You either had to play by them or become them, the only positively charged particle among a galaxy of negatives.

The clouds shifted, casting more starlight all around. I could see that I was in an oceanfront residential community. Seeing only green, I just knew that the homes were painted in the familiar pastels of beach communities spanning the entire gulf shoreline.

Time and the elements had not been kind to this place. A hurricane must have hit here sometime before. Many of the shingles were ripped from the rooftops of the surrounding homes, or at least the ones that still had roofs. Nearby, a sailboat lay on its side, its fractured mast jutting through a once extravagant home. Bay cruisers lay about like toys covered in debris. One was jammed inside of a house, outboard engine first. Using her keel as a ramp, I climbed aboard the *Reel Magic* onto her side. I woke up the tablet, casting light all around, illuminating the dirty sailboat hull and what was left of a ripped mainsail that lay draped over the hull. The GARMR was moving, but I couldn't tell from where. I panned its stabilized camera around to get a sense of its surroundings.

"Checkers, stop," I said into the Simon's internal microphone.

The full-motion video stopped moving. I panned the camera behind the GARMR and waited. Sure enough, the ghostly shapes of the undead began to form in the distance as they came into range of the machine's optics. I aimed the camera back around and sent the GARMR behind a nearby overturned boat.

"Checkers, stay," I said, causing the GARMR to collapse into its compact standby state.

I stowed the tablet and checked my wrist compass before sliding quietly down the mold-covered keel. My gun was at high ready, its magazines fully replenished from *Solitude*'s respectable armory.

Turning the corner north, I made out a street sign that was nearly covered with debris. The same went for the tall oak trees all covered with gunk at about nine feet off the ground.

Could the hurricane surge have reached that high? The answer to my mind's question could be heard in the trees.

Small branches snapped, forcing my attention upward. A dozen writhing undead were tangled in the gnarled branches, backs broken, arms and legs contorted into horrible positions of pain. One of the creatures had a fence post rammed entirely through its chest, another a small branch growing through its neck and shoulder. Alerted to my presence, they groaned and shook the branches, dropping acorns onto my head and back. I moved swiftly away from the trees of tormented souls, hoping that I'd finally seen it all.

I was able to go a mile, much of it uphill, before I started to feel tired. Instinctively, I pressed follow on the watch. The GARMR would be a few minutes behind me, so I made for the subdivision just ahead. The surge water didn't seem to have invaded this far above sea level.

I picked out a large cottage-style home and started my methodical process. Unkempt palm trees waved in the seaward breeze. The grass was two feet high in the front yard. Sapling oaks jutted up, vying for sunlight against everything else. Another gap in the clouds illuminated the area, revealing undead that stood unmoving in the dark streets, between cars.

I slowly climbed the stairs to the wraparound porch. The boards slightly squeaked from the weight they hadn't borne in ages. In both directions, the porch was covered in leaves, dead palmetto bugs, and palm bark husks. Hurricane shutters blocked the windows, and large sections of sheet metal barricaded the front door. I tried to reach behind the metal to try the door latch, but the sharp edges persuaded me to stop. Tetanus treatments required refrigerated storage, so there would be none to be found—anywhere.

I walked down the porch, staying low to avoid detection until I made it to the corner leading to the back of the house. As I crept, I heard a bang in the distance, something metallic falling on concrete. I knelt, guarded on two sides by high metal rails. Checking the tablet, I could see the GARMR was okay and advancing. Slewing the camera, I saw the overturned boat from earlier. The machine was getting close.

I got up and continued. At the end of the porch, I stepped down to ground level and onto the driveway in front of the detached garage.

A bright spotlight came on, whiting out my NOD.

"Goddamn security light!" I grunted under my breath while I raised my rifle.

I pumped two rounds into the lamp assembly, missing the LED on the first shot but disintegrating it on the next. My NOD returned to its normal state. This happened to me once before, when I was making a run to the mainland not far from New Orleans and was walking down a newly discovered dock. I'd triggered a solar-powered security spotlight, and in no time a horde of highly irradiated undead spilled onto the dock and chased me back to *Solitude* with my Geiger nearly vibrating out of my pocket.

Right now, though, I remained in the middle of the driveway, taking advantage of the open area. I waited for the creatures to come, nervously scanning over my shoulder. After some time, I could hear the GARMR's feet click quietly down the concrete drive.

I moved toward the massive screened-in atrium that encompassed the backyard pool deck and back-door area. Branches and pine needles punctured the remaining screens in almost every panel. The pool was half empty, filled with untold sludge and a motionless, bloated corpse. I opened the screen door and propped it open with a coil of garden hose, allowing the GARMR to enter the atrium. Once inside, I heard the shuffle of feet coming down the driveway around the corner. I kicked the hose out of the way and quietly closed the screen door.

"Checkers, stay," I whispered into the watch.

With the GARMR in standby mode, I moved to the chest in the corner of the pool deck and crouched behind it. I watched two lumbering figures round the corner and step onto the driveway where I'd tripped the light just a few moments before.

As if on cue, the clouds shifted overhead; the NOD-magnified moonlight revealed ghastly details of the creatures through the ripped and tattered atrium screens. The first corpse must have been a weight lifter in his previous life. It was massive, standing well over six feet tall. Its lips had long ago retracted, giving it that trademark undead nightmare look I had become unfortunately all too familiar with. I stared at it from behind the chest. Expectedly, its eyes didn't reflect IR light back at me through the NOD. The enormous walking corpse stood there for a moment, craning its head from side to side, searching. After a few moments, the gargantuan creature shambled back in the direction it'd come from; its adolescent undead companion followed it in the direction of the street.

The hurricane shutters were all in place over the windows, but the sheet metal cover was missing from the back door. I reached for the handle and turned, expecting it to be locked. Thankfully it wasn't, as it would have been near impossible to get through the robust hurricane door quietly. Remembering the GARMR, I again propped the screen door open with the garden hose and went back inside the abandoned home, shutting the heavy door behind me.

I raised the NOD away from my eye and turned on my carbine light, illuminating a vast kitchen area. I pointed my barrel up at a large and ornate chandelier that hung over the center of the kitchen. The bright light bounced in a million directions from the hand-forged iron-and-crystal monstrosity.

I concentrated on the dancing crystal refractions and imagined for a few precious moments that nothing outside wanted to kill me. The nine-foot granite island below the chandelier was covered in a thick layer of dust. Something that could have been an apple had nearly disintegrated in the center of the slab. I ran my fingers across the granite, clearing away the dust and showing the blue stone concealed underneath.

An oak spiral staircase led up to a dark loft above the main floor.

I'd nearly forgotten.

I pointed the light to the floor to check for footprints. I saw nothing to indicate that anything had been inside this house for a long time. With the master bedroom and guest rooms cleared, I walked over to the dust-covered spiral staircase and looked up into the darkness.

I crouched down to see the bottom step. Concentrating, I thought I could see the outline of a shoe print somewhere in the layers of dust. I traced the outline of the print with my index finger . . . right foot, size 9, give or take. Could be male or female. Studying the next step, I saw another. I doused my light and brought the NOD down over my right eye, allowing my left to adjust to the darkness. My gun was at the ready. I could feel the warmth of the doused weapon light with my left hand while I climbed the staircase. As I ascended, I noticed a pair of skylights recessed into the twenty-foot ceilings. They spilled twin oblong rectangles of starlight onto the floor below.

Round and round up to the loft.

At the top of the staircase, I saw something I never would have expected.

An elaborate train set. Not a plastic, mass-produced children's toy; this was a model that someone had put hundreds of hours of their life into creating.

I folded my NOD back on top of my head and again hit the light on my gun. Although covered in dust, it was a spectacular sight to behold. A huge table sat in the center of the loft, encompassing all but a narrow walking path around the table. Tunnels, bridges, pastures, cities, and countryside were all depicted in the two-hundred-square-foot model.

The level of detail was staggering. I picked up one of the train engines and marveled at it for a moment. It was hand painted, right down to exhaust stains and weathering imperfections. Some of the cargo cars had tiny spray-paint graffiti on the side. I placed the cars back where they were on the maintenance tracks and just stared at the large table. Wanting to see the other side, I rounded the corner and entered the narrow walkway between the table and the wall. Walking sideways, I noticed a pond in a cow pasture. I dipped my finger into the pond, imagining it was full of water, and it probably was before. The miniature hay bales looked as if I could pick them up and break them apart like shredded wheat and feed them to the cows that drank from the dry pond. Transfixed by the train table, I moved awkwardly down the narrow walkway before tripping and falling down between the table and wall.

I'd fallen on a corpse.

I screamed and jumped, bumping my head on the side of the table, seeing stars. I bolted away from the corpse like a spooked animal.

It didn't move.

I shone my light on it and noticed the bright silver revolver in its right hand and the hole in its head.

It was holding something in its left hand. I moved toward the corpse with my gun trained. I reached down and peeled the fingers away, cracking the bones like dead branches.

There was a control box connected to a golf cart battery under the table.

The power switch was in my hand and I just couldn't resist.

I flipped the power switch on and the world on the table was set in motion. The battery was weak but still putting out enough current to power everything. The streetlights flickered and dimmed as a small engine emerged from a tunnel, its headlamp dim from the battery's neglected state. As the engine rounded the corner, I could see something tucked into a logging car just behind three coal cars. The table lights dimmed once more, this time dramatically, before browning out. The engine stopped moving and the glow of its headlamp began to fade forever. Just like that. Something that someone put countless hours into building would never be used or enjoyed again. Fuck this world.

I set my carbine on the table's pasture between the hay bales. Its light shone over the terrain, casting a comical shadow of a cow onto the wall beyond.

The logging car held a note.

My name is Dudley. I had a long life and lived it well. I walked the earth for seventy-three years before the dead. My sympathies to the rest of you poor bastards on your trip to seventy-three. Warm Regards, D. Wildes

A bolt of jealousy struck me when I realized that I was one of those poor bastards.

I wrapped Dudley in a blanket from the nearby coat closet and placed his note on top. He didn't want anyone feeling sorry for him; he felt pity for me before pulling that trigger.

"I'm gonna take something for my daughter, okay, Dudley?" I asked aloud.

I took one of the cows from the table and placed it in my pack. Dudley's wheel gun was empty, so I let him keep it.

I went slowly back down the creaking oak staircase, now leaving my own set of footprints. Perhaps an explorer might happen upon this place in a hundred years and find Dudley, his note, and his spectacular train set. My money was on a Category 5 hurricane finding it first.

The pantry was full of canned food and something that used to be a bag of potatoes. The sack of spuds had sprouted roots that dangled down over the cans and had woven through the wire racks. Some bottles of water remained in a twenty-pack at the bottom of the pantry. I had learned to just leave the refrigerators closed in situations like this. A can of warm Coke wasn't usually worth what you had to endure to drink it.

With the home secure, I made camp in the master bedroom. Sitting on the soft king bed, I nearly unlaced my boots; this was a bad habit formed from living in the relative safety of the Keys. Taking my boots off would be the fastest way to have a hundred corpses smash through the front door, because Murphy.

Comfortable on the bed, I checked the tablet, as it had a lot more GARMR control options than the Simon watch. I tapped on sensors and was given a plethora of options. I was surprised to discover that the GARMR had an onboard Geiger. I checked it, verifying its radiation levels were in line with my last readings. Ignoring the other sensors, I tapped IR. The GARMR's head unfolded and the real-time feed began to stream to the tablet. I panned the camera around the atrium to see if anything was out of place. All clear. Satisfied with the situation in the backyard, I put the machine in standby mode again.

I woke up to the violent sounds of thunder. On my back in the bed, I could see bright flashes of light through the open bedroom door coming from the skylights. Rain slammed down in sheets. My watch said 0312. It would be a few hours before sunup.

Storms have unpredictable effects on the creatures. I could wake up in a few hours, walk outside, and have the entire undead neighborhood back there. Thinking of that, I had an idea.

Taking advantage of the storm, I activated the GARMR's sensors via the tablet, selecting IR. I tapped on the video feed and hit *Go*. The machine went to the spot on the feed I'd touched a few seconds before: the patio outside the atrium. I sent it down the driveway toward the street. Lightning whited out the machine's vision just before another boom shook the house. I saw static on the video feed as it came back into focus. I panned the GARMR's camera to the street, watching the undead.

They were frenzied. A group of them seemed to be making noise in front of a home three houses down on the other side of the street. Gesturing on the tablet's screen, I zoomed the GARMR's optics. Those things were pounding on the front of the house and door, trying to get in. Hitting the thermal filter, I saw very little color variation between the undead and their surroundings. With the GARMR's eyes trained on the door down the street, I jumped when I saw the GARMR's camera jolt on the screen in front of me.

The GARMR began to move rapidly.

I panned the camera over the machine's shoulder and saw the massive corpse from before shuffling for the machine. It had a two-by-four in its hand. It must have struck the GARMR with it. The machine didn't seem damaged, as it executed some sort of evasion protocol. As it retreated, I realized the reason it was attacked.

The GARMR was the warmest thing outside right now. Its RTG power source was giving off heat, and these things could detect that in contrast to its cooler surroundings. As the GARMR evaded, I watched its video feed, looking for a hiding spot for it to ride out the storm and the undead. Its wide-angle camera saw everything as it ran. Ducking through a section of downed privacy fence, I saw its savior: a storage shed positioned in the corner of a backyard could provide cover on three sides. I tapped the spot on the feed, hoping the machine would comply.

The movement on the feed slowed and it shifted directions. With two more taps, I eased it into its hiding spot and turned it around. I instructed it to crouch in the dirt but leave its sensors on so that I could observe.

The storm continued to rage, whiting out the GARMR's feed every few seconds. The video seemed more staticky than normal, possibly indicating that I'd reached the outer limit of the machine's video link with the tablet. I wondered what would happen if it went too far out of range.

No time to worry about machines, though. The sun was on its way. I hoped.

North

Day 5

I woke up, and checked the GARMR feed. Other than raindrops or condensation covering its lens, nothing appeared different from when I turned in after putting it behind the shed. Reluctantly, I cracked the metal door slightly to get a peek outside. The backyard was clear, except for the bloated corpse in the pool. I hadn't noticed last night, but it was still moving slightly. A blue rain barrel sat overflowing under the gutter outside the atrium. With my carbine in hand, I headed to the barrel with the half bar of soap and twisted rag I'd found in the shower. After washing up, I went back inside to check my maps.

I cracked the back door again and looked out. The bright Florida sun beamed down between the branches of a tall oak tree and through the damaged screen. To my right, I saw a rusted ladder leaning against the atrium frame. The screen above was covered with pine needles and I figured that Dudley was in the process of clearing them off when the shit hit the fan.

I exited the open screen door, ignoring the creature in the half-full pool until it started making noise. Its watch or bracelet hit the ladder inside the pool, making a high-pitched ring. I shot it from a sideways perspective, penetrating the skull and the pool liner behind it. The corpse slumped and bobbed in the deep end.

I rounded the atrium to get to the ladder. Slinging my carbine over my back, I moved it over to the edge of the roof and began to climb as three corpses rounded the corner from the carport onto the patio.

The big one looked familiar.

They didn't notice me until I got to the roof and accidentally kneed the gutter. Their heads snapped in my direction at the sound, and they began to move in a straight line toward me. They acted as if the screens weren't even there as they barreled through them, ripping them from their aluminum frames. I paid no attention to them and climbed farther up onto the roof. Some of the red architectural shingles were missing. I went over to the convex skylight and looked down into it, reminiscing about how nice it was to sleep in a bed behind reasonably secure doors.

Before heading to the apex of the roof, I left a mark on the plexiglass skylight:

Kilroy Was Here

I could hear the creatures inside the atrium below, tripping over vacuum hoses, deck chairs, and whatever else Dudley had on his pool deck. At the top of the roof, I pressed *Follow* on the watch before verifying the motion video on the tablet.

The GARMR was on the move.

I saw it exiting the section of downed fence and entering the street. Turning on the audio feed, I could hear its synthetic paws clicking on the concrete as it trotted my direction. I sat on the roof, sweating from the growing hot sun, and watched the video.

The GARMR's movement protocol was swift. It somehow calculated how close to get to one of the undead before sidestepping slightly, avoiding its grip. The paw clicks on the tablet began to give way to the real thing, and I could finally see the GARMR coming my way up the street with a small following of undead far behind but closing. Now was the time.

I slid slowly down the front side of the roof and reached over the edge for a pillar. After finding it, I carefully dropped my bag into a pile of leaves and slid down the pillar. On my way down, I saw a horribly decomposed and naked female waiting on the porch. It turned to face me, but my rifle was slung over my back. It was upon me before I could get to the railing. I pulled my automatic knife from the Kydex holster on my belt and pressed the button. The razor-sharp five-inch *tantō* blade rocketed out of the handle just before I rammed the cold steel into the creature's temple. Even with all my force, it still only penetrated halfway into the skull.

Apparently enough.

The corpse's lights went out and it fell, taking my knife with it.

The GARMR stood like a sentinel in the front yard, facing me.

It took some strength to extract the knife. I wiped it against the exterior of my pack before pulling the cocking handle in preparation for the next time I had to use this last-ditch weapon.

With the GARMR's fan club getting close, we then headed north to an area I'd found on my maps.

After leaving the hurricane-stricken waterfront community, I was careful to avoid the main thoroughfares. The Morse signal was still too weak to copy. My pack was heavy from the food I'd taken from Dudley's house, so I loaded some of the contents into the GARMR saddlebags. Now I moved a lot faster with the lighter pack and made good time.

After a few hours of concealed movement, I came to a fork in the road, with both options being northerly. I instructed the machine to check the right fork as I waited inside a nearby gas station that had long ago been looted. As the GARMR scouted, I cleared the station, not wanting a terrifying repeat of stock boys climbing out of the refrigerator. Near the back, there was a single green glass bottle on its side in the refrigerator. Something the looters missed. I enjoyed carbonated water as I watched the GARMR feed.

At first I deemed the right fork a waste of time, until the machine was on its way back through a small suburban neighborhood.

I'd nearly missed it.

Right there on the feed was an antenna mounted on a roof alongside a satellite TV dish. The top of the antenna extended beyond the machine's field of view. I pointed the electro optic sensor up to get the full view, at least sixty feet above the top of the roof. Thin steel cables anchored the antenna on four sides.

A HAM radio operator's house.

I moved the GARMR into a ditch and put it in standby. I'd

recently figured out how to check distance on the tablet. The machine was 0.9 miles from my location down the right fork.

Leaving the gas station, one of the undead ambushed me from a blind spot behind a large energy drink sticker on the glass door. I swiveled and began to squeeze the trigger.

A small girl.

I kicked it firmly in its chest, sending it sprawling backward into the storefront glass, spiderwebbing cracks in all directions. I began to run down the right fork, looking over my shoulder only once.

I have a daughter, too. I just couldn't.

Tears trickled down my face as I opened the distance between myself and the frail but deadly creature. I attempted to evade it, not wanting to take the shot. All I could think about was my baby daughter, my Bug. That thing was someone's universe; who the fuck was I?

I ran down the overgrown road until I was out of breath. The weeds, saplings, and grass were at least chest-high on all sides of the concrete. A white pickup truck sat broken down with its hood up and jumper cables hanging out just ahead. I checked over my shoulder as I began to run again. I could see the contrast and movement of red shorts a quarter mile back.

Dammit, she wasn't giving up. ~~She~~ It never would.

As soon as I looked forward again, I could see the grass begin to rustle. I imagined an army of undead children erupting from the grass, all wearing similar red shorts, reaching for my flesh. I raised my gun to the ready and was about to empty a magazine into the brush when the attacker charged. A large boar. I got off a single shot before it hit me, but I only nicked her. On the ground from the impact, I barely had the time to get to my feet before it came at me again. Using up all my good luck for the day, I sidestepped it like a matador and sprinted to the pickup truck, hoping the bed was empty. I blindly jumped into the back, landing hard on the spare tire. As soon as I hit, I could feel the truck shaking from the boar's assault.

Half a dozen piglets then flew from the brush, squealing and running. The sound of their hooves reminded me of the GARMR. I attempted to climb over the cab and leave the truck, but Momma Pig was pissed off and tried to climb under the hood to get at me. She was bleeding on her hindquarters from my shot, but it wasn't enough.

I wasn't planning to kill her, and anyone reading this would think that was absolutely insane. But killing her meant the piglets might die. Not killing her meant the piglets would probably live and go on to be survivors just like their mother. If that razorback would charge me for walking down the street, what would she do to a mindless moving corpse hell-bent on eating her young?

I was about to find out.

The undead girl had finally caught up and drew the attention of the razorback. I sat on the cab watching the train wreck play out. At first, the boar wouldn't divert her attention from me; I was the one that had hurt her. All that changed when one of the piglets caught the eye of the small creature and began to get curious.

It all happened so fast; I couldn't believe the blinding speed in which Momma Pig moved in order to protect her young.

FWAP!

The sound of wild pig impacting rotten flesh turned my stomach.

The creature was on its back with the boar on top, ripping decaying meat from the bone. The piglets moved in and began to pick and savor their share of undead flesh. My stomach bubbled, sending bile up to the back of my throat. Holding it back, I quietly jumped from the truck and ran up the right fork to the GARMR. I didn't want to be anywhere near that boar or her piglets when they decided they wanted seconds.

I thought I'd heard the snorts of the pigs behind me a dozen times before reaching the dormant GARMR. My nerves were just shot from the mental chess game I'd been playing since encountering the boar. Without my gun, she was the top of the food chain in these parts, an eater of the dead. And one scrape or bite from her would turn me—a chilling thought.

Kneeling at the GARMR, I felt somehow less alone. Although this combination of carbon fiber, titanium, and silicone wasn't alive, it served its purpose as some strange facsimile of man's best friend. I wondered what John's dog, Annabelle, might think of it. I didn't realize I was patting the machine's back until I felt the heat from the RTG's steady decay cover my hand. Those pigs must have really scared the piss out of me.

"Checkers, follow," I said, hoping that the machine had some sort of anti-pig programming tucked away somewhere deep in its processor stack.

The house with the antenna on the roof was just ahead. Weeds and saplings shot up where lush green lawns once soaked in gallons of sprinkler-delivered and precious freshwater. The GARMR struggled through the tall grass but adjusted its stride, wobbling through the thick growth faster than I could. The front door was heavy duty and shut tight. A security camera greeted me above it, staring down at the welcome mat with its dusty array of IR LEDs.

The sound of leaves crunching startled me.

I slung my gun around and nearly blew apart a cat. It'd seen better days; most of its tail was torn off and part of its left ear was missing. The undead had probably cornered it. I thought about feeding the poor thing, but it bolted away when I moved in its direction. I hoped it would be okay.

Feral or die, just like everything else out here.

I pulled firmly on the garage door handle. No luck. The opener that was no doubt attached to the sun visor of the Jeep in the driveway would probably still work if there was power. Making my rounds to the back, I was careful to check every possible entry point. All clear. With the first level secure, I went back to the Jeep and opened the unlocked passenger door. I released the e-brake and put it in neutral.

I could hear the sounds of multiple creatures beyond the chest-high grass and privacy fence. I rocked the Jeep back and forth until its axles broke through the rust, allowing me to push it forward. As it hit the garage door, I mashed the weak brake and put it back into first gear. The privacy fence began to shake and buckle in response to the noise.

I jumped onto the hood of the Jeep and tossed my pack onto the roof above, then struggled to pull myself up. I wasn't in my best shape. A few months in paradise will do that to a man. The rough exterior grated into my forearms and shins as I flailed my way up.

Once on the roof, I could see the dozen or so creatures that began to build up on the other side of the wooden fence, attracted by the noise I'd made while using the Jeep as a stepladder. I made for the nearest second-story window, only to find it locked. Peering inside the opening, I could see light coming from a room on the other side of the house.

I broke the top part of the window with my rifle stock and unlocked it from the inside. Loud cracks from failing wood posts signaled the end of the fence below. I climbed gun-first into the window and put my foot down inside the dry toilet bowl of a dark upstairs bathroom. The light from the other side of the house I'd seen was from an open window.

I didn't need to make so much goddamned noise, I thought to myself.

I stepped out of the bathroom onto the hardwood floors of a bedroom. Throwing my NOD down over my eye, I scanned the dark, foreboding corners. There were no monsters under the bed or hiding in dark closets filled with dusty clothes and rat droppings.

As I moved around on the top floor, the ancient wood below my feet creaked. The sounds made me think of the people who used to occupy this place and how these noises would have been familiar to them. They probably would have avoided that part of the floor.

I quietly scrambled down the stairs to check the bottom floor. The house was empty; no food and only a couple inches of water inside one of the toilet reservoir tanks. The water looked bad, so I'd save it for its intended purpose along with the diminishing luxury that was toilet paper. Unless someone got a shit paper factory up and running again, this stuff was going to be worth a lot someday.

The house was eerily quiet. The creatures hadn't started pounding on the doors or windows yet. I checked the GARMR and moved it near the Jeep.

"Checkers, stay," I said into the Simon.

I began checking the bottom floor for the HAM equipment. I turned the area upside-down for the radio connected to the antenna towering above the second-story roof. There was some radio equipment in the den, but nothing that would utilize the large array outside.

I leaned my gun against a nearby hutch and sank into a dusty leather chair covered in fine copper rivets. Out of old-world habit, I reached down and to my right for the lever I just knew was there and threw it back, tossing my feet up as I reclined.

I didn't know I was exhausted until my eyes began feel heavy. I lay there in a state of relaxation somewhere between sleep and full awareness. Just as my mind began to let go, I heard a very distinct sound.

Creak.

The same creak from just a moment earlier.

Something was inside the house with me.

I began to force myself awake, climbing up the rungs of my subconscious until I reached blindly for my carbine and sprung to my feet.

Creak.

I walked slowly over to the base of the stairs and looked up. Like something out of an Alfred Hitchcock movie, a silhouette passed by the vertical spindles under the wood handrails. I frantically pulled my NOD down to get a better look.

The obese corpse wore denim overalls and a white T-shirt covered in congealed blood. The floor creaked under its heavy steps, sending chills up my spine. How many times had I walked past the foul thing upstairs earlier?

As it reached the head of the stairs, it turned and looked down. I tried to duck behind the leather recliner, but it was too late. It began its descent, stumbling four steps down to the first landing. I raised my gun and fired off a single shot, hitting it in the face, tossing brains and hair onto a group of family photos arranged neatly behind it. The corpse teetered for a moment before falling forward and crashing into the stairs with great force. It slid all the way down to the bottom, hitting with a thud and spilling nasty, putrid liquid onto the floor. I pulled my shemagh over my face to lessen the stench and stepped over the large corpse back onto the stairs.

On my way up, something began to bang on the front door. Once upstairs, I realized that an open door had concealed another door and I'd missed an interior office in my initial check. I stepped into the dark room and hit the light on my gun.

I'd found the last Radio Shack on the planet. Everything from vacuum tubes to old solid-state sets were tucked into tubs or stacked in corners like old shoe boxes. They weren't necessarily important, but the antenna connection damn sure was. I pointed the light around where the ceiling met the walls, eventually finding the white coaxial cable meandering down beside a window and into the back of a multiplexer that sat on a small desk full of equipment.

CRACK!

The floor shook from the impact to the front door. I left the office and went back downstairs to ensure the door was locked before continuing with the comm mission. After making sure the bolt was secure, I went over to the stairs to see if I could move the corpse in front of the door. There was no way I could drag it, given its weight, so I was forced to painstakingly roll it over to the entrance and leg-press it into place.

Back upstairs, I sat down in front of the dust-covered desk and unhooked the antenna line from the mux. I removed the portable radio from my pack and powered it on. Attaching the antenna lead to my radio, I heard strong Morse code fill the room from my small battery-powered speaker.

I began to copy.

"We have a cure. South of Atlanta, Wachovia Tower, CDC site B. Need assistance, position compromised. Doc, TF Phoenix sends . . . AR. BT BT."

I kept reading it over and over again.

A cure? Impossible, isn't it? I thought.

It must really be Phoenix; no one else knew about the task force. And Doc—I knew that name from the debriefs I endured after the Hourglass mission. Doc was the one in charge of the four-man team sent back to Hotel 23 to secure the remaining nuclear weapon. Doc had made the tough decision to launch that missile, disintegrating a group of lunatic eugenicists and potentially saving what was left of humanity from annihilation. Even the possibility that he was now alive in Atlanta and claimed to have a cure made this a rescue mission, and one that could not afford the wasted time of a round trip back to the Keys. There was nothing that could convince me to turn back now.

I was startled by another loud crash coming from the front door and rushed down to see what was happening. As I reached the bottom of the stairs, I could see daylight peeking through the cracked door.

White, bony knuckles gripped its edges, like massive hermit crab legs creeping from a shell. The late-afternoon sunlight shone on the bare teeth that flashed through the opening. I went over to the door and stood on top of the portly corpse I was using as a doorstop. I put my suppressor through the crack. The creature reached to grab it and I fired into its face, sending it to the ground. Another stepped up to the plate and received a similar fate. I repeated this six times, using the heavy front door like a medieval arrow slit.

I hurriedly returned to the HAM office and tossed the desk for extra paper. I then made two copies of the Morse decipher and put one in the bottom of my pack and the other inside the headband of my ball cap. With the sun low in the sky, I snuck out into the overgrown backyard and through the side gate to check on the GARMR. It sat undisturbed next to the Jeep. I commanded it to follow me through the gate and into the backyard, and then put it back into standby in the thick grass near the patio. The tall privacy fence kept undead eyes from spotting me. Not wanting to clear another house before sunset, I went back inside, locked the back door, and barricaded the stairs behind me with furniture as I went up.

As the light began to fade, I knew I needed to somehow find transportation. It had been well over a year since the refineries stopped turning crude oil into gasoline. Most of the gas sitting in the abandoned fuel tanks now was ethanol mixed, meaning the shelf life was very poor compared to real non-ethanol gas. Finding vehicles was the easy part. Finding good fuel and a battery with decent cells was the hard part. The GARMR had been hooked to that soldier's radio when I first discovered it; with any luck, I could put the GARMR to work on my battery problem in the morning.

Distant thunder coming from the west: another Florida storm.

Someone else had survived here for a while some time ago. Half-burned candles sat near the bedside table. A two-year-old pocket HAM repeater directory was in the middle of the bed, covered in dust. A shotgun was propped in the corner near the head-board with a piece of toilet paper stuffed into the barrel. I'd have taken the old wood and blue-steel scattergun, but it was heavy and there weren't any shells besides what was already loaded in the gun. Inside the drawer were a few loose 9mm shells that I placed in my cargo pocket, along with fingernail clippers and a pack of AA batteries. I thumbed through the repeater directory, paying special attention to the highlighted repeaters. They all had hand-written scribbles beside them saying simply, *solar*. I placed the small book in my pack; it would make a good fire starter, if any-thing. There were magazines in the head, along with a yellowed local newspaper dated January twelfth.

> There remains no explanation to the epidemic currently gripping our nation. Authorities have instructed residents to remain in their homes. If you or someone you know becomes infected, dial 911 immediately and wait for authorities to respond. Floridians should install all available hurricane wind shutters to residential windows and doors.
> The following has also been recommended by FEMA and the CDC:
> - Secure enough potable water for 96 hours of service disruption (one gallon per person and pet per day).
> - Barricade ground-level windows and doors with plywood or furniture.
> - Do not approach any infected persons.
> - Do not discharge firearms.
> - Remain calm and quiet.
> - Turn off all non-essential electrical equipment.

All the corpses I kept finding, barricaded in their homes . . . they were told to stay. Even with the best of intentions, this was mur-derous counsel. Every home in this part of Florida was likely full of the undead: People sat huddled in corners with candles and high hopes that the authorities would somehow save them. No government on the face of the planet could have helped their peo-ple through this. The elected officials must have known that they were turning all these suburban homes into tombs when they gave their directive. After all, it was much easier to move in after the outbreak to clear the streets if most of the former residents were locked inside.

I checked the top floor for other artifacts or anything that could be useful. The rain began to fall and the thunder boomed outside. I used this opportunity to toss the upstairs. In the guest room, I found a hunting rifle with a box of twenty 7mm mag shells. I also found a woman's diary and reluctantly opened it to the last written page.

January 19th.

I closed it and put it back where I found it, not wanting to read the private words that likely talked of the undead all around and the large corpse that wore overalls. Those words were not meant for me.

I placed the shotgun and the rifle together, wrapped in trash bags and duct tape to keep them safe from the elements. I'd mark them on my map and place them under the propane grill on my way out tomorrow. They weren't worth the extra weight right now, but perhaps someday I'd come back for them.

With the heavy rain pouring down and the daylight getting low, I sat at the guest room window that overlooked much of the neighborhood. I could see the creatures milling about in the streets. After every flash in the sky and crack of thunder, they jolted and changed direction, as if somehow they could bite the lightning. These things were nothing more than biological machines running a kill program. Walking viruses looking for healthy cells so that they might replicate until there was nothing left to infect.

I had to reduce them to this. Looking at them in any other light was terrifying.

Skylight

Day 6

Dawn came, sending beams of sunlight into my face from the east window down the hall. After forcing myself out of bed, I took my boots off and soaked my feet in collected rainwater, along with the salt I found downstairs. I hated sleeping with my boots on, but I also hated the sounds of doors splintering and the undead spilling into the house while I tried to lace up my footwear.

Although the water was cold, it felt good on my swollen feet. I enjoyed the warmth of the sun on my face. I could hear the undead somewhere out there, stimulated by something, a cat or perhaps a butterfly floating on the morning wind. I dried my feet on a clean towel I'd found in a closet. In a moment of optimism, I turned on the upstairs shower but heard only a puff of air sucking back through the pipes. The gravity tower had long been drained.

I put on my freshest pair of socks and laced up my worn boots. I yearned for the flip-flops on the deck of *Solitude* but knew in my heart that the comfort of my boat was days away, if ever.

Taking advantage of the morning light, I dumped my bag onto the bed and began to re-sort. What worked yesterday almost never worked tomorrow when it came to kit. About the only thing that stayed in the same place was my sleeping bag.

In the assortment of things laid out in front of me was something I'd taken from Hourglass but never reported in debrief. A curious item from a time that I'd never know or could try to imagine. I kept the thing secured in an old leather holster in the bottom of my pack.

After arranging everything, I shouldered my pack and went downstairs. The smell of the overall-wearing corpse was stronger, prompting me to hurry up and leave.

Opening the door, I nearly shot Checkers. I didn't expect it to be standing there in the doorway, looking at me with that spinning sensor. Catching my breath, I used this opportunity to examine the machine's casing.

It didn't appear to have any way to draw from its nuclear battery that I could see, but I'd remembered connecting the solar panels on the saddlebags into the machine. According to the manuals, the RTG fed four integral-to-the-frame lithium polymer batteries that the GARMR used to pull any surge power requirements. Also feeding the batteries was the experimental and flexible solar array on the saddlebags. The combined power from the solar panels and the nuclear battery gave the GARMR a range above and beyond what I could cover on foot in any given day. I planned to leverage some of this power to somehow start a vehicle.

I then headed north in the general direction of Atlanta, out of the coastal suburbs. I kept a safe offset of a few meters to the undead-infested road. Up ahead through the trees, I could see the familiar signage of a Walmart. It took two hours to get there; I had to stay low most of the way to avoid being spotted by the creatures. There were too many of them near the road, and the rusted chain-link fence that separated us would not hold them back for long. With the GARMR slogging through the tall grass behind me, I had to find a way to get over the fence. The GARMR was too heavy (and radioactive) to attempt lifting it over the six-foot barrier. I began my attempt to cut through the chain-link material, but had to abort as six creatures walked up to me on the other side. I ran down the fence line to escape their attention and came upon a damaged section with just enough clearance to get the GARMR over.

I came through the fence behind the store, seeing the delivery trucks that had been backed into the loading bays for over a year now, never to be loaded or unloaded again. They were covered in green mildew and grime; one of them sat unevenly with a flat front tire.

The undead from the fence were getting close and beginning to moan. They'd draw more if I didn't take care of them. At a hundred yards, I took my shots. I didn't normally try to take them out at this distance, which is why my first shot hit the lead corpse in the chest, knocking it farther back in the advancing pack. I remembered to compensate for the slower subsonic round and aimed six inches above their heads.

Bang, and half a second later I'd hear the wet impact of the heavy round penetrating a skull. A pattern: the suppressed round, skull impact, and then the sound of a body hitting the pavement. In post-apocalyptic drum solo fashion, this rhythm was repeated until no more corpses advanced. The GARMR stood nearby observing, analyzing the situation in real time.

With nothing else between the semitrucks and me, I ran to the tank of the nearest one and thumped it with my rifle to listen to the sound. I removed the fuel cap and used my gun light to look down into the tank.

Half.

I moved on to the next semi.

Quarter.

I didn't have a hose or any tools beyond the multitool in my cargo pocket. I jumped up onto the running boards, causing my weapon to smack up against the exhaust pipe, and had a look inside. The main cab was neat and empty, but it was dark back in the sleeper part of the cab. Who knew what my noisiness would bring. I pulled the handle; it was unlocked. A folder with a fuel card and a set of keys sat in the passenger seat across the cab. The name signed on the fuel logs was *Chuck*. The truck smelled clean on the inside, with a hint of pine from the freshener attached to the vents. I slowly closed the driver's-side door behind me and switched on my gun light. A short-barreled rifle was handy in tight spots like semitrucks and crashed helicopters.

Crawling into the back, rifle first, I saw nothing out of the ordinary. The small bed was neatly made and a case of diet soda sat on the floorboard along with a roll of TP and some gun magazines. I ran my hands under the bed and felt something plastic. Pulling it into the light, I could see it was a green case marked *Ruger* on the top. I flipped open the two plastic clasps and lifted the lid, revealing a Ruger Mark III .22 pistol with two empty magazines. I scoured the back of the truck for any signs of ammo, but there were none. Useless; the gun might as well be a hammer. I placed it back in its case and tucked it under the bed where I'd found it, right next to the fast-food french fry that had somehow escaped the driver's neat tendencies.

I returned to the front of the cab, swiping the keys as I sat down. I'd only seen someone drive one of these a few times; they were a bit more complicated than your run-of-the-mill soccer dad standard transmission.

I attempted to start the truck but nothing happened. After fumbling for a few minutes, trying to figure out how to get the hood up, I pulled the battery and walked over to the south side of the building.

There were corpses standing two hundred yards away near the other corner of the building.

"Checkers, stay," I instructed.

Its legs retracted as I ran over, carrying the heavy battery against my hip. I worked quickly, unplugging the solar panels from the GARMR and using zip ties to secure the leads to the semi's battery. I adjusted the panels southerly and placed dead leaves and pieces of a pallet over the GARMR to conceal it while I moved on to the second stage of my vehicle plan.

Checking the toolbox on the rig, I found a thick yellow nylon tow strap. I wrapped it around my body several times like a mountain climber. I took what I needed from my pack and tossed it into the cab before I found my way onto the trailer. Not being a trucker, I had no idea how to disconnect the trailer from the cab. Wherever I'd be taking this rig, I'd be doing it with the trailer behind me, whether it be full of ammo, blue jeans, rotted produce, or empty. As I walked the length of the rectangle roof, the weight of my body caused the metal to buckle in places. This noise resonated down the trailer and into the store beyond. The semi was fully backed up into the loading bay doors; there would be no way inside without moving the truck and no way to move the truck without a charged battery.

I slowly climbed the slick drainage pipe leading to the roof and strained to negotiate the slight overhang before rolling onto the hot tar cover. I was getting old too fast. I lay there for a moment, catching my breath, before getting up to secure a way inside.

The surface of the roof was monotonous, like the moon, with skylights as convex craters spaced evenly in a grid. The milky white translucence of the skylight covers didn't allow for a view into the store below. Using my fixed blade, I began to pry the nearest cover. After a few minutes of work, I was able to pop it off and get my first whiff of the rot contained inside the abyss below. With trepidation, I stuck my head and rifle into the hole and flipped on the powerful 500-lumen torch. Hanging my torso over the opening, the sweet smell of food rot met my nostrils along with a hint of human decomposition.

I wouldn't be alone.

The skylight I'd chosen wasn't ideal; it would put me down on the white tile between aisles—basically hot lava, according to the children's game. Upside down, the blood rushed to my head while I looked in all directions for a better option. I counted two skylights over and one up, choosing a drop that would put me down on top of the shelves instead of on vulnerable ground level. I could see dark figures moving in the recesses beyond, but I didn't shine my torch on them for fear of attracting company.

After removing the other skylight, I secured the towing strap to a pipe on the nearby air circulator. After tying a few knots in the yellow strap, I tossed it down into the darkness and watched it unravel and snap two feet from the top of what looked like cases of . . . bottled water.

Incredible.

I couldn't believe that bottled water hadn't been looted this long into the grid failing and the dead walking. I reached into my cargo pocket and pulled out one of the green chemlights. I snapped it and attached it to the strap near the skylight opening. I'd want an easy visual reference I could find with my NOD if need be.

I'd be going down into the well of souls with the bare minimum; otherwise, I wouldn't be able to climb back up the strap to the roof.

It was time.

I dangled my legs down into the dark opening and felt for one of the knots with my boots. Hand under hand, I let gravity do its thing until my feet felt the end of the strap. I'd been looking up into the sunlight the whole time and still did so even after I felt the cases of bottled water under my boots. Up there was safety and security; down here was something different.

The sound of something hitting the floor below pulled my eyes away from the bright opening.

I eased the NOD down over my eye. A two-liter soda bottle was spraying its contents all over a long-dead woman. I ignored it and stayed low, careful to maintain my balance on the cases of water. As I took the high ground, I began to understand why this valuable resource remained. The looters couldn't reach these top shelves and fight off the undead at the same time.

The soda-soaked creature now shadowed me below. I was hesitant to take it out. Suppressed gunfire would only bring more of them. I edged myself to the other side of the shelf, out of the creature's sphere of stimulation, and began looking for the signs spread out over the cavernous building. The place I needed was halfway across the store.

Automotive.

I walked low on top of the creaking water bottles to the end of the shelf. I could still hear the corpse on the opposite side, which was unaware that I'd moved farther away from it. Reaching the end of the shelf, I had no other choice but to break the hot lava game rules and step on the floor. I reluctantly slung my gun across my back and climbed down the shelf. As my boot touched the tile below, I was terrified by the fresh tracks in the dust all around me.

There were too many of them.

I kept to the darkness, avoiding the areas under the skylights, places the undead would see me and somehow realize in their primordial synapses that I wasn't one of them. I stayed low, crouching below the racks of cheap clothing as I scurried toward the tall shelf full of tires about fifty yards ahead.

Rounding a rack full of clearance clothing, I was stopped in my tracks by one of them facing away from me. There was something unnerving about a human form that didn't move, didn't breathe, soulless. It was like being in a wax museum full of sculptures that would kill you on sight if given the opportunity.

I peeked up over the clothing displays, making sure that nothing else would hear my attack. I reached for the switchblade I kept on my belt and pulled it with a soft click of Kydex. I quietly approached the creature and positioned my thumb over the fire button. I pressed and the strong spring fired the razor-sharp blade out the front of the handle. The creature started to react, but it was too late. I rammed the five-inch *tantō* spike into the creature's temple and put my arms around its torso from behind. Lowering the corpse to the cold floor, I could smell the sickening necrosis.

Staying low, I moved quickly to the next department.

Toys.

As I walked down the aisle I could see a single set of footprints in the dust. I looked back to the other side of the store, to where I'd dropped down. I could clearly see the chemlight dangling from the tow strap through my NOD; the device auto-gate kicked in, dimming the night vision to compensate for the skylight above me. Rain began to pour through the opening, down into the store. I moved to the next shadow between skylights and discovered the decayed remains of a large dog fused to the floor.

At least humans have a shot with our intelligence and our ability to reason. I hate it when I find a dead dog.

Automotive was two shelves away. I began to move to my objective when I heard the squeaking of shopping cart wheels nearby. I crouched low, clutching the aluminum rail of my M4 so tightly that I could feel the sharp edges dig into my hands. The squeak continued on the other side of the shelf. Slow, deliberate, and maddening. There was no other way to Automotive; I had to pass by the next aisle. I waited in anticipation for the squeaking to stop. A few seconds of silence would pass by, getting my hopes up, before the squeaking started up again. I circled the long way to the other side of the aisle and slowly stuck my head around the corner to see the source of the terrifying noise.

The corpse of an old woman dressed in a nightgown stood behind the cart, nudging it forward as she moved. Old blood covered the front of her dress all the way down to her knees; a pair of reading glasses hung around her neck on a lanyard. Most of the right side of her face was torn open. I couldn't be certain, but I suspected that the large bag in her cart was dog food.

The aisle was shrouded in darkness, giving me no reason to think she could see me from this far away on the opposite side. I waited until the corpse looked down and then I bolted to the next aisle, right into the waiting arms of a goddamned stock boy.

We fell to the floor, grappling as we went. I held the creature's cold, snakelike throat, keeping its snapping jaws at bay. As I strained to reach my knife, I could hear the squeak from the shopping cart approaching . . . now faster.

I bucked the stock boy off; its skull thumped the hard tile floor like a ripe melon, giving me time to pull my knife. I fired the spike just before jamming it into stock boy's eye. I yanked the blade from the eye socket and darted behind the nearby service desk.

I waited in terror, holding my breath, listening to the shopping cart approach.

It stopped for a few eternal seconds and then moved again, louder and nearer.

I crouched, trembling, my back to the L-shaped service desk, as the cart squeaked closer and closer.

I felt a slight vibration as the cart bumped the counter from the other side. First the papers fell to the standing mat next to me, then a pen. I looked up to the lip of the counter but dared not prairie dog my head above it.

The ghastly face appeared suddenly above me, looking down on me from over the counter; it began to screech and flail for my flesh. My carbine was pointed up like a mortar tube when I pulled the trigger, sending the creature's brains flying into the air and down all around me. The shot was thunderous, echoing in the aisles of the massive store. A chorus of undead responded to the intrusive noise. I heard clothing racks being knocked over and merchandise hitting the floor all over the place.

Fuck it. Sprinting, I was in Automotive in no time. I grabbed a nylon towrope, two red gas cans, and a length of hose. Using the rope, I secured the cans and hose together and slung them over my shoulder.

I made for the chemlight, but just as I was about to hit my stride, I noticed a corpse sprawled out in Sporting Goods with a rifle jammed in what used to be its mouth. A year of decomposition nearly flattened the remains, leaving an outline of clothing and skeletal limbs.

With the undead converging, I sprinted over to the corpse and found a brick of .22LR ammunition sitting open nearby. The .22 rifle was held securely in place by bony hands; I didn't have time for it.

With the .22LR ammo now in my cargo pocket and slamming against my thigh, I ran as hard as I could for the chemlight.

The undead spilled out from all sides into my aisle. I let out a burst of gunfire that knocked many of them down and turned the dim lights out on the rest. They couldn't see me as well as I could see them.

I was in the shadows, zigzagging through the darkness between skylights. My M4 bolt locked to the rear as I engaged a dozen corpses. With no time for a mag change, I threw my carbine over my head, letting the sling place it across my back alongside the gas cans as it dropped.

I drew my Glock.

The bright tritium glow from the night sights streaked across my NOD before the auto-gate stabilized the images. I took three ear-ringing shots at nearly point-blank range, dropping three of the undead to the white tile for keeps. Juking by two more, I was at my shelf.

As I began to climb, the aisle filled up from all directions. Within thirty seconds they were shoulder to shoulder, reaching up, shaking the shelf. I jumped from case to case until I reached the tow strap. Rain poured down from the opening above, trickling down the strap. I secured one end of the new rope to the tow strap and tied the other end to the supplies I'd just risked my life to acquire. I also secured a case of water to the rope's extra slack.

Taking advantage of the adrenaline coursing through my bloodstream, I ascended the knotted yellow lifeline, leaving the gear and water on the shelf below. I tried my best not to look down as I climbed into the light. Every inch I ascended, I thought about my toprope anchor. Would it hold?

I was sucking wind as I pulled myself over the lip of the skylight fitting and onto the roof. Drenched with sweat and rain, I began to heave the haul up from the darkness. It wasn't long before the two gas cans, a length of black hose, and the case of water were on the roof with me. I downed three bottles before deciding on my next move.

Horde

Day 6

The rain was coming down in sheets as I tossed my haul from the roof onto the top of the semitrailer. It impacted with a thump, attracting the attention of a char-grilled corpse, blackened from some previous fire. Climbing down the pipe to the top of the trailer, I saw the blackened corpse begin to pound its fire-hardened limbs against the side of the truck. The miserable creature's fingers were fused together, forming curved flippers. Its eyelids, lips, and ears were long gone; the thing stared up at me through the rain, unblinking and gnashing its jagged teeth together with a snap that I swear could be heard over the rain. My rifle was empty, so I pulled the storage compartment from the carbine grip that held three rounds, yanked the mag, and dropped one into the chamber before releasing the bolt and jamming the empty mag bag in. Leaning over the side of the trailer, I tried to aim at the corpse, but the rain was too heavy. I couldn't see through the red dot optic. I lowered the gun as far as I could, firing the round with one hand about a foot from the charred skull. The round impacted its dome, splitting it open to the elements and sending it down into a puddle formed by weathered concrete. My bolt locked back on my rifle, prompting me to involuntarily release the empty mag and reach for another that wasn't there.

With the rain falling like it was, I took my haul with me off the top of the truck and escaped by climbing into the cab of the truck I intended to bring back to life. The smell of the air freshener was welcome. I closed my eyes and imagined that I was sitting in my car a few years ago. I smelled the pine and listened to the rain be interrupted by bouts of thunder. The moment of Zen didn't last long. The flash of lightning illuminated the adjacent field for a few seconds. Out there among nature's rage was a horde of creatures sweeping across the landscape of hills and trees. In moments I would be overwhelmed, trapped. Hurriedly, I reached for a full mag from my pack and slapped it into my carbine, racking a round into the chamber. I checked my suppressor for tight fit and sprinted out into the relentless storm.

At the GARMR, I pulled my knife and sliced the zip ties that connected the GARMR's solar saddlebags to the truck battery.

"Checkers, follow!" I yelled over the rain at the Simon watch.

I ran to the truck and the GARMR stood and began to trot in pursuit, dragging its red and black charging leads like entrails. The rain masked their smell. I had no time to fuck around; part of the main horde had now broken off in my direction. They didn't yet see me, but that would change rapidly if I remained outside any longer.

I placed the battery under the cab and crawled under the trailer, leading the GARMR behind me before instructing it to stay. It went dormant as I was climbing up the running boards into the driver's side of the truck.

They were at the fence. I dared not slam the door, closing it only enough to hear a click. I sat in the comfortable seat and watched the horde as the windows began to fog from my hyperventilated breathing.

Wiping the condensation from the glass with my sleeve, I watched the corpses march over the field, buckling the nearby chain-link fence when too many of them grouped together. The fence held and worked as sort of a guide, herding the mass east. I took the magnifier from my carbine to get a better look at them. All sorts marched together in hellish union. A sparse number of recently dead shambled along with corpses that likely had only a few nerve endings remaining from their decaying brains to their slogging legs. The massive, tireless group moved east.

It took three hours before the tail of the corpse army came into view. The mass became noticeably less dense and was populated by severely decomposed corpses missing most of their skin and tissue. Some walked on near stumps, getting stuck as their sharp bones sank deep into the rain-soaked soil. I felt no pity for them, not after losing so many, most likely my parents, my fellow officers, and Will.

The sun was low in the sky when the clouds finally broke. Birds flew by overhead as if nothing was amiss down here among the tsunami of walking corpses. The new ecosystem gave the birds an unfair Darwinian advantage. They could fly above the dead and sleep in trees. The natural enemy to their young crawled on the ground and slithered with the worms. The undead would eat snakes just as fast as they would any human. Who knows—perhaps one day they'll take over as the new dominant species on the planet.

I pressed the window button, simultaneously realizing that there was no battery to power the truck's systems. With night approaching soon, I again organized my kit and switched out the batteries on my NOD with a fresh set. I reloaded my empty magazine and drank my fill of bottled water.

With the rain subsided along with the passing horde, I could hear faint sounds coming from inside the store. The angry dead still thrashed and searched wall to wall for me. The image of the corpse of the old lady looking down on me from the opposite side of the countertop was burned into my brain.

As the sun dipped below the hill, I exited the vehicle and moved the GARMR to a safer area next to a fire hydrant surrounded by four concrete pylons. I lugged the battery over to the GARMR and reattached it to the saddlebag solar panels. Protected by the darkness of a moonless night, I started the onerous task of siphoning diesel fuel five gallons at a time from the disabled semi to the one that I thought I could get running. After two hours, my mouth burned of diesel but the tank was full on my rig. The tank I'd been pulling from belonged to the semi with a flat front tire. I didn't have an air compressor nor did I have the equipment required to change the tire of one of these behemoths, so I was forced, via NOD, to compare the visual condition of the trucks before I began sucking diesel. The tanks were cross-connected but I still alternated between filling the right and left tanks in case there might be a cross-link blockage. Afterward, I was completely exhausted and nauseous from the fumes and diesel blisters in my mouth. I knew that diesel was far less refined than ethanol-laced gas, so there was a shot that it was still good fuel.

With nothing more to do tonight, I decided to head for the truck's sleeper and turn in. With any luck, I'd have this beast running by the afternoon. I was comforted by the fact that the truck cab sat high off the ground and that the windows were well out of reach of all but the most irradiated attacker. With the doors locked, I collapsed in the bed with my carbine across my chest, just like a scared child clutched his blanket while a monster lurked somewhere below.

Dawn

Day 7

I woke at daybreak in a panic. I'd slept so soundly that I'd forgotten where I was the night before, even without an empty bottle of scotch at my feet. It took a few seconds, but the previous day's events began to play back at a blinding speed in my mind, catching my consciousness up to the bed I sat in, sweating. It was already warm and the humidity was soaring. My chest was covered in no-see-um bites and I was dehydrated. I downed two bottles of water and filled one up with fluorescent yellow piss and tossed it out the side window with a *thunk*. The only undead that remained were those nearly rotting corpses that were stuck in the mud in the adjacent field. Reaching under the seat, I pulled out a lead-filled wooden tire checker with a lanyard of olive-drab paracord routed through the handle.

I recovered the Ruger pistol from its green plastic container under the bed. I pulled the action a few times, the slide painfully pinching my thumb and index finger. I could smell a thin coat of minty lubrication on the gun. The barrel wasn't threaded, but it really didn't matter. I only had a 7.62 can that wouldn't fit the threads even if the pistol barrel was silencer ready. I loaded the ten-round magazines and inserted one into the gun before racking the slide and engaging the safety.

The front seat was peppered with empty water bottles, giving me an idea. I took the magazines from the back and began to tear out pages, stuffing small shreds into one of the empty bottles. Once it was full, I poured some water inside and split the mouth of the bottle. Taking a zip tie from my pack, I carefully secured the bottle over the pistol barrel.

The door opened with a creak as I hopped down the steps

onto the weathered concrete unloading area. Before I forgot, I positioned the solar panels southeast to maximize power to the battery. At the fence, I could see the damage done by the passing horde. Three stuck corpses leaned their heads in my direction and began to gurgle noisily through their shredded windpipes. I hopped the fence and approached one of the flailing sacks of rotting meat. I placed the water bottle on its head and selected *Fire* on the Ruger.

I pulled the trigger.

Pop.

It was loud, but not as much as my suppressed carbine. I repeated the process, eliminating the immobilized undead until my magazine ran dry. The shots got progressively louder as I blew out the guts of my makeshift silencer with each round I sent into the skulls of the creatures. I yanked the bottle off the end of the gun and tossed it into the mud, disgusted. A bulky silencer effective for only five or ten rounds wouldn't do me any favors. I stuffed the warm pistol under my belt and splashed through the dark mud back to the semi.

I had lunch on the roof of the trailer, glassing the area all around me with my binos, seeing nothing but the occasional corpse stumbling through the fields in the distance. Once back in the truck, I placed the brick of .22 ammo and the Ruger pistol in the GARMR's saddlebags and again adjusted the panels into the rising Florida sun. As I crouched below the trailer, I could hear a faint thumping on the aluminum walls.

One of them might be inside, or it could just be from the creatures in the store.

Feeling like a million dollars for a multimeter would be a fair trade, I ignored the noises and focused on organizing the cab of the truck as well as my gear. I hadn't scavenged the nearby truck with the flat tire, so I methodically worked that from the back to the front, taking tools, ropes, and everything else that might come in handy from its exterior. The cab was locked, but there didn't seem to be anything useful inside, and this one didn't have a sleeper compartment. Breaking the window wasn't worth the trouble or the noise.

Thump, thump, thump came the sound from the other trailer.

I hoped it would go away. I looked up at the bright sun that beamed down onto the copper-tinted solar panels.

"Shine, you bastard," I said aloud, willing the photons onto the panels and the electrons into the precious battery.

At about ten thirty, I decided to give it a shot. I disconnected the battery and lumbered up onto the engine compartment. I replaced the leads and nearly fell from the truck as loud static began blasting from the speakers inside the cab. I jumped off the engine and raced up into the cab, shutting off the source of the dinner bell static. The key wasn't even in the ignition. The trucker had his CB wired to work without the key.

Thump, thump—the sound from the trailer continued.

I worked quickly, preparing for a mob of undead to round any corner without notice.

As I worked, a question formed in my mind: *How am I going to get the GARMR in the cab?*

Pushing the problem out of my head for the moment, I plugged the panels back into the GARMR's lithium polymer battery frame, tucking the cords out of its way.

"Checkers, follow."

The machine walked gracefully over to me in the shaded grass. I told it to stay and ran back over to the truck. Up in the cab with the door open, I went through the steps I remembered. The machine started on the second attempt, blowing dark smoke from its stack and over my hood. I let the long-dormant engine spin and lubricate for a minute before putting it into gear and edging forward.

Something fell behind the truck. Looking back into my rearview mirror, the creature began to get back on its feet. I gave the truck some gas and parked near the GARMR, leaving it running. I jumped down off the truck and nearly twisted my ankle, sending off an unwanted shot into the brick facade of the store. As the round zinged off the wall, I put another one into the corpse's face, disconnecting enough nerves to put it down, but not enough to stop it from moving. The thing jerked and twisted uncontrollably as I focused on the open loading bay doors and into the deep black.

Nothing came for me.

The truck was still running when an idea hit me. I ran to the back of the trailer, hoping to see pallets of ammunition and dry food but instead found rotted lettuce. I pulled one of the aluminum-undermounted ramps down from the back of the truck and pressed the follow button on the beacon watch. As I came up the ramp, I heard the sounds of several creatures rounding the outside corner of the store. The other truck was between the advancing creatures and me. They didn't notice me yet. The GARMR clicked and clacked up the ramp into the trailer; I told it to stay and stowed the ramp before getting back into the cab.

All at once, the things poured into the loading area from both corners of the store, no doubt attracted by the CB static and engine noise. They began to quickly fill the area. Not wanting to damage my ride, I kept it in first and rolled slowly through the growing crowd, crunching some under the massive weight of the truck and knocking others to the side. After passing the majority of them, I upshifted, eventually getting to twenty miles per hour as I rounded the corner past the automotive bays and into the front parking lot. Coming out of the turn, my tire took out a concrete guard with a loud clang, sending it flying under the semi.

I departed the store lot and turned out onto the road, towing a trailer full of rotten lettuce. As I straightened the rig out on the overgrown road, I checked my mirrors and saw a hundred creatures marching out behind me. I gave it some gas, banking around abandoned cars and road debris. My companions in the passenger seat were the two empty fuel jugs and a length of hose sitting near my carbine. As I stayed slow and attentive to the hazards of the road, I tuned through CB channels, hoping to miraculously land on some intel. I found nothing but silence and static as I tuned the dial back and forth along every citizens band frequency.

I was having luck navigating around the deep potholes and wrecked cars until I came to a roadblock up ahead consisting of a giant red conex box. I stopped the truck, grabbed my rifle and binos, and headed for the roof. I lay prone on the top, glassing the roadblock. The heat coming off the blacktop caused mirage distortion. I saw movement, figures walking back and forth in front of the red box. I got back into the cab and idled ahead for a closer look. When I got to within two hundred meters, the situation became apparent.

The roadblock was abandoned.

There were half a dozen animated corpses chained by their necks to the base of the conex. As I crept to within a hundred meters, I could make out the faded black spray-painted letters on the front of the metal box:

YOU'RE DEAD!

I rolled up to the roadblock slowly with my carbine sitting across my lap. Scanning left and right, I saw no indicators of ambush or other shenanigans, so I stopped the truck in front of the conex, just out of reach of the incarcerated creatures. I listened to their chains drag and scrape against the ground; the sounds sent me back to a memory of the undead chain gang I was once forced to deal with. My handwritten record of that encounter was lost in some Hourglass lab somewhere too secret for my pay grade.

The creatures here, though, converged on the truck, the slack in their chains pulled taut just out of reach. With duct tape from the truck's toolbox, I attached my five-inch *tantō* switchblade to the tire thumper. The corpses were dispatched quickly and quietly without incident. There was a guard shack (if you could even call it that) sitting out of direct view behind a van. It consisted of a tarp for a roof over a few rusted folding chairs and one of those plastic folding craft tables. Using one of the chairs, I climbed up onto the red conex box and looked over to the other side.

What I saw caused me to drop to the roof, melting into it in order to get as flat as possible. The other side of the roadblock was crawling with the undead. I slunk slowly off the box and went for the yellow tow strap I'd used to fasten rope down into the store. I didn't waste any time attaching one of the undead's chain collars to the front bumper of the semi, not even bothering to free the cadaver. I jumped up into the cab and put it in reverse. Backing slowly, the heavy-duty yellow strap took the slack from the chain, raising the body off the ground in a grotesque pose. The truck stopped moving, so I gave it more gas, causing the large metal box to screech across the surface of the road in my direction.

The adrenaline flowed, brought on by the corpses coming at me from both sides of the box. I gave the truck more gas, yanking the box from its long-held spot on the road, revealing a rectangular outline of rust where it sat before. I barely got the truck parked before jumping out and retrieving the tow strap. I took a parting shot at one of them just before it grabbed me by the shoulder.

It got that close.

I was up in the cab just before the mass of creatures surrounded the truck. I couldn't close the door now; there were too many trying to climb up into the cab. I edged the truck forward, kicking wildly outside, tempted to empty a precious mag into the ones that blocked the door. Rolling past the roadblock, I saw two of the undead wearing severed ears as necklaces. They had guns slung tightly across their chests, FN FALs. Might as well be on a different planet; there was no salvaging them from the sea of undead that surrounded the rig. These guys were probably bad news when they were alive. I kept rolling on, away from the creatures, rounding two more bends before losing them.

An hour after the roadblock, I came to a long straight stretch in the road with nothing for miles in both directions but a few abandoned cars. One of them had an open side window with a small oak tree growing through it and out the shattered front glass. In fifty years, that car would be high off the ground and someone like me would wonder how the fuck that could have happened.

Perspective.

I took this time to shut down the rig and regroup. I was fairly sure the alternator would have charged the battery over the past few hours of hauling ass at a brisk twenty-mile-per-hour average. I checked the atlas I'd found wedged between the seats; I was on Highway 319 heading north to Tallahassee. Using the scale on the map, I estimated that I was more than two hundred miles away from Atlanta. Part of me wanted to turn back right now and head for the gulf, for *Solitude*. The other wanted my wife and child to live in a world where they would never have to worry about a corpse climbing into their window at night. I knew Tara would be concerned and pissed; I missed both her and Bug more than anything in the world.

But my idea? I just had to try.

Everything that gave me happiness in the world was at the mercy of the undead.

As I penciled my route north onto the road atlas, I imagined what these parts might be like thirty years from now. Anyone handy with a gun and a few rounds could make it out here if they were smart and not too brave. Guns got you food and water and everything else left abandoned to the undead. If you had guns, you could waste enough of them to loot an entire warehouse full of food and water. What would happen when the guns wore out and all the bullets resided in the skulls of a hundred million corpses turning to dust out here? Then that will be the age of the mountain man, the true survivor forced to learn to make it out here without endless ammunition and food that hasn't expired. Right now, we're making it off the back of fading technology and production capacity that died along with most of the population. With no refineries, we're all pretty much on foot within a few years. Ammo will probably become currency. I've scavenged spare sails from other derelict boats in my travels, putting them in a safe place along with riggings and extra parts. I've thought this through as much as any man could. We're beyond peak oil now. Beyond peak everything.

I hadn't made much progress since the roadblock. Even this back-road highway was in pretty sad shape. I've had to stop and pull three cars out of the way, some of them filled with hungry corpses. I heard them but couldn't really see them inside their vehicles; the glass was translucent, too glazed over with whatever slime sunbaked corpses secreted. As I slowly edged north, I came to a large lake just off the highway to the east. Rolling forward, I nearly turned the rig around from what I saw. There were dozens of corpses on the banks of the lake walking into the water, trying to get at something. The noise from my engine peeled a few off from the mass at the shore. They lumbered in the direction of my rig with their arms reaching out, as if they had no depth perception that I was over a hundred meters away.

As I watched the advancing creatures, I caught something out of the corner of my eye. The water flashed white near the beach and a dozen corpses were knocked over like bowling pins in a strike roll. A few of them turned over onto their backs and stood back up. They again advanced into the water nearly up to their knees. The other stricken corpses were flailing miserably on the beach, covered with mud.

Something had broken their legs. Through my binoculars, I could see white bones from compound fractures poking through the gray and rotting skin of their thighs and knees.

The creatures that ventured out into the water were agitated by something.

I watched one as it was taken under in a violent blast of white and black water. Then it happened again. I kept watching the battle between the creatures and the lake, still unsure of what I was seeing. I hadn't been this entertained and mystified in a damn long time.

I rolled the truck farther down the road. Fixated on the water, I nearly ran the truck off the road. I slammed the brakes, throwing me forward into the steering wheel as a massive fourteen-foot something partially beached itself and grabbed one of the undead in its powerful jaws, pulling it back into the black, death-rolling the creature into pieces.

My mouth hung open at the fearlessness of the alligator.

It wasn't working alone.

Two other alligators showed themselves just in front of the group of corpses that were dumb enough to wade into knee-deep water with thousand-pound reptiles. The beasts tore into them, ripping their decomposing bodies to pieces by sheer jaw pressure and lacerating death rolls. The large alligator came back for more after its smaller companions took their enemies under the water. Unafraid, the alpha reptile charged the beach. It was completely out of the water, swinging its large tail at lighting speed into a fresh group of advancing creatures. The undead didn't stand a chance. The alligator's tail impacted with a sickening *thwack*, tossing broken bodies like rag dolls into the water near the muddy shoreline. Similar to the wild boars I'd encountered, these half-ton reptiles were well fed and not afraid to use the weapons that millions of years of evolution provided them.

My concentration on the spectacle was broken by a thumping on the driver's-side door. Four corpses stared at me from the ground below, unsuccessfully attempting to climb the steps to the door. I reluctantly put the rig into gear and rolled forward slowly, past the scene of reptilian carnage I'd never forget. Just like the birds, alligators were suited to survival against the dead. The birds could fly over unthinkable hordes; the alligators could simply swim away or feast on rotten flesh from the safety of the murky waters they dominated.

"*Eat every last one of the fuckers!*" I screamed out the window as I drove past.

1700

I'd only made about twenty miles of progress since leaving Alligator Lake. Fuel state looked good, but I'd be looking out for somewhere to siphon some diesel tomorrow if possible. I found a mansion off the road with a wide turnaround driveway to park for the night. At probably five thousand square feet, I didn't have the inclination or energy to clear the place. This fact was hammered home by the corpse I saw inside looking out at me and clawing at the window on the second floor. There was no telling what horrors awaited me inside.

I climbed up into the trailer to check on the GARMR. It had slid a couple feet from where I'd put it on standby. I began to toss out pallets of rotted lettuce and was assaulted by flies and mosquitoes for my effort. I kept clearing the trailer. The pile of lettuce boxes outside grew larger as I moved closer to the front. As I got rid of the rest of the rotten food, I felt the cool air from the trailer's refrigeration unit blowing against my face. I figured out how to disable it, hoping to save a few precious drops of diesel.

I slid the aluminum ramp down and hit the follow button on the GARMR. As it exited the trailer, I pulled out the tablet and began to direct the machine through the tall, unkempt grass leading behind the mansion. Like the spiral staircase house I'd used for shelter, this one had a large screened-in back area with a pool. I watched the high-definition feed streaming onto the tablet as I sat in relative safety inside the cab. The GARMR feed showed five or six corpses standing in the field behind the house. There was also a detached three-car garage in the back near the pool.

I recalled the machine, waiting until I heard the soft clicks of its synthetic hooves on the driveway outside the door. I could handle half a dozen of them. With no swarms in the vicinity, I stowed the GARMR and listened to Willie Nelson, the only CD I could find in the truck.

2145

The thing in the window kept rapping on the glass, trying to get out. I pulled the NOD from my pack, dialed my red dot down to the lowest setting, and rolled down the passenger window. The moon was reflecting its bright eight-minute-old light showdown, illuminating the area.

Through my optic I could make out the female corpse standing there with a bandolier of something hung across her body. Possibly shotgun shells. She'd been dead a long time; her eyes were sunken and her lips shriveled, allowing the moonlight to shine from her jagged and broken teeth. I took aim with my SBR and squeezed the trigger. The round impacted the glass, shattering the pane instantaneously, sending the corpse to the floor with a thump. I couldn't hear anything else coming from inside the house. I sat there in the cab with my NOD still on, watching the smoke slowly rise from the ejection port.

Higher Education

Last night I dreamed of alligators, hundreds of them chasing me all over God's green earth. At some point, I thought I'd gotten up and checked the window again, seeing the curtain move as if something was inside. Now my back aches and I'm fatigued from tossing and turning. Something about the nearby house puts my hackles up.

At about 0700 I had put my boots on, stretched, and checked my surroundings in the morning light. Satisfied that nothing would grab me on the way out, I jumped down to the running board and to the driveway below. Without even thinking, I pressed the Follow button on the Simon and watched the empty lettuce boxes I'd stacked fall away from the sleeping GARMR. Its sensor spun up and its head tracked me as I began to walk, waiting until a space of ten feet was between us before its electrical and hydraulic servo motors sent it trotting after me. I don't know why I told the machine to follow; I just did. It wasn't a dog, but it was something that filled some primal void in my brain that didn't like being completely alone. The machine was utterly efficient in its movements, rationing every joule expended. I'd only seen cheetahs walk like that on TV. With the African population being what it was before the dead walked, I doubted that any cheetahs remained. Perhaps they weren't nuked and the corpses were all being picked apart by the sand and birds of the Sahara.

I edged forward toward the large house. Its curtain-filled win-

89

dows and disheveled appearance gave off an unsettling vibe. I walked past the front of the house as the GARMR clicked behind me down the vintage ribbon driveway. Nourished by the heavy rains, huge mushrooms sprouted in the center of the driveway between the ribbons that led to the garage up ahead. Reaching the driveway, I could see the tall grass waving beside the garage. Thinking of the wild pigs, I raised my carbine in defense.

The GARMR advanced ahead of me onto the slab in front of the three closed garage bay doors. As it reached its spot, an extremely decomposed corpse emerged from beside the garage and began to come for me. The GARMR walked in front of the pseudo-skeleton, causing it to stumble. As it began to recover its balance, I studied the corpse. I could not see one square inch of skin remaining on its body. Sinew and tendons worked its limbs in plain view like a see-through grandfather clock. Its one milky white eye locked onto me. I could see the individual bones in its hands and even exposed ribs. I squeezed the trigger, impacting the thing at the top of the head. The rotting corpse nearly fell onto the GARMR as it hit the concrete driveway with a wet splat.

Birds flew up and away from the brush in reaction to the gunshot. I reached down and tugged at the center garage bay door with no success. It was locked down pretty tight. With the other two doors also secure, I rounded the side of the garage between it and the screened-in area behind the house. There was a side door underneath a massive wisteria plant that wrapped around a pergola post like a python and covered the pergola's roof. The unkempt wisteria trunk was in a black pot next to the pergola post, but it had long forced its roots through the bottom of the pot and deep into the ground. It had already dominated the pergola; it was slowly breaking the thinner boards on the roof and beginning to invade the garage soffit. In several years' time, it would no doubt cover the garage and begin to wrench its way through the nooks and crannies, eventually compromising the roof.

The side door was locked tight as well. With some hesitation, I placed the muzzle of my Saker suppressor up to the doorknob, trying to center the bore on the keyhole, and pulled the trigger. The 300 round hit the lock with a loud bang and blasted through, knocking the inner components through the other side into the garage. I again gripped the doorknob and forced it to turn, crunching what was left of the lock mechanism. After some elbow grease, the lock finally gave and the door creaked inward, revealing the pitch-black inside. I flipped on my gun light, blasting photons through the swirling dust. Quickly, I reached over my head and pulled the plastic handle on the end of a string, disengaging the garage door opener motor from the door. I tossed my rifle over onto my back as I raised the door.

Before I got the door fully up, I knew I was in trouble. The smell arrived just before the shadow, and then the creature wrapped its arms around my chest, tackling me to the floor. The piercing pain of the gun's receiver digging into my back took my breath away. I quickly grabbed the corpse by the neck, feeling its individual vertebrae wobble on cartilage between my fingers. I marveled for a millisecond at the coldness of the rotting meat as I instinctively squeezed its throat, as if somehow that would help. I reached for my automatic knife, as my fixed blade was on my belt behind my back. I wasn't going to chance the pistol bringing an army down on me unless I had to.

The creature snapped its maw open and shut like a factory press when I put the knife to its temple and pressed the fire button. I heard the *thwack* of the blade leave the handle, but the goddamned spring was too weak, causing the blade to hang fire. In a fit of panic, I flicked the knife with my wrist, throwing the blade out of the handle into its locked position. Just before the damned thing sank its teeth into my neck, I pushed my blade into its eye socket and twisted, turning out the lights. Immediately its muscles relaxed. I could feel the vertebrae loosen in my left hand and its jaw went slack. I pushed the creature off me and onto a dry spot of oil on the garage floor, and yanked my knife from its brain. The GARMR trotted up between the corpse and me, as if nothing out of the ordinary had just happened, and then out the mostly open garage door.

Breathing heavily, I retracted the blade, readying it for the next near-death experience. So many things I wouldn't be telling Tara about when I got back. The humidity was creeping up along with the sun, and the mosquitoes were also out and about. I often wondered what would happen when they landed on a walking corpse, looking for a sip of blood. Serves the bastards right. Malaria was in the Keys right now, or was before I left.

With the light beaming in through the open garage door, I noticed a car covered in the third bay. *25th Anniversary* was embossed in silver letters on the white cover. I yanked the corner of it, scattering dust into the air. Underneath was the object of every Generation Xer's fantasy: a red Lamborghini Countach. I was stunned by the beauty of the vehicle. I went over to the window and looked inside, admiring the hand-stitched leather seats but otherwise Spartan interior. This was a super-car, not a Cadillac. It was not designed for driver comfort, only pure speed and handling. I still remember the poster on a high school buddy's wall stating boldly, "Justification for Higher Education," depicting a five-car garage filled with sports cars, one of them being a Lambo like this one. *If I could just find the keys,* I thought before reminding myself where I was and what I was doing. It was a hard fall back to reality.

I searched the garage, careful not to ding the Lambo. While dumping tubs and looking through the industrial shelves, I found some two-cycle gas, some power tools, and a charger for the tool batteries. Exiting the garage with what I'd found, I noticed the array of solar panels at the south side of the house on the roof, concealed from the road. The rig needed diesel, so I pushed back the urge to clear the mansion and took what I'd found back to the truck. No need to hang out here any longer than necessary. Marking the house on my atlas, I started the rig and continued north down the desolate road.

I'd nearly been killed twice since leaving the mansion, both times because I couldn't get my trailer around the abandoned cars and had to push or pull the land hulks out of my way. The undead homed in on the screeching metal sound as the rig wrenched on the obstacles, forcing me to either run them over or waste precious subsonic ammunition. After passing through a particularly sticky situation involving an overturned bus and me emptying a magazine, I came upon an industrial park off the beaten path and hopefully away from the undead.

Lonnietown Tool Factory looked to be a hundred thousand square feet and two stories. I pulled the rig into the factory's shadow and rifled through the glove box. I had to get rid of the trailer or risk a repeat of what I'd just gone through. The wind was blowing in great gusts, hitting the trailer broadside and causing it to shake.

I knew that one of the steps was to release the fifth-wheel lock from the driver's side. I'd seen it done once before. Everything after that was trial and error. Paranoid, I checked all around the rig, making sure that I was alone. I reached under the trailer, grasping the greasy metal ring, and gave it a solid pull. The lock released with ease. So far, so good.

I knew I'd need to crank the landing gear down on the trailer so I could drive away from it, but doing so would mean I was committed. If the gear was down on the trailer and I was attacked, I'd be on foot.

I began to crank.

I turned it over and over, making little progress on the gear until I accidentally pushed the bar a certain way, changing the gear ratio. From then on, the gear dropped rather quickly. When the foot pads were on the ground, I switched back to the low gear and torqued it a few turns, listening to the creaking steel. As I turned to jump up into the rig to move forward, I noticed the two air hoses and the electrical connector attached to the trailer. I pulled those as well and attached them to the back of the cab.

Back in the rig, I put it in gear and edged forward.

The landing gear made a horrific screech as it scraped forward, gouging the parking lot concrete.

Creatures began to pound the metal walls inside the factory, sending out great drumroll rounds of noise across the parking lot and into the industrial park all around me.

What the fuck am I doing wrong? I thought.

I looked at the panel of switches in front of me and flipped the one labeled *Air Suspension*.

I could feel the truck tilt slowly, lowering the back. Jumping out of the cab, I heard air rush from underneath and saw the back end creep downward, away from the trailer. As soon as I saw the kingpin clear the fifth wheel, I scrambled back in the cab and cringed as I put it in gear and edged forward.

I was clear of the trailer.

I couldn't see them, I couldn't hear them, but I knew they were coming.

I then sprinted to the back of the trailer, my gun painfully hitting my side, and pulled the ramp.

"Checkers, follow!" I shouted.

The machine stood and began lumbering down the aluminum ramp onto the concrete. I hurried back to the cab and the machine trotted after me. With its ten-foot human standoff protocol in place, I had to grab it by its chassis and guide it up the steps behind the cab. As I tied the GARMR down for travel, the first of them broke through the tall grass across the parking lot. I nearly bugged out and left, but I remembered the fuel cans and hose in the back of the trailer. I retrieved them, dropping the red plastic gas cans twice along the way. This sound caused the undead to move forward with even more determination. They knew something living was nearby, something warm and good. I tossed everything into the cab and climbed up inside as the first group entered the parking lot.

I put the rig into a wide arc, as if still pulling a trailer, and turned out onto the access that led back to the main road. Leaving the tool factory, I watched the abandoned trailer get smaller in my side mirrors as the dead overwhelmed the area, and felt the difference in acceleration. If I had a welder and some power, I'd turn this beast of a rig into something Mad Max would be proud to drive.

I came upon the outskirts of a town as the sun threatened to dip behind the trees. Driving slowly, I passed by a small gas station. The inside didn't interest me; it was more than likely looted down to the last bag of black licorice (the worst candy remaining on the planet, before, during, and after the dead returned). I turned the rig widely into the station, still adjusting for the trailer that wasn't there. I left it running when I jumped down.

The gas hoses were all lying on the ground around the pumps. I managed to get one of the lids off the diesel tank access and put my nose down to it. There was fuel inside, but I didn't know how far in it was and didn't have a pump to get the precious fuel aboveground.

A crashing sound pierced the droning of the rig's engine, causing me to bring my carbine around. It was trapped behind the shatterproof gas station doors. I wouldn't be getting diesel here.

I was back in my seat and rolling north as the sun threatened to touch the tops of the trees ahead of me. I was about to stop for the night when I neared another rig jackknifed on the road, blocking one side of the path ahead.

A fuel truck.

I could clearly see the diesel markings on the side. I screamed a triumphant "Fuck yeah!" in the cab as I got closer. But my excitement was cut short when I noticed the string of bullet holes that tore through the fuel trailer from top to bottom. I rode up to the wreck, cursing at my bad luck, and parked on the other side of the unintentional roadblock.

I headed straight for the fuel trailer. I had no idea how old the bullet holes were, but the sound attenuation from hitting it with my gun told me it was dry. The fuel was robbed by evaporation, probably even before I escaped San Antonio a lifetime ago. A corpse decayed inside the cab, killed by multiple gunshots puncturing its face, neck, and shoulder. The holes were bigger than 5.56 and the impact pattern suggested automatic.

A crew-served machine gun.

Whoever Swiss-cheesed this trucker and his cargo were either military or someone bad enough to take an MRAP or other armor from them. Three matted-hair-covered skulls surrounded by a jigsaw puzzle of bones were scattered near the driver's door. Two of the skulls had bullet holes in them.

I pulled the handle on the trucker's door; the weight of the corpse inside flung it open, spilling what was left of the trucker onto the asphalt. Gripped tightly in the trucker's bony right hand was a small snub-nosed revolver. The glass pattern on the driver's window suggested that a lot of rounds had come in, and some had come out. Whoever this guy was, he was returning automatic machine-gun fire with a fucking revolver. Hard-core.

The guy still had skin left on his forearms, revealing an Airborne infantry tattoo. I couldn't let him get eaten by coyotes like the rest of the poor bastards at my feet, so I tied some cordage to the corpse and dragged it to a nearby pickup truck, placing it inside. The trucker's semi interior was covered with nasty dead-body shit from months in the elements. Maggots squirmed on the seat, hungry for what was left of the trucker. There was nothing useful remaining inside, and I was about to give up and get back in my rig, when I decided to check the fuel truck's regular tanks. I had to put some torque into getting the cap off, but the effort was worth it: There was half a tank waiting for me.

I rushed back to the semi to recover the gas cans and hose; as I rounded the front of the rig, I saw a mass of corpses moving south across a distant bridge, and heading in my direction. At any moment, they'd be within hearing range of the humming diesel engine. I got low, nearly to a crawl, and headed for my rig's passenger door opposite the horde's line of sight. Opening it slowly, I crawled in and closed the passenger door with a single click. I quickly cut the engine and checked the locks before getting back into the sleeper compartment and drawing the curtains, cutting me off from the nightmare that approached in lockstep with the darkness.

I frantically checked my gear, getting any noise that needed to be made out of the way before they were upon me. I pocketed two magazines and made sure the one in my gun was topped off. I was running low on suppressed 300 and didn't stand a chance of surviving if my engine didn't start and I was surrounded. In a final act of preparation, I placed my pack on the passenger seat and sat on the bed with the curtains parted just enough to see the sun dip below a nearby billboard.

The creatures were already here.

The lesser of the decomposed led the mass of what must have been thousands. As the river of corpses flowed around on both sides, I could not help but notice their interest in the rig.

I could feel the cab move slightly from side to side as they nudged the truck.

As I sat back in the sleeper, looking through the curtain opening, I saw a head pop up into view on the driver's side and then fall away into the crowd.

One of them actually made it up the step.

I looked behind the cab: I saw the creatures keep marching south, disinterested in the fifth-wheel portion of the truck. Up front, they clumsily hit the hood and grille and tried to embrace the shielded exhaust pipes.

Heat.

The bastards were somehow attracted to the heat, to anything warm that might be alive.

The rig shook harder as thousands of them gathered around, distracted by the warmth radiating from the engine and exhaust. Risking a peek through the right curtain, I saw the other semi. I'd left the door wide open. The things were not paying that much attention, probably because it hadn't run hot in a while. Jan was right: These things could see heat up close. The horrifying experiment playing out before me proved just that.

Just Capital

Day 9

The river of undead corpses seemed to flow for hours. I remained in a place somewhere between consciousness and sleep, twitching at the sound of the chrome door handles being pulled throughout the night, or the sleeper walls being rapped on by bony hands. When the sounds began to fade, so did my consciousness. I dipped into restless sleep and awoke at sunup, slowly parting the curtains, revealing yet another wasteland created by untold thousands of undead footfalls. The grass on both sides of the highway was worn away down to mud for as far as I could see down the road through the morning haze.

Heat attracts them.

Body heat, the barrel of a gun, engines.

I started the rig a few minutes after sunrise and positioned it close alongside the other derelict truck. With the length of cut hose, I began transferring fuel from one truck to the other. All was going well until the fuel stopped flowing from the other truck. Siphoning only works when the destination tank is lower than the source. I thought for a moment, dismissing the stupid idea of letting the air out of my tires. But I could let the air out of the truck's fifth-wheel air bags. I flipped the same switch I used yesterday to release the kingpin from the trailer, lowering the truck a few inches. With my rig now lower than the other one, gravity was able to help me siphon the rest of the diesel out of the tank.

After jumping back into the cab, I checked the fuel gauge and was happy to see it climb back up above three-quarters. Aside from a tank, this was the least efficient vehicle I could have chosen, but it was also a few feet off the ground, had its own sleeping quarters, and always seemed to win the law-of-gross-tonnage chicken game with the undead.

I left my highway camp site at about eight, rolling over the disabled undead as they dragged their broken legs behind, following the horde that abandoned them. Approaching the bridge, I wasted no time in pushing a small blue car out of my way, crunching it into the guardrail as I passed by. I've learned not to get curious if I see a car seat. It's bad for your soul, if one believes in those sorts of things. Leaving the bridge, I wished for one of those Green Goblin faces on the front of my truck like in *Maximum Overdrive*. The stupid shit you think about when you're on the road . . . I also wondered what it might be like if I could trade the undead for murderous machines.

It was still early when I crested a hill and saw the skyline of Tallahassee in the distance. Up ahead a few miles before the city was a strip mall, followed by a hardware store. Passing lumbering undead, I mischievously bumped them into the ditches and abandoned cars as I passed, but not without purpose.

I pulled into the hardware store parking lot and took the rig around the side. There was a tall razor wire fence that protected the lumberyard from petty theft. A lock connecting rusted chain drawn between two gates kept the honest folks out. I could bust through the fence in the rig with no problem but that wouldn't help me in my quest for sanctuary before entering the outskirts of Tallahassee.

I leapt from the truck, nearly into the arms of a female corpse. She was visibly excited at the sight of a warm piece of meat and reached out for me as if to offer directions to the nearest gas station. I front kicked her to the gravel and shoved my fixed blade with great force into her eye socket. With more undead no doubt drawing near, I ran to the gate and placed my muzzle against the lock face. I pumped three rounds into the brass lock before enough of its internals were blasted away that I could remove the lock. Kicking the gate open, I hurried back to the cab and pulled the semi through.

Ten creatures were rushing the fence as I got the gate closed and wrapped the chain over and over between the bars of the gate. With nothing else nearby, I cut the cordage that secured the

GARMR to the rig and used it to secure the chain keeping the undead at bay. Soon, ten became twenty and I had to do something. I was running dangerously low on 300 subsonic and trying to kill them up close with my knife would only result in losing it, violating my number one rule.

Never be in the badlands without a fixed-blade knife. Never.

I ran to the still-running semi and recovered the Ruger Mark III from its cheesy green plastic case. Open to the late-morning sun, I could see the fiber optic sight inserts shining in their storage vial. I didn't have time to be picky and I wouldn't be making ranged shots. I quickly loaded the ten-round magazines, earning a thumb blister from retracting the magazine springs.

The creatures were beginning to buckle the fence when I took my first point-blank shot. I placed the Mark III up against a nearby creature's head and pressed hard before squeezing.

The report was miraculously muffled by the corpse's skull.

I repeated the process through two full mags, forcing a reload caused by poor shot timing. I squeezed the trigger before the muzzle was pressed tight against a skull, causing a loud blast, bringing more of them. After forty rounds of .22LR were expended, the onslaught ended with a pile of corpses stacked high on the other side of the fence. The Mark III only jammed once, which is remarkable for any rimfire gun no matter the maker, especially considering the circumstances. I topped off the mags and tucked the Mark III in the small of my back and went on about my business inside the yard.

Stacks of wood were placed neatly by dimensions in their two-story-high bays. If not for the grass shooting up through the cracks in the lumberyard's concrete, I could almost see the builders loading up for the day's contracts. There were plenty of wood planks available but absolutely no plywood; people probably bought it all up to cover their windows and doors from the undead before things got real bad.

I headed for the office in the back of the hardware store and peered inside the single-locked glass door. No skylights cut the darkness inside; it was pitch-black. Before figuring out my B-and-E plan, I peeked around the corner at the secured gates. Two corpses milled about in the street but were not aware of my presence; I'd shut down the rig before blasting away with the Mark III. Noise brought them here from somewhere distant, but they didn't know exactly where to look.

Good.

I went back to the locked door and decided that I wouldn't be able to get inside without pulling it from its frame with the rig, but the window ten feet away was cracked. A long-idle oscillating fan sat in front of the window plugged into a nearby overburdened power strip. I cut the screen away with my knife and raised the window all the way up. Peering inside with my weapon light, I could see no movement.

I squeezed my large ass through the opening and clumsily fought a rolling chair before planting my boots on the dusty tile floor. I listened for any sounds before grabbing the stapler off the desk and chucking it as far as I could into the dark hardware store. A couple seconds went by before I heard it knock something from a shelf. I looked down at my watch, counting the seconds, and listened. After sixty seconds, I was satisfied that if one of those creatures was inside, it would have told me in the way that the undead speak, through desperate noises of hunger and wanting.

They do talk. You just have to know when and how to listen.

The back door was unlocked, so I zip-tied it so I could kick through if I needed a fast getaway, but one of those crafty undead bastards couldn't just pull it open.

I headed into the dark opening, letting my eyes adjust to the smorgasbord of useful shelves inside. First, I found some heavy-duty zip ties to replace the ones I'd been using. Never thought these things would be so damn handy for securing doors, gates, whatever. I tossed them into a nearby empty shopping cart and made for the next aisle. There was no sign of footprints on the dust-layered floor, no signs of activity. It sort of makes sense, though, as hardware stores are not known for having food or water. I left the cart behind and went to check the front of the store.

Another chain secured the double doors from anyone getting inside. Whoever ran this place before they abandoned it probably locked the front, hightailed out the back, and secured the gate on their way out. The same type of lock was on the front door. Through the double-door glass, I could see half a dozen creatures outside across the street in the strip mall parking lot. Keeping this in mind, I continued shopping.

Spray paint, bolt cutters, cordage, duct tape, 12-volt inverter, battery-powered nail gun, bit driver, Sawzall, and some extra li-poly batteries were among the many items that filled my cart. Wheeling past the generator aisle, I lugged one of the Honda EU2000 generators into the cart along with all the fuel treatment and oil on the nearby shelf. I grabbed an extra gas can for the generator and marked it with a *G* so as to not confuse it with the cans I used for diesel. I grabbed a stack of coffee filters sitting on the counter at the back office and cut the zip tie I'd attached to the door. Blinding sunlight hurt my eyes as I shoved the door open with the cart. Satisfied that I wasn't noticed by the undead, I began to shuttle the supplies back to the truck.

After the transfer was complete, I ran back behind the store with my new gas can, coffee filters, and a Phillips screwdriver and made for the nearby flatbed pickup truck. Using the chock sitting on the flatbed, I drove the screwdriver into the gas tank underneath the truck. Before removing the Phillips from the punctured tank, I placed a coffee filter into the opening of the gas can to filter out the tank's bottom debris. I yanked the screwdriver from the tank and precious liquid energy streamed out into the gas can along with flecks of rust and sediment that were trapped by the coffee filter. I lay there on my chest for a long while until the tank dribbled dry, giving me about two and a half gallons of fuel. The truck's fuel light must have been on when it was parked here long ago. Replacing the cap on the gas can, I hurried back to the rig, the precious fuel sloshing as I went.

I checked the oil on the Honda generator and added some from the stash I'd liberated from the hardware store. The tank was empty, as the unit was on display, so I poured three bottles of fuel treatment into the genny and filled it the rest of the way from the gas can using a fresh coffee filter to double filter the old gas. The small generator took nearly a gallon before fuel spilled over the side. I had just over a gallon remaining in the gas can, so I poured the rest of the fuel treatment inside, hoping it would stabilize the no-doubt-ethanol-hobbled fuel. I replaced the cap and shook the generator to mix the fuel before securing the unit to the rig's frame with cordage and zip ties. The small, lightweight generator offered two 110-volt outlets with 2,000 watts of power, if the damn thing worked. I ran an extension cord from the generator into the side window of the rig's cab and attached the tool charger.

With that little side project out of the way, I activated the GARMR and helped it down the small steps onto the ground. Running another Geiger scan out of paranoia, I was satisfied that the radiation levels were the same as when I'd first recovered the machine. After shaking a few cans of spray paint from inside the semi to suppress the rattle, I spritzed the GARMR with a makeshift camo pattern to break up its outline, careful to avoid its spinning sensors. I was satisfied with my artwork and moved on to the truck. When I was finished, the rig had a name.

Goliath.

I secured the GARMR to the platform behind the cab and set up my transceiver. The same Morse was coming in, still faint. I scanned the spectrum on either side of the Phoenix freq and heard a faint voice drift in on a waft of RF energy.

"Outside Atlanta . . . don't know . . . surrounded."

I instinctively smashed the transmit button on my set: "This is Hourglass, just outside Tallahassee. How do you read? Over."

I listened, concentrating on the noise until the response came back.

"Hourglass . . . Phoenix . . . surrounded . . ."

The signal was too goddamned faint. I needed to get higher—fast.

After ten or so hard pulls, I brought the Honda to life from its long hardware store slumber. I left it running to charge the tool batteries sitting in the charger on Goliath's driver's-side floorboard. A Sawzall and drill could come in handy out here. The genny noise was bringing them to the fence again, so I started up the rig and moved up to the gate. I jumped out and popped them all in the head with the .22, but I was a little sloppy this time. My ears were ringing when I walked back to the rig and drove out the gate. With Goliath's big diesel humming, I couldn't hear the small Honda out back. The green light on the battery charger indicated it was still running, filling the dormant tool batteries with energy.

The radio communications I'd just received pumped me with adrenaline, pushing me in the direction of Tallahassee, to the highest building I could see on the city's meager skyline. It was idiotic and reckless, but our people were in Atlanta, possibly trapped. It was more dangerous to drive deeper inland to pick up the signal than it was to summit the high-rise in the city. I kept telling myself that as Goliath closed the distance to the city.

I kept the hammer down as much as possible, moving north until about midday, when the road became dense with abandoned evacuation traffic out of Tallahassee. Both lanes were clogged, making navigation via semi impossible. Giving up on forward progress, I pulled the rig behind a real estate agent's office building and shut her down. As the engine sputtered and quit, the Honda generator's small motor echoed off the brick building, amplifying the noise. I jumped out and shut that down too, satisfied with the charge the tool batteries had received since the hardware store. I snapped the battery from the charger and inserted it into the bit driver, placing that and a set of drill bits inside the GARMR's saddlebags. After loading the machine with things I might need, I led it down off the platform into the tall grass that surrounded Goliath.

Climbing up onto the hood, I sent the GARMR out into the field and around the building to see what was up ahead. The sunlight sort of washed out the backlit tablet display, but I was still able to make out what the machine was seeing through its advanced, multi-spectrum eye. The machine's "autopilot" weaved in and out of abandoned cars as it patrolled ahead on the highway. I'd not been using the road to travel, but I was curious what I might find if I had. As the machine moved ahead, a skeletal arm shot out to grab it, reaching too high as the GARMR trotted underneath. Panning the camera backward, I trusted the GARMR's collision avoidance capabilities as I watched the seat belted corpse flail inside an old Pontiac. Up ahead on the road was a group of them in all their pixelated glory. If the machine continued, the creatures would take notice of the movement and pursue until they realized that titanium and carbon fiber didn't taste like human flesh. I hit the recall command on the tablet, sending the GARMR into a reverse maneuver back to my position.

Reaffirming that the main road into the city was still a bad fucking idea, I consulted my maps, taunted by the view of the top of the building I needed to summit beyond the trees. I had to get a stronger signal. Either higher or closer to Atlanta: Those were my only choices. I popped a chemlight, wrapped it with a single layer of tissue, and placed it on top of the cab. The naked eye wouldn't be able to make it out, but through my NOD it would shine like a beacon after nightfall.

With the rig locked up tight and my kit stowed on my back, me and the GARMR headed for the tree line in the direction of the tallest building in the city. If I had tried this before things went jungle, I wouldn't have stood a chance. It was going on two years since anyone mowed the lawn in Tallahassee . . . hell, anywhere. It wasn't hard to find cover in the city; one had only to run to the nearest patch of green, highway median or otherwise, to disappear. Nature would own everything in a few years when the buildings began to collapse in on themselves, crushing the ancient art that sons and daughters made for their cubicle-dwelling parents. Future explorers might uncover the caricature of a smiling, happy family standing alongside one another and wonder how the hell that could even be possible on this godforsaken rock. Thinking of this invoked thoughts of Tara and Bug, and how I smiled when standing next to them, and I hoped the future families might experience all that themselves.

If Phoenix found a cure . . . a vaccine . . .

My resolve was hardened and my pace quickened into the no-doubt-infested city.

The GARMR's electrically actuated motors pushed it nimbly through the tall grass behind me. The rhythmic clicks of its movement were somehow relaxing, providing the illusion that I wasn't alone out here. Its "custom" Krylon paint job made it look like a war machine, something you might find running alongside some snake eater. I ran through the small field into a wall of taller trees.

After a bit of hacking through the heavy foliage and sharp thorns, the tall growth opened up and I spilled out onto shorter grass. A nearby sign jutted from the ground at waist level. Carved into the painted wood was the number 7. I moved around the bend, discovering a large pond with pits of sand up ahead.

A golf course.

As I waded through the grass, I came upon a green and marveled at how different it looked without the care and attention it so desperately required to stay playable. On the lakeshore fifty meters ahead, two alligators sunbathed, their menacing heads out of the water, resting on the tall grass. As I carefully edged by, the reflection off their eyes shifted and they watched, not at all interested in the flimsy biped before them. Although I felt a kinship with the wild beasts, I knew firsthand what they were capable of. I gave them a wide berth and kept moving away from the water, from their domain. Leaving the lake, I came upon a golf cart that had been turned over on its side. Rusting golf clubs were strewn around the cart like dropped matches, and a decomposing corpse lay pinned beneath the overturned cart's roof. Despite the elements, the scorecard remained attached to the steering wheel. The legs of the corpse were eaten down to the bone by whatever roamed here day or night. The upper torso was more intact but still unrecognizable, other than the fact that its neck was broken at an awkward ninety-degree angle. There were a lot of things I thought about doing back in San Antonio when the shit hit the fan, but golf was not one of them. Hats off to this hombre who decided to go out in style.

Putting my back and legs into it, I flipped the cart back over on its wheels with a thud.

The creature's arm moved.

Despite its eyes, face, and nose being gone, some basic connection between the arm and brain still existed. I dispatched the corpse with my blade before climbing into the cart. I pressed the pedal and surprisingly it weakly rolled forward. The GARMR ran behind as I rode the cart for a couple hundred yards up the fairway until the battery died completely. It was fun while it lasted. Before getting out of the cart, I checked the scorecard. "Stephen" could apparently golf a lot better than I ever could.

I could see the roof of the clubhouse, so I decided to head in that direction. After shadowing the tree line and thinking I was about to get eaten by two imaginary alligators, I finally was in the line of sight of the clubhouse. There were half a dozen undead in hibernation around the building. A bird swooped near one of them, activating its primordial programming to hunt. This started a chain reaction, waking the others up, and they all started wandering, walking across the practice green to the fence that surrounded the large swimming pool full of the same color water that was in the lake. There'd be alligators in there too if the large fence had not closed the man-made pond off to the local fauna.

I dropped another chemlight on the fairway before ducking into the trees to skirt around the clubhouse and head north into the city. The tennis courts to my right were eerily normal with nets in place, as if a match were about to start.

After clearing the courts and the country club's large parking lot, I came out into the concrete jungle of what was Tallahassee.

I dropped to one knee and raised my carbine, scanning the immediate area. Coffee shops and clothing stores extended in both directions, walling me off from the objective.

I sent the GARMR into the nearby alley and watched, hopeful the machine would not be greeted by several thousand undead. Decomposed bodies, piles of bones, and debris filled the alleyway. I was hitting the return button, sending the machine back to my location, when I heard the engine.

At first it was faint, but the noise picked up quickly when the vehicle turned the corner several blocks away. I ran back to the tall grass and waited on the GARMR to return.

"Hurry, hurry, hurry," I said under my breath, as if that would get the machine back any faster.

The machine broke out onto the street as what looked like an armored car rapidly approached. I sent the quadruped deeper into the brush and put it in standby mode.

I could hear the engine rev up before blue rotating lights illuminated on the top of the approaching vehicle. I almost stepped out from cover to flag it down before I noticed the corpse crucified across the hood.

The vehicle slowed and came to a stop. It sat there, running for a full minute before the driver's and passenger doors swung open and two rough-looking men stepped out. I retreated back to the GARMR and commanded it to follow me back, deeper into cover. The machine and I relocated to a position two hundred meters up the road from the armored vehicle before I poked my head back out to see what the men were up to. The rotating blue lights were still on and the vehicle still sat parked. After a few minutes, one man broke from cover within twenty meters of where I was concealed. From my position, I could easily make out the conversation.

"Tracks end here. Some sort of dog," said a man with a red beard.

"That wasn't no dog. It was somethin' else," replied a voice coming from somewhere nearby.

The second man stepped out from cover. He was tall, well over six feet, and wore a dirty Hawaiian shirt over body armor.

"I thought I saw someone else. Might have been one of those things, though," said Red Beard.

"We need some goddamned ammo. You should have took the shot," said the other man.

My heart began to thump, making me squeeze my carbine so hard, I thought I might crush the grip.

"Yeah, but—knowing my luck—it would just be another one of those fuckin' pussers. Why waste more bullets."

"I don't give a shit—we need ammo and chances are, if someone's out here somewhere, they have it. That, and food. Next time, you shoot. If they survive, they'll talk."

The men turned their back to me and began walking the two hundred meters or so back to the armored vehicle. Although I was dealing with psychopaths, I just couldn't make myself shoot a living person in the back, not after all the death I'd seen and had to deal out. The two continued to banter until a couple dozen undead flowed out into the street between them and their vehicle.

For a moment, I thought my problem would be solved.

Just as the mob was about to close in on Red Beard and Parrot Shirt, the hatch on the armored vehicle clanged open and a third person, a woman, rose out with a machine gun, quickly mounting it to the roof. The group sprinted and jumped into the grass as the gun began to bark rounds at the mass of creatures. I got low as the shots ricocheted in my direction with a whiz, shattering storefront glass and thumping loudly into cars. One of the rounds tagged a parking meter, exploding change onto the street like confetti. The gunfire only lasted maybe fifteen seconds.

Risking a glance out into the street, I could see the bewildered men stumble toward their ride.

"Hurry the fuck up—that's gonna bring the city on top of us!" she screamed from atop the armored car.

The two men increased the pace, dodging the remaining undead before reaching the vehicle. Two car doors slammed and they executed a three-point turn, speeding back in my direction. I remained low as they approached. As the vehicle passed by, I watched the crucified corpse on the hood swing its head from side to side and snap its jaws. Its legs were long worn to stumps by the friction from being dragged along in front of the vehicle. There could be no mistake—the driver had terror in his eyes when he sped past me down the road, back from wherever he'd come. As the vehicle escaped, the gunner again squeezed the trigger, sawing across the remaining undead at chest level, knocking them to the ground.

I had little time to prepare. A great chorus of moans now echoed through the streets.

"Checkers, follow," I commanded before sprinting from cover to a nearby alley.

Once in the alley, with the GARMR not far behind, I risked a glance over my shoulder. The streets filled with the undead, attracted by the loud machine-gun fire from just moments ago. Glass shattered like pressure relief valves from untold hordes leaving buildings, agitated by the artificial noise. Although I'd never experienced it firsthand, I felt as if I was in a great draw in the dusty Midwest and a flash flood was nearly upon me; I just had no clue as to what direction this deluge of undead would come from.

Taking a chance, I rounded the corner and saw a vine-covered fountain ahead in the middle of a park. I ran to the fountain, ignoring the splintering doors and shattering glass all around me. To the east, not far from my target building, was a hotel. Waiting would mean suicide, so I fled toward possible safety with every burst of twitch energy I had.

Over my shoulder, a dozen undead were locked onto my movement and began their pursuit. The sight of the growing mob shot adrenaline through my system, pumping my legs faster and with more resolve. My pack and gun bounced painfully all over my front and back. My rifle's stock struck my chin hard; I checked it with my right hand and my fingers were covered in blood. I slung the rifle over my head across my pack and just kept running, applying pressure to my chin as I did so. The closest door to the hotel was a side entrance. The undead, now numbering a couple dozen, were about a hundred meters back but closing fast. The weeds and brushes all around them shook, prompting birds to take flight in protest.

I slammed into the door and pushed the thumb latch to open. Locked.

Without thinking, I ran to the GARMR and retrieved the drill from its saddlebag and inserted the largest bit in the set. At the door, I rammed the bit into the lock and squeezed the trigger. The drill tore through the softer metal and began to churn up the tumbler inside.

The undead were at about fifty meters.

I overzealously drove the bit into the lock at multiple angles to be sure to tear up anything that would hold the locking mechanism in place. Using the still bit, I canted the driver, releasing the lever inside the lock, and pulled the door outward.

The undead were almost on top of me when I met the GARMR to corral it inside the hotel. The smell of decay inside was overwhelming. I shot one of the creatures in the face and kicked it back into the group behind it before slamming the door shut and heading for the nearby stair access.

The GARMR had to slow down to climb the stairs, but it handled them a lot better than I thought. Its artificial feet were loud inside the enclosed stairwell. The creatures rampaged outside the side door on the first floor, slamming their bony arms into the metal door. I didn't think it would hold too long, not after I disintegrated the lock internals to gain access. The GARMR and I were on the second floor outside the door leading to the guest rooms. It was dark in the hallway, so I put on my NOD and peered through the vertical rectangular door window.

The door shook as a corpse smashed its face into the glass from the other side. *Jesus.* I checked my drawers before putting the muzzle of my suppressor up to the glass and ending the thing. The shot boomed in the stairwell; I could hear a door bang open from above and something tumble down the stairs.

I opened the door and walked over the corpse I'd just shot. The GARMR followed, stumbling over the body but quickly gaining its footing. I secured some cordage around the horizontal bar to an adjacent door handle. It would stop one or two, but not the mob outside. The hallway went on for quite a distance and broke off halfway down at the elevator access. I suspected the hotel was shaped like an *H* from above, based on what I saw on the outside as I approached the building. There was likely a whole other wing beyond the elevators.

I checked the locks on the first six doors as I advanced down the hallway in the direction of the elevators.

All locked.

I didn't know how centrally controlled electronic locks worked, but I assumed that they reverted to their locked state in the absence of power. It didn't take long to give a door the drill treatment. The guest room locks were flimsy compared to the metal door below. I was inside in less than thirty seconds. I checked the hallway once more before the GARMR and I ducked into the guest room and closed the door.

I swung the door's steel security latch over, providing relative safety for the time being. A small sliver of light illuminated the area. Satisfied that nothing inside wanted to eat me, I led the pseudo-radioactive GARMR into the bathroom, put it in standby mode, and closed it off from the rest of the room.

Shaking from adrenaline, I stood quietly for a moment before catching sight of myself in the mirror. My chin had stopped bleeding, but the front of my shirt was splotched with blood. In the room's low light, I resembled one of them. Looking away from the train wreck in the mirror, I diverted my attention to the dimly lit room.

Aside from the dust, the place was in pristine condition. The tightly made bed was inviting. The refrigerator was stocked with warm beer, and small bottles of alcohol sat atop the bar on a tray along with stale packages of potato chips and other snacks. I risked a glance outside the curtains and saw a hundred undead spaced almost evenly in the fountain park I'd run through on my way here. If I closed my eyes and slowed my heart rate, I could still hear the faint thumps of them trying to gain access below. But as far as I could see, the hotel was not surrounded.

While studying my situation outside, I heard another round of machine-gun fire. With my second-floor vantage, I observed the undead react like a flock of birds in formation flight. Nearly simultaneously, they changed direction and moved toward the source of the noise somewhere in the distance. It was freaky to behold. Below my window, I watched the corpses that amassed outside the side door peel off and join the horde in search of the gunfire.

I dropped my pack and collapsed on the bed, smiling at the luck brought on by the sheer stupidity of other men.

I lay in the dusty bed until after nightfall, unaware of the actual time. I don't remember closing my eyes, and when my senses returned, they were still open. A sliver of bright moonlight shone through the curtains. I stared at the ceiling and the metallic sprinkler, barely noticing a sign below it that probably warned guests not to hang their clothes on it. My bones and muscles ached when I stood up. Without thinking, I went to the bathroom and tripped over the GARMR before lifting the lid and emptying my bladder into the dry toilet. The tank was bone-dry when I tried to flush. In the darkness of the bathroom, I could see a dim green LED status light blinking somewhere inside the GARMR.

I took the time to draw the curtains tight and lit a small candle. If those bandits had night vision, they'd pick the candlelight out from across the city through an open window. I sipped on a small can of soup concentrate and drank a bottle of water, then checked out the tall building across the way that was about to block out the moon. There were some undead outside the window, but a fraction of what was there earlier before the gunshots rang out. With the undead dispersed, I decided it was time to make my move.

I was down to only four magazines full of subsonic ammunition. Finding 300 Blackout ammo somewhere out here in the ruins would be nearly impossible. I had hundreds of rounds of scavenged .22LR remaining, but I didn't want my survival coming down to a .22 pistol. I topped off my carbine mag and placed two precious full magazines on my belt in their Kydex holster. I put the last one in the outside pocket of my pack, hoping I'd never need to reach for it. With my pack organized, I woke up the GARMR and stood by the guest room door for a few seconds before disengaging the steel lock, slipping on my NOD, and stepping out into the hallway.

The smell of rotten flesh hit me like before; I ignored it and went back for the stairwell, stepping over the creature I'd shot, and peeked through the vertical window. I could hear something moving somewhere down the hall, perhaps trying to get by a cleaning cart.

With the stair platform clear, I slowly clicked the door bar and stepped inside the stairwell. The GARMR slowly negotiated the stairs as I made for the first floor. Nearing the bottom, I had to pull my knife to dispatch one of them coming up the stairs. I kicked it hard in the chest, throwing it backward into the wall and onto the ground. With full force, I stomped down on its orbital socket with a loud crunch. I repeated that until it stopped moving; I stood out of breath by the door leading to the first-floor hallway.

I barreled through the door, seeing three of them turn down the hall and head in my direction. It was pitch-black and they bounced off the walls like pinballs, gravitating to the noise of my escape. I held the door open for my mechanical companion and ran out the side door into the tall grass outside.

The side door closed automatically but the undead were soon upon it, pleading for it to open with their thumps and moans. I stayed low, below the grass, and crawled away nearly on hand and foot. I prayed that I wouldn't run into the legs of one of them out there in the night. I was out of breath and sweating profusely when I looked back at the hotel. The undead were congregating around the side door, unaware that I was already long gone. Looking ahead, I realized that I stood in the long moon shadow of my objective.

The small courtyard was empty in front of the tall building, so I ran for the front revolving door. Only a bloody piece of rope outside kept the spinning door from giving entrance to the building. I gave the rope a swipe with my knife and stepped inside, pushing my way to the other side. The GARMR looked at the revolving door for a moment before stepping in as well, allowing me to turn the door so it could follow. The rope I'd cut reminded me to do the same, so I threaded two heavy-duty zip ties together and secured the door to a handrail inside.

I passed the brass door elevators on my right, wishing that they were in service. The buttons told me that the building had twenty-two floors, not counting the basement levels. It was going to be a fucking beast of climb. See you at the top, Zig.

Before finding the stairwell, I nearly ran into the architectural model of the building I was currently occupying and read the brass plaque attached to the front of the case: *Florida State Capitol Building*.

"That figures," I said aloud to myself.

I was actually dumb enough to pick the state capitol building as my communications relay high ground. Of all the buildings to choose, this one would have probably been the most fortified, and occupied when the dead began to walk.

The mockup in front of me was a detailed exterior model of this structure, as well as the old capitol building oriented to the building's east. I shook my head, hoping for the best before stepping into the stairwell that hopefully would take me to the top.

The smell of rot was incredible, even worse than the hotel. I put the GARMR on standby and took the drill out of its saddlebag. Thank God for night vision. I found an old bloodstained shirt in the corner of the stairwell and covered the machine's chassis before abandoning it for the duration of my climb. The wind was blowing in gusts outside, causing something inside the great structure to creak. I passed by the fifth floor, blown away by the number of skeletons and mostly decomposed corpses on the stairs. I had to skirt around heaping piles of bones and parts; flies and maggots still infested them, squirming under the IR illuminator from my NOD.

I made for the sixth floor and nearly fell through the steps. Someone had crudely taken out the stairs leading up to the next platform. Blast patterns on the concrete and steel indicated shaped charges. If I hadn't been using night vision, I'd have probably broken my neck, or at best my leg, in the fall. I grabbed the metal handrail and edged across the chasm to the next available step. It checked good with some weight, so I stepped onto the metal-reinforced concrete and was on the sixth-floor stairwell.

Spent brass blanketed the entire platform, rattling around underfoot. I reached down and examined one of the casings: M855 "green tip."

Military-issue.

They were trying to ban this shit before the dead walked.

I raised my NOD and panned my gun light around the platform. A terrible fight took place here long ago. The brass casings were dull from tarnish and dust. Dried blood splattered the nearby walls, and smeared handprints tracked along the bottom edge of a jagged, broken window. What appeared to be intestines were draped over the window shards like garland over a bannister. I peered out the opening to the ground below and saw a pile of body parts, bones, clothing, and other unrecognizable filth. There must have been hundreds below. It was difficult to imagine what exactly took place here, but it was a safe bet that a military unit tried to hold the capitol building. They were up against untold hordes, enough to form a human staircase up the destroyed stairs and onto this floor. I don't see how anyone could have made it out alive.

I pulled another industrial zip tie from my pack and secured the bullet-ridden sixth-floor access door before continuing my ascent. The stairs remained littered with brass all the way up to sixteen, about the same time I ran out of heavy-duty zip ties. Transiting up to floor seventeen, I saw a rifle on the stairs and picked it up. Its action was locked back, magazine gone. Peering into the action, I could see that the gas tube was melted to the point of failure. Either the gun ran dry or the shooter was doing mag dumps and the gun's gas system failed from heat fatigue. On the end of the gun was a blown-out suppressor; nothing remained but the can that held the baffle stack. This gun fought hard before its master abandoned it. I disconnected the upper receiver from the lower and placed the lower in my pack, along with the bolt carrier assembly. Could come in handy.

I arrived at the twentieth floor and noticed the door was propped open by a long-dead corpse. It was dressed in multi-cam and wore a flat dark earth-colored climbing helmet. Most of its neck was gone, probably torn out by one of the creatures. A look of terror was somehow preserved on its mostly decomposed face; its jaws gaped and its dried eyelids were slit open. A shriveled tongue hung out of its mouth. Peering into the dark hallway beyond the corpse, I could see no signs of undead, so I dragged the body into the stairwell for examination.

A large, scoped AR-10 rifle was slung across the soldier's chest. I popped the mag and verified the caliber: .308. The mag felt about half full. Reluctantly, I slung the heavy AR-10 over my shoulder and continued up the stairs.

As I rounded the stairwell, leaving the twenty-first floor, the scene of a last stand was before me. Sandbags covered the top of the stairs and shell casings once again littered the area—this time larger-caliber 7.62mm brass. As I crunched through the casings, the silhouette of twin crew-served machine guns came into view. The barrels were bent and shot out from extreme heat, reminiscent of Elmer Fudd's hunting rifle after Bugs plugged it with a carrot. The windows on the stair platform were gone. It appeared as if the soldiers gunned down the undead in waves and tossed the corpses out the window. I noticed that explosives (sans detonators) were attached to the stairs leading up to the sandbag pillbox on the twenty-second floor, where the stairs stopped.

I climbed over the sandbags into the pillbox and stepped on a female corpse dressed in full battle rattle. An M9 was stuffed into her mouth, locked to the rear from expending the magazine's final round. The 9mm exit wound was hidden by the Kevlar helmet, still chin-strapped on her skull. Sadly, both ammo cans feeding the machine guns had quite a few rounds remaining. The guns failed from high rate of fire, and the poor soldier must have pulled a service pistol, using the last round. A new barrel was sitting on the ground near the gun, but who could have possibly had time to change it out when hundreds of undead were advancing up the stairs?

I felt pity for her. She courageously held her line as long as she could. A picture of a middle-aged man hung halfway out from the shirt pocket on her camo blouse. She was the last gatekeeper to the twenty-second and final floor. The metal door behind her firing position was damaged from the unimaginable force but remained solidly locked. I checked the corpse for keys and found none, but did find four detonators and put them in my pack along with the explosives.

Drill, baby, drill.

I worked the lock, cringing at the reverberating noise it created. Taking a break, I went down the steps and looked through the smashed-out window.

The undead were getting agitated in the street below.

I hoped for more gunshots to pull them away but heard none, when the lock cylinder gave and fell out of the metal door on the other side with a *thunk*. I put the weight of my body against the door and listened.

Nothing.

Reluctantly, I kicked the door open and went in, gun leveled in front of my NOD. The bright moonlight beamed into the penthouse floor through the near-360-degree view it offered.

It didn't take long to quickly scan the floor for threats and find the roof access stairs in the back office area near a cargo elevator. Burdened by the extra AR-10 and my heavy pack, I dropped them near the welcome desk and went back outside the door to collect a few sandbags. Using about fifteen, I stacked them in front of the access door, effectively blocking any undead from approaching the floor I was on. A heavy desk was an extra reinforcement to the sandbags. The unsettling evidence of the fight outside the door indicated that hundreds if not thousands put this place under siege some time ago.

With the area fairly secure, I began a more thorough examination of the twenty-second floor. I walked the windowed perimeter, taking in the dark skyline outside. At the far end of the floor, I felt a gust of wind before nearly walking off the floor through a missing glass window. A rope made of sheets and tablecloths flapped under the open window outside. I got on my chest and looked down through the missing window panel. Adjusting my NOD, I saw that the rope only made it halfway down the building. I thought the other half of the rope was wrapped around a light pole in the street below but couldn't be certain. When the clouds shifted, I could see another pile of corpses on the ground far below the missing window in the street.

I carefully slid back, away from the window, and pushed myself onto my feet. Heading back for my pack, I noticed a pad of paper covered with writing sitting on a leather chair. The letterhead on the paper indicated that its owner was the Office of the Governor of the State of Florida.

The night sky had not given quarter to the rising sun when I started reading the account of what took place here. I was well into the early-morning hours before I looked up from those words.

January 15...
I've been directed by the Governor to document our efforts in Tallahassee in light of recent tragic events.

-The National Guard is still on the streets below. We can hear their gunshots. Five security guards remain on the ground floor. The Governor has requested that the police fall back to the capitol building and form a defensive perimeter.

-We still have running water in the city, but our radio contact with the power company has gone dark. We are seeing rolling blackouts, presumably caused by fires inside infected homes taking out transformers.

-We have not actually seen the President on TV in a few days. The Governor has been in touch with other state leadership via satellite phone and will not tell me what is being discussed. ~~I know the man and I've never seen him this shaken.~~

January 18
As the scribe, as well as the only medic in the upper floors, I've been patching up our security contingent for thirty-six hours straight. One of ours has been shot by one of the people outside the building. ~~Tag guns.~~ Only three of our ground force contingent remain. The others are missing or have abandoned the building. The streets are filled with them now. In the beginning, I could count them; I could differentiate between them and the SWAT police bashing their skulls with nightsticks.

January 19
There are rumors of a special operations force coming to help. The Governor has received word that all the capital cities are receiving aid in the next twenty-four hours.

January 21
Help has arrived. Army EOD. They've flown in a lot of explosives and guns and they've requested copies of schematics for the capitol building. Something is strange; they're not answering the governor's questions.

January 22
The Governor has asked me to document specifically that the US Army has wired the entire capitol building for demolition and that they're going to fill the building with infected and blow it. They aren't letting anyone leave. I've made somewhat of a "friendship" with one of the EOD soldiers. She doesn't agree with what's going on.

January 25
The helicopter pilots are dead. The Army SF contingent isn't going anywhere. They're trapped here along with the rest of us mortals. The Black Hawk on the roof is a paperweight.

January 27

I've learned that the assistance the federal government sent us was nothing more than one last ditch covert fucking operation. They're going to nuke the goddamned cities! Tallahassee didn't make the target list, so the Pentagon assigned a secondary cleanup operation. Codename: Benchwarmer.

- The street's completely overrun.
- The Governor is dead, suicide. Shot himself in the head.
- The special ops guys cut the fuel lines on the chopper and left the building. No one has seen them since.

My friend, Sergeant Amanda Perez, didn't leave. She's set up outside the door with the heavy machine guns and ammo the special ops guys left behind. I've offered to stand "duty" for a few hours so she can sleep, but she refuses to let me.

January 28

A loud explosion has shaken the building. Amanda told me to shut the door. I have repeatedly refused. I can't leave her alone in there, abandon her to those things. The sound of ear-piercing machine gun fire randomly erupts from the stairwell. Outside our windows, I can see what looks like a million of them converge on our building from all directions. The only ones left on the twenty-second floor are the state treasurer (acting governor), Terry the janitor, Sergeant Perez, and myself. Everyone else already tried their luck on the streets below. I don't see how on earth they could have made it through that wall of things.

January 29

I have shut the door.

I placed the notepad back on the chair where I found it. The sun is coming up very soon.

I allowed sleep to take over for an hour and awoke to the bright morning sun beaming in through the large windows of the observation floor. The story of the scribe's last stand still lingered in my head. If they'd only known the metal door would hold.

I groggily walked up the stairs with my pack to the roof access and swung the door open. Sunlight flooded in and cold rainwater dripped from the doorjamb onto my head. The roof was covered in small puddles coalescing in the low parts. I walked around the roof access structure and was surprised to see a Black Hawk helicopter sitting on the helo pad. Yeah, I read in the scribe's entries that it would be here, but it's different seeing it in person. The aircraft profile brought me back to that day I'd crashed and barely made it out alive. I still remembered waking up inside the cockpit, the pilot reaching for me from the left seat, still strapped in and very undead.

I splashed through the puddles and approached the chopper from its open-door side, careful to check for anything that might be waiting. I went in gun first and was startled back by two birds that had claimed the helicopter for their own. The passenger compartment contained a large GAU machine gun hanging out the door, nearly over the edge of the building on the aircraft's starboard side. I hadn't noticed it at first, as I'd approached from port. I grabbed the gun and swung it on its turret. Loud creaks echoed weakly off the nearby buildings. I pulled back the action halfway, scratching flecks of rust off the slide as I did so. Half a can of belt-fed ammo remained in reserve and the barrel was still good, unlike the twin crew-served guns with blown-out barrels in the stairwell down below. I'd kill to have this GAU mounted to *Solitude*'s decks with my other machine gun.

I rummaged through the chopper's kit, finding nothing of interest but a flare gun and three shells. I pushed aside two white aircrew helmets and stepped into the cockpit. Unfamiliar with the start-up sequence, I looked for a checklist before giving my best shot at starting the engines. I turned on the electrical system and was surprised when I heard clicks and saw a Christmas tree of master caution lights illuminate. Flipping the hydraulics to auto, I could hear pumps whine to move fluid into and out of their voids. I attempted to start the auxiliary power unit, resulting in a loud screech of grinding metal and then silence. The APU's demise sent echoes bouncing off every building around me; the moans of the undead responded even louder than this man-made flying machine's dead generator unit. When you're working with something that has seventy thousand moving parts, it's not gonna be nice without its aircraft maintenance spa treatments.

The flying machine's rotor remained fossilized in place above my head, probably forever. The undead protested again with a boom from the streets, and I risked a glance over the edge. Hundreds of feet below, the undead were flowing out all around the building. Their increasing concentration invoked the scribe's writings, causing my legs to shake. As I stepped out of the gray helicopter onto the rooftop, I caught a flash coming from one of the buildings.

The cockpit glass splintered as a round tore through it as well as the aluminum fuselage. I instinctively hit the deck as the shot boomed and the sonic crack split the ozone above my head.

The undead went wild as the shot reverberated off the glass buildings. Low crawling, I eventually made it to the chopper's tail rotor section. I was on the roof of the tallest building in Tallahassee, so unless the shooter mortared the rounds, I was okay. I couldn't be hit unless I stood up like a fucking idiot.

Another shot impacted the helo, penetrating its fragile fuselage. The hole in the aircraft was fucking huge, definitely a large-bore rifle. I was lucky there was a morning wind or I might be sporting a fist-sized hole in my chest as well.

I low crawled back to the roof access and slinked down the stairs. With nothing but bare windows between the shooter and me, I had to be careful. As I passed the sandbagged door access, I put my ear to the door and listened.

Nothing.

I grabbed the AR-10 gun and my pack and headed back up the stairs to the roof. Dropping the pack, I slung the scoped .308 across my back and crawled again to the chopper. Carefully and quickly,

I grabbed one of the helmets and dove back down to the ground. I scurried under the chopper and sat the helmet down next to me as I set up a firing position. Finally comfortable, I nudged the helmet out away from me with the muzzle of the AR-10.

Straining, and stretching my upper torso, I was able to get the helmet to the edge of the precipice of the building, in clear visibility of the shooter. At first nothing happened. The wind blew, howling against the building's angles and broken windows. My heartbeat began to slow and I craned my neck out to look at the cluster of buildings a hundred yards away.

The helmet launched into the chopper with a loud *thwack* as the high-caliber round impacted. I caught a glimpse of movement and pointed the rifle. Adjusting the focus, a group of three came into view. One shooter, one spotter, and one rear security. The shooter looked like he was prone behind a Barret or other large-bore sniper rifle with a huge muzzle device. The spotter was scanning the roof with what looked like a telescope, and the security, a woman, had her rifle at the ready watching their backs at the roof access.

Wasting no time, I took the shot.

The unsuppressed .308 rocked my eardrums and thundered through the valleys of the urban structures. The undead responded again. Through the scope, I saw my round impact just in front of the spotter, launching debris, knocking over the telescope, and peppering the spotter with rocks and bullet fragments. With no time to fuck with mil dots or finicky scope reticles, I applied a hold-over and started pulling the semi autotrigger as fast as I could.

My punished ears throbbed with pain.

Settling the scope back on the adjacent rooftop, I assessed the carnage. The spotter and the sniper were hit and bleeding out. The woman took aim in my direction with her rifle and began firing wildly. Some of the rounds impacted the helicopter and others flew over my head. Through my magnified eye, I could see the panic on her face as she dropped her empty gun and waved her hands in the air.

Surrender.

I calmly took my finger off the trigger. It didn't matter, as my bolt was locked back, gun empty. The woman dropped to her knees next to the sniper and started tending to his wounds. The spotter was probably dead. I could hear muffled screams and sounds of desperation coming from the other rooftop. The woman was covered in blood and applying pressure to the sniper's injuries, when the roof access door on her building flew open and the undead began to file out into the sunlight.

I broke cover and ran for my carbine.

Instinctively, I opened fire on the undead that were about to tear the woman and the injured sniper apart. The rounds struck the ground in front of the undead; I couldn't get a kill shot from this height and distance to the other rooftop. I thought I'd be forced to watch the whole thing play out right in front of me and was about to scream out across the void how fucking sorry I was when I remembered the GAU.

I bolted over to the chopper, jumped in, and charged the machine gun. I let her rip on the advancing horde, throwing body parts and torsos from the roof in a hailstorm of armor-piercing rounds. The woman hit the deck as I slewed the barrel, cutting through the creatures. I worked the gun like a fire hose and watched the destruction play out.

I could see my bullet holes tear through the metal roof access door. Chunks of cinder blocks exploded around the door. Knowing that my ammo can was running out, I began short, controlled bursts at every corpse that emerged through the damaged door.

I pulled the trigger for the last time with a click I couldn't actually hear; my ears felt as if they were bleeding.

I bailed out of the chopper door and picked up the AR-10, peering through the glass. The woman went back to the sniper, but her body language told me the man was already on his way to hell. Defeated, she stood up, covered in blood, and turned to face the undead that continued their assault on the roof. She fought with defiance, slaying them hand to hand with what looked like a lawn mower blade. She fought and fought until she became tired.

My finger eased onto the trigger of my carbine. My ammo situation was critical; I had to give pause for every subsonic round expended. The woman was just too far away. Even if I managed to aim ten feet high and score a lucky hit, I couldn't be sure that there would be enough velocity left to penetrate the undead's skulls.

I watched the woman during that uncomfortable transition when defiance transforms into fear. With the undead showing no signs of stopping, she ran back to the sniper and picked up his gun. Straining to shoulder the weapon and hold it level, I heard her scream "Fuck!" just before lowering the muzzle to pull back the bolt to load another round. Just as death was upon her, she leveled her gun and pulled the trigger without aiming. The blast from the large-caliber sniper rifle knocked her back five feet, nearly on her ass. The round tore through four corpses, pushing them all back but only taking two out of commission. The round must have severed their spines. The other two flipped over onto their fronts and started to get up.

The woman charged and kicked the nearest corpse repeatedly until she forced it off the roof, giving it a final blow with a golf swing via the large bolt gun she wielded.

That was one way to use it.

The undead on the street far below reminded me of elementary school science class, iron shavings moving along magnetic fields. My machine-gun fire pushed the shavings to the capitol building, where no doubt some of them had entered and were coming up the stairs. Her shots with that shoulder cannon pulled the iron back in her direction and into the bank building. Only, the figures below weren't harmless elements reacting to magnetic fields. They were a complex biomass engineered to kill, to wipe out intelligent life on Earth.

I couldn't help her.

Besides, she just tried to fucking kill me. They shot first.

But . . . that'll never unburn the image of that woman's last stand. Never.

She fired the final round out of the bolt gun into the oncoming crowd of monsters, to no effect. They kept coming, pushing her into the corner of the rooftop. Backing to the edge, she began to kick them, but there was nothing anyone could do. The bowels of the building released a hundred undead onto the roof.

She fell off the building with three sets of jaws clamped to her flesh, plummeting to the concrete. I watched her fall.

Unburn.

I listened to her soul-searing scream.

Unburn.

I heard the sickening crack of her body on the pavement.

Unburn.

I watched the disfigured and broken undead that fell alongside her tear into her flesh as the other lemmings from above dropped, reaching a hundred miles an hour before impacting in a grisly dog pile of bones and rotten meat. The woman was no more, buried without dirt, no ashes to ashes or dust to dust.

I watched the writhing pile of what used to be human move unnaturally, fighting for warm flesh.

A final kernel of humanity remaining inside of me began to throb and pull before I lost it over the side of the building, spewing vomit out into the glass, metal, and concrete canyon.

I lay there in the morning sun trying to mentally materialize some brain bleach to somehow unfuck my head, but lost control and went into a deep, trauma-induced sleep. My eyes were open before I woke up; I remember coming back from sleep staring at the sunlight beaming through the bullet holes in the chopper. I stood up and took in my surroundings. The undead completely dominated the streets below.

When I was twelve years old, my cousin and I went into the woods to hunt squirrels. We stayed out for hours, taking three tree rats with a hundred-year-old bolt-action .22 rifle. We talked about cartoons and video games on the way back home. Reaching the wooden steps, we each looked down at our legs and panicked; we couldn't even see the blue of our jeans, as our legs were completely infested with seed ticks. My cousin and I doused our legs in gasoline to get them off our skin, repelling the tiny bastards. The current scene reminded me of my childhood in some distant, demented way.

I stuffed some empty casings in my ears to quell the booming noise of the dead. With some hesitation, I grabbed my pack from the steps and began to set up the radio on the northern side of the building. As I worked, shattering glass punctuated the wails along with wrenching metal.

I was in a bad situation, standing on the precipice of an undead lava cauldron. Even if I had the inventory of the Remington ammunition factory up there with me, it wouldn't have been enough to dent the numbers of walking corpses. The wind lifted their stench, dramatically shifting its intensity between the two extremes of being absent and nearly watering my eyes from its pungency. Holding back a fresh wave of nausea, I tossed my antenna over the nearby light pole, missing once.

Connecting the antenna to my small radio, I heard the sound of gunfire and immediately went flat on the roof. I lay there blowing out a dry spot near my mouth so I could listen without moving.

Boom.

Boom.

Rat-tat-tat-tat.

Two explosions followed by machine-gun fire. Not terribly close, but somewhere in the city.

Whoever those people were on the other roof had friends, and those friends had radios. Either they were sharing my view of the streets below and wanted to exfil, or they were coming for me.

I worked quickly, retuning the radio to intercept the transmission.

I began to recognize the sloppy Morse and concentrated, copying the signal through the earbud.

The signal was clear.

"Tune 8.992 for recording. Atlanta has vaccine. Do not approach CDC. Go south of Atlanta, Wachovia Tower. Need exfil, position under heavy assault. Phoenix sends . . ."

I quickly tuned the shortwave freq into my radio to hear the recording.

"Atlanta, CDC site B. We have a cure. Repeat, we have a cure. We can stop . . . deactivate them. If anyone is out there, get to Atlanta, to the Wachovia Tower, and draw them out. We've got no fucking choice: We've got to make it out with what we've got. The building is completely surrounded and we're running out of resources. If you're hearing this, we are either all dead or need immediate extract from a hot LZ, and I do mean hot. This is Sean Casey, United States Navy, Task Force Phoenix. Out."

Another fucking building. I was trapped above Tallahassee

with a million screaming freaks on the streets below. If I made it out alive, my next stop was another building . . . just outside Atlanta proper. I was watching the other rooftop, when the person who'd shot at me before began to move. Through the AR-10 glass, I could see the legs twitch before the new corpse opened its eyes and lifted its head. Its head moved from left to right, as if scanning its environment before it sat up and got to its feet. I waved my arms, catching its attention. It somehow knew I wasn't dead. Somewhere firing in its still-warm brain was a primordial, possibly reptilian instinct to feed. It'd been a while since I'd seen one this fresh, which unsettled me. Upon recognition, its lips drew back and its legs took the body forward, right over the edge of the building. The creature fell, eventually knocking over half a dozen more of its kind, as it most likely broke every bone in its miserable body on impact.

More gunfire.

Closer.

An explosion.

A concussion broke windows in the distance. I could hear panes of glass hit the ground from buildings somewhere east of me. I headed back downstairs in case one of those thugs was gunning for me, which was almost a foregone conclusion at this point.

I had to find a way out, a way back to Goliath, my virtual lifeboat with ten wheels of freedom. Disregarding for now the noise of approaching combat, I headed back down to the observation floor below. The wind was gusting, causing the red tablecloths to flap on the tables near the broken glass that led straight down to the ground. The sheet hung there just as it had before, just as it had for over a year.

I went back to the stair access door and put my ear to it, listening for any signs that the enemy was on the other side. Nothing yet.

After laboriously removing the sandbags, I swung the door open. The distant shuffling of feet caused my heart rate to increase. I sat at the top of the stairs, briefly listening with my eyes closed to somehow get a better idea of what I was up against.

The GARMR's tablet glowed brightly in the dim stairwell. I navigated to the manual operation screen and turned on the machine's LiDAR turret, panning it around. The view was half obstructed by a cardboard box I'd used to conceal the machine, but it fell out of the way, revealing a stairwell full of undead, all heading upstairs to my position. The blown-out stairs halfway down would slow them.

I activated the GARMR's motor function and listened to the audio as its camouflage fell away to the ground, causing some of the creatures to crane their heads in curiosity. Moaning, they went for the GARMR, likely attracted by the heat radiating from its nuclear battery. Upon closer inspection of the machine (like, face-to-the-camera close), they lost interest and kept moving.

The creatures must have snapped the zip tie on the revolving door at the front of the building. I needed a door wedge.

I moved the GARMR slowly. All I needed was snow and it would look as if I was piloting it at the speed of an Imperial AT-AT.

After making it through the door, I pushed the machine forward via touch screen, toward the front of the building. With its sensors blinded by walking corpses in all directions, the GARMR navigated ahead, occasionally being nudged or grabbed by a curious corpse.

After the machine cleared the densest group of creatures, I could see the revolving door spinning via the machine's crackling video. I increased my pace, garnering the attention of more creatures that immediately rushed the machine, attracted by heat and movement, only to realize it wasn't edible. A steady stream of them were entering the building. Too many more, and the whole place would fill to the brim, forcing me higher and higher until I met the same fate as that woman on the other rooftop.

The revolving door kept turning and there was nothing I could do to stop it.

I panned the machine's LIDAR sensor around the room. The only thing I could control in this environment was the GARMR. Without thinking, I pressed forward on the virtual control stick of the touch screen and charged the machine into the spinning revolving door until the door slammed into the GARMR, causing a burst of on-screen static. The sounds of straining metal told me that either the door was getting over-torqued or the GARMR's hardened titanium frame was getting beat to shit. I spun the camera 180 degrees, looked down the GARMR's back, and saw that the door stopped spinning, temporarily stemming the flow of undead into the building. I put the machine into dormant mode.

The GARMR was now my shield.

I picked up the heavy machine gun, wrench, ammo, and new barrel and rushed back into the observation room. Tossing the heavy gun onto the nearby couch, I closed the door and began stacking the sandbags and furniture, fortifying the only way inside.

The undead were coming.

Rat-tat-tat-tat . . .

Another burst of machine-gun fire made me jump. It was much closer.

I set the heavy gun up facing the door and dropped the new barrel into place. I loaded the gun and racked a round into the chamber. I had about five hundred rounds remaining—not much, considering there were probably at least a thousand inside the building before I plugged the leak with the GARMR.

Checking the screen, the door was still stuck. I panned the machine's optic around to the undead trapped in the door, seeing a dozen gnashing faces pressed angrily against the heavy glass, trying to push through. Wrenching metal and great bellowing moans erupted from the tablet's small speakers.

I turned the GARMR audio off.

I rounded up my kit and placed it nearby. Crawling to the window in the prone position, I saw the first group of human OPFOR; a convoy of armored Humvees with armed men on the roof turrets rounded the corner two blocks away toward the other building. Watching through the binoculars, I saw another goddamned .50-cal-armed sniper jump out of a Humvee and sprint to the nearby building, disappearing inside after a few bursts of gunfire from his spotter and a dozen other assaulters. I remained low, watching the noise pull legions of corpses away from my building back to the other one—again, like iron shavings to a magnet, all polarized in the opposite direction.

The rest of the convoy ran down mobs of undead, stopping in front of my building, firing everywhere.

These fuckers must have a lot of ammunition stored somewhere.

I grabbed the tablet and woke up the GARMR. Thankfully it still functioned. After two failed attempts, I backed it out of the revolving door and parked it behind the welcome desk, right on top of a skeleton a few meters away. Through the camera, I could see the revolving door reverse direction as the undead began their outflow in reaction to the situation outside.

The guns seemed to fire endlessly. Staying low, I could see piles of bodies stacking up on the street below in wide arcs around the vehicles.

I kept Checkers' camera trained on the revolving door and turned the audio on. The gunfire on the screen was a half second behind what I could hear from the top floor but it was clear that the group was fighting their way inside, when the revolving door turned yet again in the other direction and muzzle flashes temporarily blanked out the GARMR feed.

I put the machine into dormant mode and ran to the metal access door. I cut out the drywall from a section next to the door with my blade and shoved in the explosives I had taken from the stairwell inside.

This was going to be crude.

I stabbed the detonator into the explosives and hunted for extra wire, quickly cutting a section of LAN cable from the wall into different-color lengths. I needed a 9-volt, so I risked standing up to look around.

Yeah, smoke detectors.

I ran around the floor ripping them from ceiling mounts, forcefully disconnecting them from the dead AC power sources. I had three batteries, one of which didn't shock me when I touched it to the tip of my tongue. I picked the strongest charge of those remaining and frantically wired it to the detonator so that it would make a connection when the door opened more than one inch. I pulled the machine gun back, away from the door, and stacked couches and anything else I could find to shield me from the blast.

With the gun repositioned, I put my pack on my back and slung my carbine. I was ready.

Well, that's what I thought, anyway.

Thump.

Thump.

Something was surging against the door. I watched in horror as it momentarily shifted away from the top of the jamb. It was nearly imperceptible the way the light along the seam between the door and the jamb changed, but it moved.

Another burst of gunfire from somewhere else in the building. *Thump*.

The fucking undead were at the doors; there had been enough of them to complete a bridge over the blown-out stairs!

If the creatures tripped the explosives, they'd just blow the door off, allowing the rest to file inside, along with whatever came after.

I couldn't approach the door; it was barricaded and could blow at any moment.

I edged back to the window where the sheets were tied together, forming the opening. I pulled the machine gun back to my position. Through my shitty barricade of sandbags and office furniture, I could see the door wiggle from the pressure exerted on the other side. My pack was cinched tightly to my back, uncomfortably cutting into my shoulders. My carbine was strapped to my pack.

I had no choice.

As I was about to step over the edge and take my chances on the sheet that led only halfway down the building, gunfire opened up from the adjacent building, shattering the glass around me into a million one-carat-diamond-sized pieces. In desperation, I stuffed two spent brass cases into my ears and turned the machine gun counterclockwise, returning fire on the other building. To an onlooker, it would have been reminiscent of two sailing ships firing broadside at one another at a perilously close distance. Half the time I didn't even look where I was shooting, as I knew they had a heavy-bore sniper with them somewhere in the other building.

Glass continued to fly along with the foam ceiling covers. Dark rust water began to flow from a ruptured sprinkler system that somehow still held some pressure after all this time.

My final round was gone. Ammo links, water, foam, and glass were everywhere. My ears rang from the mayhem as I crawled to the window opening, wet and seriously pissed off.

Shaking with fear of the overwhelming height, I edged my legs out into the chasm, clutching the dangling sheet with both hands. Even though it was soaked with brown-colored water, it was easier to grip than I expected. All the kit I carried made the climb down awkward. The power drill clasped to my rigger's belt banged painfully against my hip bone.

They say never to look down.

The mass below was punctuated only by other buildings and derelict vehicles. Every space in between was filled with the undead tsunami.

I was twenty feet down the sheet rope when the explosion rocked the building. The concussion spit the couch out of the twenty-second-floor window. Surrealistically, it flew twenty feet or so and then whooshed past me on its way down. Still in shock and not fully accepting my current situation, I had to watch. The huge couch flipped end over end until it hit with crushing impact, flattening the corpses underneath.

Forcing myself back to my current predicament, I continued my descent until I was nearly startled off the sheet by half a dozen undead that slammed against the other side of the glass of what I thought might be the eighteenth or seventeenth floor. I was inches from their hunger, feeling the vibration of their impacts against the glass barrier between us.

I kept going down.

Dammit, my arms were getting tired.

A shot rang out, hitting the building somewhere above my head, rattling the glass.

The sixteenth floor was full of undead.

I had maybe twenty more feet before the sheet ran out with a jagged and ripped end.

The fifteenth floor was full of undead.

The fourteenth floor was socked in.

The thirteenth floor had curtains concealing what was inside. I had five feet of sheet remaining.

I went halfway to the twelfth floor before seeing it was filled to the brim with angry corpses.

Painstakingly, I wrapped my legs around the sheet and slowly made my way back up to thirteen.

Wrapping my left arm through the sheet, I pulled my drill like a six-gun, jammed the carbide bit into the glass in front of me, and depressed the trigger. I punched the drill repeatedly into the glass until it formed a spiderweb. With every last bit of energy, I pressed the bit into the nexus of the window cracks and drove the bit in.

The glass exploded like before into tiny pieces, sprinkling like salt onto the hungry undead below. I tossed the drill through the curtains into the opening I'd created.

I unraveled my leg from the sheet and kicked back on the building as if rappelling.

Time slowed for a moment.

As I traveled forward into the opening feet first, my mind went over the worst-case scenarios. The dark stuff of nightmares concluded what could be behind curtain number one, but I had no real choice.

I flew right into the waiting arms of a large padded leather office chair. It spun around and the momentum tossed me onto a huge wooden desk covered with shit that would never matter again. The curtain flapped in the wind and rounds hit again somewhere above me. The opening where I left the twenty-second floor faced away from the attackers. They might not have noticed I'd escaped.

Kicking myself for not reaching for my carbine sooner, I unsecured it from my pack and raised it up to the ready position. The large corner office was adorned with plaques and pictures of a man standing next to three former presidents. Well, they're *all* former presidents now, aren't they.

The office was clear. I risked a look out the other set of windows to the building from where the shots were coming. Halfway up the building, a fire raged; smoke hugged the sheer glass face before being dissipated by wind turbulence at the top.

I waited for nightfall.

0315

The steel beams from the building across the street were straining under the extreme heat and weight of the floors above them. I could smell roasting flesh in the air, even from my holdout here halfway up the capitol building. Flaming corpses walked around on the street below, unaware they were on fire. I caught a glimpse of a flashlight beaming around below the fire-stricken floors. Whoever it was, they were looking for something or someone.

In my building, I heard intermittent gunshots; they seemed to come from above. It was dark so I dug my NOD out of the top of my pack and flipped it on. Quietly, I moved the heavy chair away from the double doors that led into the office. I heard nothing, so I proceeded into the foyer, careful to turn the handle mechanism slowly, disengaging the lock and moving the heavy door inward. I could see a corpse standing next to an empty water cooler with its back to me, swaying, hibernating almost imperceptibly against the grainy and green honeycomb backdrop of intensifier illumination. I snuck up on the corpse and rammed the blade of my switchblade into the base of its neck.

I was startled when the corpse didn't crumple to the ground but swung in a wide arc. I hadn't noticed that the body was attached by its neck to a length of dark wire suspending it a few inches off the floor. Its mouth still opened and closed; I must have missed the brain, so I pulled my carbon steel fixed blade and came down hard on the top of its skull with a crack.

Lights out.

I froze for a moment, listening.

Footsteps.

Ducking low into a reception area, I heard something approach. I low crawled away from the noise into a cubicle farm that smelled like mildew. With the sound in the foyer area getting louder, I went deeper into the maze of office desks and dividers, a potpourri of lives that once were, small picture frames holding photos of strangers alongside toddlers' works of art penned in crayon. I saw a grenade sitting on a nearby desk and eagerly reached for it as if it were a lightsaber. I swiped it from the desk along with its attached plaque, which stated: *Complaint Department: Take a number*.

Fuck.

For no logical reason, I tossed it in the top of my pack and continued into the labyrinth of the early-twenty-first-century office. The moon was in full view through the windows up ahead, its disk nearly bisected by some sort of wire that hung down over the outside of the building. The moonlight shone in, outlining the silhouette of a corpse that stood sentry over the windows.

I checked my carbine and took aim as I closed in on the creature. This one wasn't suspended by a wire necktie but, like billions of others, by some dark force that kept the terrifying things moving. The creature paid no attention to me. I pulled the drill from my belt and moved in closer, wondering why I hadn't used it earlier. I rammed it into the creature's face, simultaneously squeezing the black plastic trigger. The bit rapidly bored into the creature's head, scrambling its brain and the chemical switches that let it walk and seek out what it thought was food. Anticipating, I switched directions on the drill and reversed the bit just before the corpse fell to the carpet floor with a thud.

The sound of the electrical motor on the drill turned out to be a very bad idea.

The cubicles stirred with movement and the bright moonlight at my back shone on a dozen creatures jolted from dormancy by the interesting mechanical noise I'd just offered them. Their simultaneous moans were calls to action for all nearby undead that were listening.

The call to feed.

The moonlight was at my back. They didn't see me yet but were going off sound, like bats. Gray cubicle dividers shook and office chairs tipped to the floor as the creatures began to scramble and search. I backed away from the mob, which now numbered well over twenty. More of them stood, their heads peeking over the dividers, looking for a way out. As I edged backward, my elbow hit the cool window glass, signifying that I could retreat no farther.

The moon's light brightened the faces of the undead. More began to come into the office area from the hallway beyond, stimulated by the activity inside. I looked over my shoulder again, noticing the cable running outside the building from higher above. Taking another glance, I saw a second cable and followed it down to a platform glowing in the setting moonlight. Looking back, I was forced to take a shot at one of the creatures that came within arm's length.

All hell broke lose.

The undead triangulated the shot and began to converge. I

went full auto on the glass behind me and kicked. My leg launched through the glass and I almost fell through it before grabbing the thin frame of metal that separated the panes. I took more shots as the mob doubled down on my position. I slung my carbine and squeezed through the hole in the window, clutching the jagged, skinny metal wire. I began to descend much faster than expected because of the extra weight of the heavy pack on my back and the thinness of the wire.

The skin on my hands was torn away in places before I impacted the aluminum platform rail, tumbling hard onto the window cleaning platform. I saw stars, and it took everything for me not to scream out in agony at the pain throbbing through my hands. I looked down at them through the NOD and saw too much blood.

The first creature made it out of the opening above and hit the platform before spinning out of control, away into the void.

Another corpse hit with a loud clang but remained bent over the platform at its waist. It looked up at me and grinned, or it looked that way to me. I gave it a front kick to the chin, helping it off the platform and down to the ground. It must have been a three-second fall before the audible thud. Another fell and missed the platform altogether, but I didn't see it; the flapping of clothing fabric and whoosh of air were what gave away its passing in the night.

I could hear the crunching of glass above, but nothing else fell.

I dropped my pack and opened it with bloody hands. I pulled out my med kit and tore into the silver-laced clotting agent, spreading the powder onto my hands. The sting was nearly unbearable as I stood there on the suspended platform, holding my hands like claws to keep anything from touching the wounds. Small strips of skin hung from my palms, revealing dark tissue underneath. Eventually I drummed up enough courage to shove my hand back into the pack to get a bandage. I sloppily wrapped my left hand with my right and pressed the button on my Microtech knife for a one-handed opening. The *tantō* spike shot out, reflecting the last remnants of moonlight off the bloodstained razor-sharp blade. I sliced the bandage and repeated the process on my right hand. I reluctantly took my emergency oxycodone with a half bottle of water. Those motherfuckers are addictive; I only carried two in my kit for a reason. If it were not for Jan, I'd have been addicted to them a few months ago after a scavenging trip that went south on me.

I lay back on the far end of the scaffolding and turned off my NOD. The meds hadn't kicked in yet, but the water and the gift of temporary asylum from the undead had. I looked over at my only companion, the man in the moon, and began to speak.

"You've seen worse, haven't you?" I asked.

Yes, my subconscious responded.

"Your own catastrophic birth, the death of the dinosaurs."

It only gets worse, kiddo.

"Not very encouraging, man in the moon. Woo!" I howled.

Yes, now the meds were definitely starting to kick in.

The platform was chilly from the wind coming out of the west. I was on the back side of the building, opposite the action. Looking down with the NOD, I could see only a couple dark spots moving around below.

"Good-bye, Moon," I said as its face dipped behind a distant building.

See you soon, I hope, the voice in my head responded.

On my back, looking up to the stars, I could see evidence that the sun was on its way . . . not soon, but not too long from now it would show itself and ruin any chance I had at getting out alive.

Beams of light danced above my line of sight to the stars. I thought that I was hallucinating until shots burst through the window four feet above my head. One of the creatures slammed into the damaged window as rounds were pumped into it. Chunks of glass and corpse showered down onto the metal platform. My heart raced, and adrenaline pumped into my system, temporarily pushing me out of narcotic brain fog.

I adjusted the reticle on my NOD and began to examine the lift control panel. The flashlights waved around above my head and eventually disappeared, leaving me to the howling wind and the inevitable sun. The box had three settings: *Stop,* *Up,* and *Down.* Grabbing on to the rail, I selected the down setting and began to laugh out loud as the machine slowly lowered itself, floor by floor. It must lower hydraulically, I thought, as I doubted the machine had seen electrons in a long time. I suspected that the Down worked but the Up never would again.

As the floors slowly went by, I saw increasingly gruesome snapshots of death and carnage. The floors that had been cleared by the human raiders were slaughterhouses of dismembered corpses and twitching limbs. The floors that the raiders took a pass on were packed tight with undead. As I passed the seventh floor, I saw that the creatures were crammed so tightly inside that when they saw me, there was no room for them to even beat on the glass.

The window cleaner lift shook for a moment at about the fourth floor before it began to lower one side unevenly.

Ten seconds later, my pack flew off the now vertical lift onto the ground below, and I was hanging off the railing twenty feet off the ground like a trapeze artist. I shook my legs in a desperate attempt to get the cable to pay out more slack, but this only caused excruciating pain to shoot from my injured hands to my entire body. Looking up at the sky, my hands gave way and I fell.

But the pain disappeared as soon as my hands lost their grip. The meds.

I marveled for a moment at weightlessness and at the brief few seconds I felt nothing. And then I hit the ground like a lawn dart. Despite the meds, my ankle hurt like hell, momentarily filling my vision with rhythmic starbursts of pain. I lay on my back, trying not to pass out while simultaneously reaching for my rifle. I crawled over to my pack and used it to wedge myself up into a sitting position. I immediately tightened my bootlaces on my injured foot. My vision started to close in as if I were traveling through a dark tunnel. Every heartbeat expanded the darkness, but the time between beats became darker and darker.

"Checkers, follow, help," I said into the Simon just before blacking out.

I momentarily returned to consciousness to a dark figure approaching. The sun had not yet come up, so I knew that I hadn't been out very long. With my vision again closing in, I raised the rifle and shot the dark shape as high up as I could see. Whatever it was, it fell and didn't get back up.

The next sound I remembered was the whirring of the GARMR's motors as it neared. Half conscious, I saw it lowering its body down next to me. I grabbed its titanium frame with my less injured hand (thankfully, I can still shoot and write) and felt the warmth of its nuclear battery on my knuckles as it somehow dragged me and my pack across the grass in a straight line away from the building. It was low to the ground, its legs folded up at the top joint, giving it extra torque while it pulled. Once I felt the security of tall grass, the command was given for the machine to stop.

The rising sun was concealed by the large capitol building, but I could see its rays pass entirely through the building's windows on the second floor. I must have been two hundred meters away from where I'd fallen from the platform. I looked down at my ankle and tried to flex it. It moved but didn't feel so great. I didn't dare loosen my bootlaces or my ankle would expand to the size of a fire hydrant in the span of a few minutes. I looked over at the GARMR and caught myself patting it on the back, treating it as if this man-made beast was somehow alive.

"Thanks," I told it aloud.

The GARMR didn't respond but simply locked onto my face with its spinning sensors, not willing to miss any gesture commands it might be given. Unyielding obedience, but not unconditional love—this was the way of machines, of tools, but not of living companions.

Smoke climbed up over the buildings and I hobbled my way back to the country club, using the GARMR to support the weight my injured leg couldn't handle. The warmth of the GARMR was unsettling, but I had no choice. I could injure myself beyond the point of mobility if I got too careless.

With the majority of the undead concentrated between the two buildings in the distance behind me, I was able to get to the golf course while shooting only twice, bringing my magazine down to five rounds remaining. I stopped near a water hazard and watched as two oblivious turtles jumped into the drink and swam off. Wincing from the pain, I reluctantly reached into my pack and popped my last two painkillers. I didn't bring more because I knew myself (from past experience) and knew that addiction was more of a vicious monster (master?) than those things walking around. I couldn't really decide which was worse, my torn-up hands or my ankle. The pain from both was hard to compartmentalize, even with the strong meds that coursed through my body. I'd lost a lot of water fighting to high ground in order to intercept the Phoenix transmission, and looked thirstily at the pond after downing my last half bottle of water.

I fought off the urge to dunk my head in and drink; getting diarrhea or some other god-awful disease while being injured would definitely seal my fate. I wasn't far from Goliath, so I changed magazines and pressed on.

0800

Gunfire erupted from the direction of the capitol building, along with an explosion that shook the trees within visible distance. I watched the capitol building shed clouds of dust and glass as if about to collapse in on itself. Those dark visions of 9/11 flashed back to my mind for a brief second, but the capitol didn't give in on itself; the building lurched over like a refrigerator on an appliance dolly. Great steel beams snapped and more dust shot out of its broken windows as the building slowly toppled over instead. It fell at a tragically slow speed before shaking the earth, coming to rest at a forty-five-degree angle on top of the shorter building nearby. The shorter building was barely visible over the tops of the trees surrounding the country club golf course, but the state capitol resembled a crashed monolithic spaceship. Dust hovered all around, and sunlight glimmered off the shards of glass that somehow remained attached to it.

Pulling my binos, I watched masses of confused undead shuffle out of windows and fall away into the dust clouds below. Tracer fire beamed like a laser from somewhere on the ground up into the building, wreaking havoc on what was left of its internal symmetric lines. I watched in awe as enough firepower to sustain our stronghold in the Florida Keys for years was wasted in the span of a few short minutes. These idiots were likely trying to kill me.

There was no other fathomable reason to go scorched earth like that.

I turned away from the train wreck that was downtown and slipped away into the field that led to the area where Goliath was hopefully still parked. I knew I was on the right track, as I'd already seen a chemlight I'd dropped on my way to the interior of the city. The GARMR's heat was now freaking me out, so I found a walking stick along my path in the form of a small tree poking up out of some old mulch like a weed. I took out my blade and chopped the green wood at the base and cut the branches off, forming the crude implement.

With one hand on my gun and the other on the oak stick, I hobbled ahead to the building, careful to not attract too much attention. As I approached, the hellish faces of undead stared back at me through the glass of the office building. They opened and closed their mouths and beat on the glass in protest. Beat all to hell and high on meds, I didn't give a fuck.

The warm leather seats of Goliath were almost as nice as the sound the electronic locks made when I engaged them. I was here: not my home but a home insofar as this world would allow. I had a working diesel engine under my feet, fuel, power, water, ammo riding shotgun in the passenger seat, and a robot dog on the fifth-wheel steps.

1600

Sometime before noon, I downed another bottle of water and started up the rig, turning the air conditioner on full blast. Finding my gear, Goliath jerked forward into the grass. I flipped it around back onto the road out of Tallahassee. I slalomed between abandoned vehicles, watching the broken capitol building burn through my side mirrors. I almost looked away when I noticed the flash of something move behind me in the road. Easing off the gas, I concentrated on the mirror.

Because I was not paying attention to the road, I smashed into the fender of a compact car, sending it hard into the guardrail of the small bridge I was crossing. Looking back again, I saw them. A pair of motorcycles shadowing me, maybe three hundred meters back. I kept cruising for fifteen minutes, watching them and trying not to hit another car on the road while I careened between obstacles. My pain meds wore thin and my ankle and hands were becoming a problem. Even my hair follicles somehow hurt. I needed more oxy in a bad way; my right hand shook when transiting between the wheel and the gearshift. I looked back and could still see the flash of motorcycles swerving, one red, one white.

I slowed to a stop and waited. The hum of the bike engines soon overtook the rumble of the diesel as the bikers approached. Kitted up in full motocross gear, I saw one of them reach for a long gun from a scabbard mounted to the handlebars. I found reverse and hit the gas, throwing me forward into the steering wheel as the huge rig rolled backward. The biker got off a shot, sending a round through the chrome exhaust pipe at about my eye level. I nearly redlined the engine and swerved to line my rear axle up with the red motorcycle.

I looked away just before hearing the crunch of the bike, but it could have just as easily been bones and tendons. As the rig slowed again to a stop, I put it in first and hit the gas, spinning the tires and throwing motorcycle parts out behind me. The other biker stayed behind the cover of an abandoned car. I couldn't tell what he was doing and didn't much care. I was getting the fuck out. I glanced over at my mirror again and saw the white motorcycle resume pursuit.

Behind him, a large crane rounded the corner and barreled through a group of vehicles, tossing them aside like empty cardboard boxes. The biker gestured to the crane to follow, as if the driver didn't notice me in the rig up ahead. Upshifting, I scanned ahead on the highway and began to change lanes, smashing through a small group of undead that were chasing a buzzard around the highway as the large bird attempted to feed on them. I barely missed a propane vehicle as I sped past, changing lanes again to dodge an overturned log truck. I saw stacks of logs spilled out into the median and forest, probably thrown by the trailer when it overturned.

Why weren't they shooting at me?

Up ahead, a long-abandoned police checkpoint came into view. An MRAP sat across the road, surrounded by sandbag pillboxes and tattered tents. I noticed the strips in the road just before it was too late.

Spikes.

I spun the wheel and hit the brakes, skidding sideways into the grass on the right side of the highway. My rig stopped next to the checkpoint as the white motorcycle hit the rusty road spikes. Its tires shredded and its front wheel locked up, sending its rider face-first into the MRAP at sixty miles an hour. Like a bug to a windshield, the heavy MRAP didn't even shake from the impact of the human projectile.

Getting my bearings, I realized that I had spun around, facing the approaching crane vehicle. Putting the rig into first did nothing but throw mud behind me. I rocked it back and forth between reverse and first until I could find traction, getting it around to the other side of the roadblock. I could hear the large tires on the crane explode on the spikes, and I edged the rig forward down the road until I was sure I was out of range of any rifleman on board the crane. I was damn lucky to notice those spikes; thank you, 20/15 vision.

At a safe distance from the checkpoint, I idled the rig and stepped out onto the side for a better look. I could hear cries for help from the other side of the checkpoint. Someone was screaming into a radio. At first I thought the crane driver had found his motorcycle buddy spread out all over the side of the MRAP and was freaking out, but the booming moans of the approaching undead were all I needed to convince me otherwise.

I heard some clinking and finally saw a man climb into the crane control seat just before a second motor started up. The tattered FEMA tents and bullet-ridden sandbags obscured a lot of what I saw, but when the crane woke up, extending its metal neck, and the ball dropped, I realized what the man was doing. The ball on the end of the crane was full of spikes. I had to stop watching to kill three creatures that rounded the front of my rig, so I missed the first impact, but the second was spectacular. The crane operator swung the spiked steel ball with impunity, catapulting corpses over the tops of trees and sending them smashing into the sides of cars, nearly folding the doors in half.

The wrecking ball definitely qualified for the top ten of most screwed-up things I'd seen since this started. I wish I'd had a camera, because no one would ever believe this. I had to give him credit: He was actually doing a decent job at keeping them away from the crippled crane until a thousand more corpses stepped out of the woods. The crane operator swung the ball 360 degrees in a last-ditch effort to repel boarders, but he was just too outnumbered.

I was done here. I boarded Goliath and put it into gear, heading west, away from the insane crane man and then eventually north toward Atlanta.

Mountain Man

Three days have passed since I left Tallahassee. In a fit of blind luck, I actually made good distance. I took a secluded and nearly clear highway to within sixty miles of Macon, Georgia, to a storage facility. I ran into some trouble along the way when the shakes, pain, and stupidity got too severe. Pulling the rig into the remnants of a nameless small town, I made a beeline for the drugstore and killed the engine, coasting the rig a quarter mile before rolling it up onto the sidewalk. Opening the rig's door, I carefully made my way down the steps to the concrete, wincing in pain as I did so. The wound on my hand opened up as I attempted to balance myself on the rig's handrail, and my ankle felt as if it would snap anytime.

I limped to the front door of the drugstore with a chain and a climbing carabiner in my cargo pocket. Using the drill, I worked the lock until the batteries went dead. Cursing, I twisted the chuck and pulled the drill free, leaving the bit stuck in the lock like a sideways Excalibur. Footfalls behind me tipped me off to the things that were approaching. I limped over to the rig and pulled my pack from the passenger seat.

I had time.

Digging in my pack, I found the sheathed bayonet, naturally at the bottom, and sat it down on the steps near the tied-down GARMR. I reached over my shoulder and pulled my rifle in front of me as the first corpse rounded the front of the truck. Its lower jaw was missing and its tongue hung tragically slack and wiggling from the gaping hole below its upper set of teeth. Straining against the pain, I detached the silencer from my carbine, putting it in my back pocket before fixing the bayonet to the lug. The long, thin shank of carbon steel gleamed, and I wasted no time in bayonetting the first creature through its eye as it advanced, letting it fall from the skinny dagger just as easily.

Three more now approached. I hobbled to them and managed to spike them all through the head, with the last one getting it in the roof of its mouth; that one fell forward onto the bayonet until the tip of the blade hit the skull from the inside. Off balance, I cursed in pain while forcing the bayonet out of the skull.

I went back to the drugstore door and flicked out the pliers on my multitool. Using the teeth of the pliers, I backed the blood-stained but precious drill bit out of the lock. Replacing the battery in the drill with another, I was able to defeat the lock and get inside the drugstore virtually unnoticed by whatever undead no doubt lurked in the alleys and strip mall across the street. I secured the door behind me, attaching the two ends of hardened steel chain together with the carabiner. Inside, I began to clear the store, bayonet affixed to my SBR. The weight of the suppressor in my back pocket reminded me what would happen if forced to fire indoors.

The place was picked over, devoid of food and other essentials. There was some carbonated water, so I grabbed it and drank deeply from the greenish glass bottle. The hint of lemon in the bubbly water was nice. Too bad I hadn't found it during winter, when it might have been cold.

Halfway through the store, I realized that I'd forgotten to let the GARMR off the truck. My hands shook again, reminiscent of the pain and onset of addiction I felt a while back in the Keys. That's another story. Against my better judgment, I decided to leave the GARMR secured and continue on into the back of the store, where the drugs were usually kept. Looking out over the ravaged shelves to the front, I nervously checked the windows and the chain wrapped between the two front doors. Although a poster covered the glass on one of the doors, I could see through the other.

Still clear.

The counter and floor behind it were covered with pills of all kinds: purple, blue, and everything in between. I clicked on my light, clenching it in my mouth as I swept a handful of them up in my hand to read them; my hands were shaking too much to make any of them out. Rounding the corner to the back room of the pharmacy, I nearly tripped over a skeleton lying facedown with a syringe embedded in its head. Some half-red, half-clear liquid still remained inside the syringe. I nudged the skeleton aside with my foot and continued into the pitch-dark area behind the pharmacy.

NOD on.

Another corpse lay on the ground in front of a large safe. A pistol with the slide locked back was clutched in its skeletal grip and I could see bullet dents on the safe.

The lack of undead inside the drugstore and the hole in the back of the pistol-packing corpse's head pointed me down a depressing path. The poor soul at my feet had needed so badly what was inside the safe that, when it wouldn't yield, self-destruction was the only option.

True addiction.

My hands shook from the pain and from my own desires to get inside the metal box and the treasures within. I had a tool kit on Goliath that I could use and I could probably drill the lock. I was far enough into the interior of the drugstore that the noise would be muffled to any undead lurking outside. I pulled the drill and adjusted the settings. I inserted the bit into the keyhole on the safe and began to dig into it. Sparks flew, flashing brightly through my NOD.

The bit bore about halfway into the lock, when the sound changed as if it hit a different medium. I backed the drill out and brought it closer. Tiny pieces of glass were embedded in the valleys of the tip of the carbide bit, a mechanism fail-safe to avoid brute force entry. The glass would shatter to thwart any would-be thief's plan at over-torquing the lock.

Just like I did.

Desperately, I pushed the drill into the jagged hole and the bit went all the way through the door to the other side. The drill whined loudly with no resistance to slow it down. I pulled the drill out and then turned the safe handle with no success; it was locked tightly in place, untold numbers of steel cylinders engaging all around the door into the steel lips on the inside.

I dropped the tools on the desk and went back to the truck. As I quietly moved to Goliath from the storefront, I noticed two undead at the intersection. They rotated their heads at a predictable cadence.

I'd been around them long enough to know they were searching for food, and more would be on the way.

I quietly took the pry bar and hammer from the truck's tool kit and limped back to the safe, careful to chain the doors again on my way in.

I attacked the safe like those things attack living humans. I wanted the oxy as bad as they wanted me. What would Tara think if she could see me now? The thought brought on overwhelming guilt, worsened by the thought of my daughter. I wasn't thinking straight; the pain, coupled by the early onset of what was likely addiction, pushed me into an anger-fueled rage. I jammed the pry bar into the top left corner of the safe and began to tug. Using the drill, I perforated the corner of the safe door, running the battery dead in the process. Now working the weakened door with the pry bar, I was able to peel it away and reach inside the steel box. At first, I could feel only an empty shelf, but after getting my arm inside up to my shoulder, my fingers grasped a plastic tub. I gripped it and began to pull it to me, to the opening I'd created.

I was so fixated on what was inside that I hadn't noticed the banging on the glass coming from the front of the drugstore. I mean, I knew it was there: I could hear it. I just hadn't noticed it. My incessant drilling and prying and cursing had attracted their attention. I didn't care.

"Give it to me," I growled at the safe, ignoring the sounds of cracking glass. I pulled the heavy tub to the opening and yanked, dropping the tub back onto the shelf inside the safe. The opening was too small.

"Fuck!" I screamed.

My hand and arm shook ferociously as I reached back inside the safe. Unable to pull the whole tub out, I grabbed handfuls of whatever was inside and hastily brought it in front of my NOD.

Tylenol #3. Codeine.

Just as soon as I saw the label on the plastic bags, I could hear the shattering glass. I stuffed my cargo pockets with painkillers and hobbled out from behind the pharmacy counter. The undead had not yet broken completely through. My hands shook as I detached the bayonet from my carbine. I knew I was running low on ammo. I painfully ratcheted the silencer onto the muzzle brake with a series of clicks and took the gun off *Safe*. I limped to the front of the store to assess.

I counted five of them trying to smash their way inside. Part of the entrance was already giving way to the left and a near-skeletal head peeked through, its white-orb eyes locking onto me as its arms began to flail on the outside of the glass. I limped over and shot it at point-blank range; it plugged the hole in the safety glass like a cork. The sound of my gun increased the excitement of the others as they began to beat the glass and doors, rattling the chain that held them together. The sharp pain in my ankle and hands briefly dissipated my brain fog, allowing me a few moments of clarity.

Bandages.

Antibiotic cream.

Idiot! What the fuck were you thinking?

I hurriedly grabbed a shopping cart and went around the store, dumping bandages, ointments, and anything else I could find inside, along with the remaining carbonated water. Not wasting any time, I shot three more undead before my carbine bolt locked back, indicating I was empty. Using the bayonet, I waited for the last creature to put its head behind a weakened portion of the glass before ramming the spike into its skull, my hand searing in agony. The body hung there, balanced on the blade, using the glass as its fulcrum. Strangely, through the smeared glass, I could see the creature's white eye move about, searching once more before its body went limp. The large poster-covered glass pane shattered as I pulled the blade, revealing the approach of more creatures from down the street. I quickly unchained the door and wheeled the squeaky cart to the passenger side of Goliath, tossing the contents haphazardly inside.

I climbed up into the rig and reached inside my cargo pocket. Tearing the plastic, I half chewed, half swallowed one of the pills laced with codeine. I sat there for a moment letting the drug be absorbed into my system, reminded of what pain can make a man do. The drug took, but not nearly as strong as the oxy. I put the truck in gear to the sounds of countless undead beating on its exterior, clawing for purchase to get inside the cab with me.

I remember the pain fading away and my eyelids sinking as I traveled down the road a few miles until I discovered a closed off-ramp that led somewhere away from the main thoroughfare. Smashing through the orange and white barrels with dangerous disregard, Goliath coasted along the ramp into an overgrown parking lot with a small building. The sign in the front said:

REST AREA
CLOSED

One of the last things I remember was shutting down the rig and fading out into drug-induced sleep. I remember the heat as well as the tall grass and the tree I saw that seemed to grow into the rest area office window and out the skylight. Like so many places along the way, the green was winning alongside the undead. Give it enough time and there would be no trace of us, unless whoever was looking got into it with an excavator.

I woke up to pain when the moon was high in the night sky. Coyotes howled and carried on somewhere beyond the rest area.

Not smart, not at all. They should know better.

Grimacing, I reached in my cargo pocket and popped a pill, swigging it down with half a bottle of water. I needed to piss pretty badly, but the shadows moving around outside kept me in the rig. I attempted to go into the water bottle but got most of it on my pants and hands. I screwed the plastic lid on the half-full bottle and tossed it onto the passenger seat floorboard with a thump.

I tried to make sense of the shadows but knew better than to turn on my headlights. I was asleep again before I could put too much thought into what I thought I was looking at.

The morning sun rose over the roof of the rest area, warming my face and awakening me to more pain. My hand instinctively reached for my cargo pocket and pulled out the already open plastic bag. Using every atom of willpower, I stopped myself from taking another pill.

I had necessaries that needed tending.

Checking the windows, I could see no undead save for a few specks moving about on the highway three hundred meters distant. I quietly opened my door and stepped down onto the cracked concrete being slowly separated by grass and ice. Rounding the front of the rig, I threw open the passenger door and pulled out my drugstore haul. I made for the concrete picnic table; its benches were concealed, its tabletop slab being the lone platform in the center of a tall grass sea. I sat on top of the table and began to sort the bandages, ointments, and other tinctures I had taken in a hurry. I dealt with my hands first, as I'd need to use them for everything else.

I soaked bits of bandage with rubbing alcohol and cleaned my hands. The alcohol stung like a motherfucker; no other way to put it. I dug into the wound with the soaked bandage, routing out the pus and dirt and whatever else was in there. After cleaning them thoroughly and painfully, I filled the holes with antibiotic cream and wrapped both hands with clean, dry bandages. With that out of the way, I unlaced my boot for the first time, allowing my ankle to breathe. I cleaned it the same way I had cleaned my hands. This didn't make medical sense, as there was no open wound on my ankle, but the cool, fast-evaporating alcohol felt good. Small spider veins were visible around the bone that jutted out on the inside of my leg where my foot met the ankle.

It was severely swollen, but after doing some mobility testing with my shaking hands, nothing seemed broken, although of course I couldn't be sure. After cleaning it, I wrapped my ankle up tightly, fighting against my urge to take another painkiller, and slipped my boot back on. Unable to fully lace it up, I wrapped the laces around and tied them off loosely. I scraped up the drugstore haul into the front of my shirt, holding it like a bowl, and waded through the grass back to the rig.

Rounding the front, I could see one of the undead coming up the ramp to the rest area. Its hand pointed at me, and it quickened its pace to a trot. I again thanked Christ I wasn't in an irradiated zone now; that thing could have been coming at me in a full-on sprint. I didn't feel like fucking with this right now, but if I climbed up into the truck to rest, it would just bang and bang on the door until I took care of it. Reluctantly, I trampolined the haul out of the front of my shirt into the truck and went through the routine of fixing my bayonet again.

I just stood there next to the door, impatiently waiting for the biobot to close the distance so I could get high and go to sleep.

Please.

The horribly disfigured female corpse seemed to walk in slow motion. Its hair was gone in patches and its clothing was badly torn. The only shard of humanity that remained was the huge diamond rock it still wore on its left hand. The light reflected from the ring like a disco ball, and she finally came within striking distance of my bayonet. With zero motivation or patience, I simply held the blade up, letting the instinct-driven corpse walk right into its sharp carbon steel tip. My shoulder and upper torso did the rest. Not long after the thing thudded onto the asphalt, I was safely in the cab, swallowing painkillers.

The previous day melted into the next without any noticeable seam. I wasn't yet well enough to drive out of my little rest area enclave, but I was running low on water. Skipping from one cloud to another every few hours was a battle, one that I kept losing.

I should only take a half pill next time—that's what I told myself after taking the last one.

When the pain came back with a vengeance, I convinced myself I needed a full dose, only to make another broken promise even before the medicine hit my lips. My hands felt a little better, and I was able to grip my carbine without gritting my teeth in the process. My ankle still hurt pretty badly, but only between meds.

I recovered the GARMR from the back of the rig and activated it. I watched it wake up and then instantly lock onto my face, slewing its complex sensors to get the best angle. What I used to think was creepy I now strangely looked forward to seeing.

I limped over to the building being slowly overtaken by unchecked plant life and stood in front. A fountain was positioned in the middle between the restrooms, filled with black water and tadpoles. A smashed-out vending machine was near the main office. Nothing remained inside. I had no way of knowing for certain, but I thought this place had been closed to the public even long before the undead walked.

Armed with this new confidence, I went door-to-door, lightly knocking and checking the locks. The men's room was shut down tight but the women's restroom door and the main office door were only closed, not locked. After verifying the unlocked restroom was clear, I opened the office slowly, enduring a long, low creak like that in a horror movie. Inside the office were a desk, a candle, a chair, and a propane lantern. A Georgia road atlas lay open on the desk.

I closed the door on the GARMR and went in for a closer look. After ensuring I was alone, I pulled up the chair. It was dim, so I shook the small green propane tank attached to the lamp. Half full. I ignited the propane and watched as the egg-shaped mantles glowed to life. They had holes in them as if chewed on by some unseen moth, but they were serviceable and filled the room with a bright glow.

I heard the GARMR's movement servos flex, causing me to shoot up from the desk, knocking the chair back against the wall as I bolted for the door. I opened it and jabbed the bayonet through.

The GARMR was only tracking a plastic shopping bag as it floated past the derelict fountain like a post-apocalyptic tumbleweed. I watched the unnatural white shape catch the breeze and expand on the wind, reminding me of the white-hot mantles that burned inside the office. With my heart rate spiked, sending blood to my extremities, my ankle again made me reach for my cargo pocket, but I resisted. I didn't know how long my resolve would last, but it was a start.

Recovering the chair, I sat back down at the desk and examined the atlas. As it was covered in Sharpie notes, I could clearly see the current position indicated by the shape of a diamond.

The rest area.

There were notes written in small letters all around the page, and circles indicating places that the owner had checked and found something, or found wanting.

I traced the bold black letters and markings with a dirty index finger, absorbing every word as if I'd written it myself.

I looked south and west at the horizon and saw the great fireball. The radio said they'd do it and they sure as hell did. The sky lit up for a moment and it looked as if an ungodly sunrise flashed from unnatural direction. The ground shook under foot and after a few minutes the wind shifted and the owl in the tree outside ended his sonata. My dog is whimpering under the desk, licking my hand.

I followed the writings clockwise around the map where the owner had used the city callouts on the edge for scratch paper, never intending to visit them.

I've shot all game within a mile of the abandoned rest area and harvested the edible plant life to the point of local extinction. I'm out of food. Had to eat Roy to make it through the winter. Wasn't an easy choice, but I did it like a man. My dad would have been proud. I . . . took him round back, and looked him in the eyes, and said I was sorry before putting him down. I used what I could and buried the rest after saying a few words.

I scooted the wooden chair back away from the desk and shined my flashlight under; was what I'd read inside the pages of a five-year-old edition of a Georgia road atlas reality or fiction? Spent .22 casings and Roy's dog hair stuck in the grout lines of the office floor told me that the author had spent time here. I could almost see Roy curled up under the table, a loyal companion to a master who did what had to be done.

My gaunt frame tells me that I'll die soon if I don't eat. Ten miles through the fields to the Anderson farm. I wouldn't make it one mile with those things out there. I saw one running on the road yesterday, leading a few slower ones north. It came from the direction of the flash, I just knew it. Just after the nukes, a congressman broadcasting on the AM band warned about radiation and what it did to these things. They're out there.

I turned to the next page and was greeted with madness on paper.

Lizards, lichen, leather. Ate my shoes, ate my belt. Thinking of eating one of them, they are a plenty on the road just down the ramp. It's getting close to that time, the flu? I don't know, hunger is enough without it. Think I'll lock myself in the men's room, but not before I finish what I need to say. Fall is upon us all in the north. I used my last bit of caloric energy, a Hail Mary attempt for food inside aban- doned cars. I still remember them in the beginning. Their hazard lights worked for days. One of them blinked and blinked, for nearly a week through the trees.

I found a case of water, but I had a whole closet full of that.

JUST NO GODDAMNED FOOD!!!

Unless you count the stick of Wrigley's I'd rationed for three days.

I dream of Roy, but not in the way I should.

To me, this atlas felt cursed. It represented a true darkness and desperation, and was not to be read again. I closed it and tossed it across the table, hoping I'd never become the same kind of author. Become desperate, become small.

This was not a place I wanted to stay at for too long. It had been looted thoroughly by Roy's master, the man with no name. The one who lay dead inside the locked men's room.

I doused the propane lantern and left it on the desk near the atlas and departed the office for fear I'd be the one to take my place at the wooden desk with the GARMR curled underneath to keep me warm.

Opening the office door, I was greeted by the machine as it tirelessly stood watch.

The GARMR had seen better days since rolling off whatever experimental production line from which it had been born. Not even the fresh Krylon paint job I'd given it could hide its battle scars; I could see that its frame was dented, scratched, and shot from untold badland adventures with its former master. Still it functioned with the same boring reliability as a bicycle or calculator.

I could depend on it.

The GARMR would do what it was programmed to do, independent of self-preservation or petty emotions. It had already pulled me out of the shit back in Tallahassee and knee-checked undead that came for me before that. I patted its titanium head and hobbled back to the rig, away from the office that once housed Roy and his doomed master. The thought of breaking into the men's room for a look didn't even cross my mind.

Emptying my pack onto the bed in the back of the rig, I took stock of my stores, realizing that I was running out of food. I repacked my kit after setting aside a dehydrated meal. I'd already eaten everything heavy along the way, lightening my load down to the dried stores. Rain began to spatter the windshield up front, so I gathered up two empty plastic bottles and sat them outside under the roof of the rest area building where runoff was already starting to drip.

My hands were definitely healing. It still hurt to grab door handles or pull up my pants, but it was starting to become bearable to wash my hands.

After collecting enough water from the bottles outside, I poured some into my canteen cup and lit off the Sterno fuel, heating it to a near boil before adding the food. I didn't have the luxury of boiling it for fifteen minutes to ensure the food was properly cooked. I'd run out of cooking fuel too fast if I did that.

Lasagna wasn't supposed to be crunchy, but it was far better than eating my belt and shoes.

The sun disappeared below the trees. "What a horrible night to have a curse," I said aloud. I looked outside my window and saw the GARMR folded into itself, dormant, just outside the door. It was my night-light.

I pulled the road atlas from the back of the seat and began to chart my way north, away from here. As my dirt-crusted fingernail traced a potential path, I came to the realization of what I was doing and placed the atlas back in the pocket on the back of the seat. I wasn't ready to become Roy's master.

The sun was gone, but some of its light still cast dark shadows over the rest area. Large pin oak trees loomed over the rig, providing shade in the day and a cavelike atmosphere at night.

Hearing the snap of a twig outside through the cracked window, I turned on my NOD and scanned both sides of the rig, seeing nothing. It wasn't worth deploying the GARMR. It might get stuck or make too much noise and draw more in from the highway.

Checking my watch, I was still half an hour until my dosage time but snapped one of the pills in half, justifying that it would be fine taking a half dose a little early. My ankle hurt but didn't throb constantly without medication anymore—a good sign. I was starting to heal. Excellent, because I needed to find more food, and an easy mark at that. I couldn't go rappelling into a Walmart skylight in my condition. It had to be easy.

Painstakingly, I climbed into the front of the cab. I turned the rig's electrical system on and rolled through the AM band. Nothing. I thought I could hear a British accent somewhere in the static, but it was probably my imagination. The mind sometimes heard what it wanted to hear. With a half-full stomach and painkillers coursing through my blood, I started to embrace the possibility of sleep.

At about 0500, I secured the GARMR and started the engine. I clumsily turned the rig around to get back on the highway the same way I had come in. The rest area exit was blocked off with construction barricades, and I didn't want to hurt my ankle more while trying to move them out of the way. I crunched over a corpse that lay rotting in the road before turning a sharp right to get back on the highway.

As previously noted, the road was clear to Macon. I only had to stop the rig once to attach a cable and pull some wreckage apart to pass through. I wouldn't take any chances with driving the rig on the grassy shoulder with how much rain has been falling. Getting stuck out there with a hurt leg was so much more than a death sentence.

Before leaving this morning, I took one pill from the codeine stash and intentionally put the rest in the GARMR's saddlebags outside the truck. As I rolled out, I took half a pill. I wanted to take the other half too, but I was making my first attempt at reversing my pain med dependency. Approaching Macon, I nearly stopped the rig, limped out, and recovered the rest of the meds but forced myself to rein in those feelings. It didn't hurt that bad. It didn't hurt that bad. It doesn't hurt that bad.

It was simple: If I left the truck to get the meds, I was addicted. If I stayed behind the wheel and kept on mission, I wasn't.

On the outskirts of Macon I turned off the road, following a sign:

ZERO MOUNTAIN COLD STORAGE 4 mi

The only reason for cold storage was preservation, and preservation meant food. Probably none of it was unspoiled, but food meant food trucks, which meant diesel. Goliath's tanks needed a drink. Unlike a big-box grocery store, the masses of panicked people at the start of all this wouldn't have rushed a place like Zero Mountain. Hopefully.

I cruised down the road, edging around a jackknifed rig and down a street cleverly named Zero Avenue. The opening to the facility was set into a hillside with trucks parked near rows of loading bays. I parked Goliath among the dozens of other rigs and shut off the engine. I climbed down, ignoring the urge to get to the meds in Checkers' saddlebags.

Listening for any signs of undead, I got down on the ground and looked under and around the hundreds of tires belonging to the Zero Mountain trucks scattered about the parking lot. I picked up a piece of concrete and chucked it far into the group of trucks. It impacted metal with a loud bang and returned a few echoes back and forth between the hillside and me. I again got down to the ground, watching for any movement.

There. A pair of legs started a slow shuffle from behind the tractor toward the rear of the trailer. Then another rounded the hood of a red truck. Both figures moved to where they heard the noise.

These bastards had the uncanny ability to know where sound came from.

I painfully fixed my bayonet and met the first creature with its point. The second was dispatched in the same way. After double-checking the area, I walked around from truck to truck, tapping on tanks with my rifle. There was more than enough fuel to fill Goliath's tanks. I went back, led the GARMR to the ground, and started the rig. I pulled in close to the trucks I'd identified as having fuel and began siphoning tank to tank until Goliath overflowed with diesel. I filled my spare fuel cans with as much as I could hold and stowed them away for a rainy day, which was any minute now, judging by the clouds gathering overhead.

Two trucks were backed up into the loading bays. I limped over to them with the GARMR in tow, clicking its feet on the cracked pavement. At the bays, I grabbed onto the rubber bumper, wincing a little at the stiffness of my hands, and slowly climbed up onto the platform. I reconfigured my carbine with its silencer and flipped on the light to look through the crack between the truck and the bay opening. It was relatively high off the ground and a tight squeeze to get inside the bay. I could hear the thunder rumble and reverberate off the hillside.

I climbed back down and parked Goliath near the bays, careful not to smash the GARMR in the process. It seemed to have basic self-preservation programming: It moved out of my way when I backed into my spot. Now inside the loading bays, I was safe off the ground and I could get to Goliath by jumping from one truck to the other if I absolutely had to, although my ankle ached at the thought of it.

Two massive rolling shutter doors with chain pulleys separated the bays from the interior of Zero Mountain. After checking the immediate area for anything useful, I began to tug the chain, sending the metal doors up a few inches.

A hundred bony hands reached in unison through the opening at the bottom, gripping the door, pulling up with all the power left in their decaying muscles and tendons.

I couldn't let go of the chain; the creatures were actually nearly bringing me off the ground. I held on to the rusted heavy-gauge chain, hanging by all my weight, and still they managed to pull me off the ground in a bid to raise the shutters and get to me.

I gave the chain one last pull before letting go and exploding out of the bay like a scared animal. I could hear the door roll upward behind me, so I hurried as fast as my ankle would allow for the box-shaped opening ahead. Pallet jacks and banding rolls crashed to the floor, giving chase to the warm body in flight. Squeezing through the opening, I had to go slow or risk hurting my foot in the descent. As my leg touched the ground outside, one of the creatures appeared through the bay opening. I covered my face as it fell toward me.

The thing was too big to get through.

Stuck at the waist, it flailed and gave a raspy moan as whatever was in its unused lungs began to spill out of its mouth and down the side of the trailer, down to the rubber bumpers. For a moment I thought I'd been lucky, until the rest of the cast of horrors appeared behind the portly ghoul, pushing it forward toward me like a Looney Tunes character. The GARMR looked at me and at the creatures. I know I'm not crazy and I know it's only a machine, but I got the feeling the GARMR was contemplating, *Okay, what now?*

"Run!" I told it as if responding to the machine's imaginary communication.

Back at Goliath, I heard the large creature hit the ground below the bay with a crash, followed by lesser thumps from the rest of the ones that followed. I quickly loaded up the GARMR and jumped into the rig.

The engine turned over but didn't start.

I sat in the rig and listened as every creature hit the ground with a thud and watched in disbelief as they began to surround Goliath in numbers I could not defend. My carbine had barely over a magazine remaining. Thirty-something rounds were useless against the numbers I saw outside my windows, unless I could get them all to be accommodating and stand in line. I tried to start Goliath again. The battery was strong but it didn't fire up.

I sat there for a moment, lamenting on how screwed I was, until I remembered the pistol I'd found in the sleeper when I first discovered Goliath. As I was about to jump into the back between the two front seats, a gruesome face appeared in the window next to me. Amazingly, part of the creature's head was missing but not enough to stop its animation. It was in advanced stages of decomposition but had still found a way to climb up and take a look inside at its prey. I pulled out my Microtech, deploying the blade as soon as my hands pulled it from the sheath. I timed the power windows so that it couldn't see the spike coming. I jammed it into its head with boxer-like quickness, sending it back down into the developing mosh pit below.

More were trying to get up.

I put the window back up and went back to find the Ruger Mark III .22.

Recovering the heavy steel pistol, I checked its action. Nothing was binding and the sights seemed pretty close to lined up in the rear of the gun. I spilled part of the brick of .22LR out onto the passenger seat and inserted one of the mags into the Ruger.

Putting the window down to half-mast, I squeezed the trigger on the blaster as fast and accurately as I could. At the distance I was shooting from, the .22LR penetrated skulls with no problems. The first ten rounds were spent fairly quickly, so I slapped the next mag into the gun, tossing the empty in the seat on top of the ammo brick. My ears rang, so I stuffed them with 9mm rounds and continued pulling the trigger. Microscopic brass splinters shot into my right arm and face, and the bright fiber optic sights on the Ruger sent my rimfire projectiles true to their targets.

I shot, and shot, and shot.

My thumbs were blistered nearly all the way through from loading the Mark III magazines, which became difficult to load after a hundred shots. The spring tension button on the magazine feeder was nearly impossible to hold back with my thumbs as I inserted the tiny rounds into the metal magazine. Piles of human remains littered the area around Goliath, creating a problem. The remaining dozen or so undead were using the fallen corpses as a stepstool to walk up onto the rig's running boards. I kept blasting through the pain in my hands.

With few malfunctions, the Mark III eventually put down all of the undead in the immediate area. The dashboard was full of spent shell casings and smelled of a gunfight. My shooting hand ached and my thumbs throbbed in agony. The Mark III's barrel was warm to the touch when I sat it down in the seat with nearly half a brick remaining.

I nearly vomited, thinking of loading the empty Mark III mags; the pain was that intense. With more undead spilling into the parking lot now, I began to pray for the first time in a long while.

"Dear Lord, walk with me in this valley. Please make the truck start," I whispered with eyes closed and clasped hands.

I pressed the clutch and turned the key slowly, not daring to touch the accelerator.

With twin puffs of black smoke, Goliath's engine roared to life. I had only a smidgen of food and water left, but I had divine intervention and two full tanks of diesel cross-feeding into the engine, giving me enough range to get to where I pointed the rig.

Atlanta.

Paradise—that's the only word I can use to describe this. And, like the Garden of Eden, I couldn't keep it. Only a short reprieve from what was outside the walls.

As I made my way north along a back road highway, learning Goliath's gears and quirks, something caught my eye in the trees to the right. Movement. I slowed the rig to a stop and fished the binoculars out of my pack. Turning the eyepieces into sharp focus, I could clearly see a small wind turbine above the trees, probably a mile or so in the distance. I put Goliath back into gear and pulled off onto the next road leading up the hillside.

After a series of wrong turns, I found what I was looking for: a closed wrought-iron gate that looked as if it'd held back great hordes. Fat, gristle, and general slime coated the gate, which appeared solidly holding on to the rock pillars. Nothing short of the rig I was driving could pull that gate off its hinges, and without sufficient weight holding down Goliath's tires, that might not even be enough.

I popped half a codeine pill, putting the rest of the meds in the glove box, and stepped out of the rig. The asphalt, though covered in leaves and dead grass, looked recently resurfaced. The gate to the property didn't have initials on it; only a solid copper crest, a vertical dagger, the tip pointing down and wrapped with a snake in front of a shield. The wall was high and I was about to turn around, when I heard the faint sound of music from the other side of the fence.

I painfully climbed back up inside the rig and put the grille about an inch away from the iron gate. I released the GARMR, tossed a knotted line to the other side of the fence, and climbed onto the rig's warm hood before I stepped over the top of the fence and down the rope to the other side.

The music was barely audible. The click of the GARMR's heels told me it didn't like being fenced off. Inside the GARMR's tablet menu, I programmed the gate area as a new "return home" waypoint for the GARMR, just in case something went wrong and I had to escape the area from another point. I commanded it to wait and began walking down the meandering drive that cut between what looked like a forest on both sides. The path eventually brought me to a large two-story home. The porch lights were still on, likely powered by the wind turbine I'd seen from the highway. Three dead dogs remained on the sidewalk leading to the front door. They were either Dobermans or rottweilers; decomposition made discernment impossible to my eyes.

Classical music played from an artificial rock sitting in a flower bed overgrown with weeds and saplings. Although it'd been a while since I'd heard the sweet sound of music, I flipped the stone over and yanked the wires, killing the tinny sound.

The front door was unlocked, and the blast of clean cold air from the inside told me that something besides a tiny wind turbine was juicing the place. There was no way air-conditioning could be powered by it. I reveled in the coolness, something not really practical or even allowed in our outpost in the Florida Keys. Even the two Westinghouse nuclear reactors that provided power to our islands couldn't supply air-conditioning to the whole colony without brownouts. Electrons were rationed and limited.

I closed the door behind me, taking in the ornate design of the house. It was relatively clean, the air filters reducing dust and other debris that settled on the floor. I took a few minutes clearing the house and the grounds all around the fence perimeter. The home was surrounded by walls and tall iron fences, impervious to undead assault in small to medium numbers. A large concrete water cistern was positioned at the top of a hill above the house. Walking the ten-acre perimeter, I found no gaps in the fence line and saw only one corpse on the other side, facedown in a dry streambed. I called out to the creature and threw rocks at it to make sure it didn't move.

The detached garage was also unlocked, so I shouldered the door open, ready to fight a platoon of them. The garage held no undead. My luck couldn't hold forever and finding a place like this was more than good fortune. The large garage held a full-size Land Rover sitting uneven from a flat tire. The thin layer of dust indicated that it had been there since the beginning. I put my NOD down over my eye and proceeded inside. Nearly past the Land Rover, I thought, *The house actually has power*.

I went back to the door and flipped on the switch, illuminating the abandoned garage with clicking fluorescent lights. Industrial racks lined the other side of the garage; they were filled with diving gear, motorcycle helmets, and even a few parachutes folded neatly in a bin. Although the Land Rover was appealing because I could actually change the tire on it myself, it lacked the extreme range of which Goliath was capable. I would have needed to find fuel more often, and regular fuel was laced with ethanol, a substance neither good for gas nor internal combustion engines. The Land Rover was locked, but that didn't stop me from throwing a dive tank through the passenger window and getting inside. I didn't dare open the door for fear that the battery would still hold a charge that powered the vehicle's alarm system. I carefully negotiated the sharp glass and reached to the visor to recover what I was after.

The gate remote.

With the small device clipped to my belt, I slowly hoofed it back to the main gate. Rounding the last corner before the gate, I could see the GARMR standing there, looking down the path in my direction. I'd told it to wait, but something had woken it up: a small group of corpses milling around the rig. The creatures paid no attention to the GARMR; they must have jarred it from standby out of curiosity and left it alone after figuring out it wasn't something they could tear to pieces. With only three behind the fence, I rapped the butt of my rifle on the iron bars and called out to them. As soon as they got into range, I stuck them all in the head, careful to do it so I wouldn't have to drag the heavy meat sacks out of the way when I reopened the gate.

Depressing the button on the remote, I heard the electric motor tension the chain, swinging the gate inward with a wrenching squeak. I stepped back to avoid getting smashed in the face by the gate, allowing the GARMR to trot inside. I told it again to wait uselessly, expressing that "I meant it this time."

I got inside the truck cab and turned the diesel over. Careful not to sink the heavy tractor into the grass, I executed a three-point turn, backing it inside the property in the event I needed to make a quick getaway. With another press of a button, the heavy gates met in the middle, sealing off the property from the monsters outside. Instead of walking down the leaf-strewn path leading back to the house, I took another pass around the gate perimeter. Same as before, same dent in a section of gate caused by a lawn mower, same corpse facedown in a dry creek bed, and the same hot Georgia afternoon.

Checkers faithfully followed, staying ten feet behind me so as to not soak me with RTG battery radiation. Back at the house, I told it to sleep outside the door. It would be easier to recover the GARMR if the house got overrun and I had to exit via the second-floor window. I cursed under my breath for even having to think that way and went inside to the cool refuge of the home.

That creeping pain started to set in again, making me reach for my cargo pocket to no avail. I'd intentionally left the meds at the end of the driveway. If I braved the heat and limped back to the truck for my fix, I'd know I was still under its spell.

In the medicine cabinet, just inside the great hall, I found some aspirin and took a small handful, washing it down with cold beef stew from the pantry. I stood by the front door, palming the door handle, trying to talk myself into heading back to Goliath for the meds.

You're in pain; you need them.

Only take half a pill, it's not a big deal.

No.

After about thirty minutes, the aspirin and beef stew kicked in, dulling the sharp edges of pain. I fell back from the door to the couch, talking myself down from the prospect of braving the heat for the little pills in the glove box a half mile away. Keeping my mind off the meds, I pulled out the GARMR tablet and began clicking through menus. Finding the one I wanted, I set Checkers' sensors into a sector scan, keeping an eye on the driveway. If it detected movement, it would make the tablet beep and send full-motion video to the screen.

After turning on the GARMR's sentry mode, I took a look out the window at the machine. Its body remained dormant in a rectangular shape, but its sensor turret remained active, sending out LIDAR to its assigned sector, looking for movement to report to the tablet. It was a rather genius design chock-full of military applications. I had never seen one like this before the shit hit the fan . . . the closest to it being the machines made to carry heavy battlefield loads powered by loud gas engines or conventional batteries. With the GARMR on watch, I checked the home a little more thoroughly. Raising the lever on the kitchen sink faucet, I was floored to see water spew from the gooseneck opening. Dirty for the first few seconds, it then cleared up. I put my head under the sink and just stood there. It must be falling down the pipes from the cistern up the hill I'd seen earlier.

I swung the lever over to the side marked *H* and waited. I

heard something sounding like a hot-air balloon coming from another room down the hall, and soon hot water came spilling from the gooseneck faucet onto my damaged hands.

Glorious. My eyes literally began to tear up with joy. If the sink had hot water, then, oh God, so must the shower. I immediately slammed the lever down, cutting off the water flow, not wanting to take any chance of missing out on a hot shower, which was something even rarer than unicorn gills.

Cruising down the hall to the bathroom, I checked the linen closet. Nothing inside but sheets and the home's air circulating unit. Multiple copper pipes snaked out of the slab, entering the circulator. Curious, I pulled the panel and touched my hand to the coils. They were cold.

The shower was a massive walk-in with no door, tiled from wall to wall in fancy marble. I wasted no time in turning on the rain nozzle, letting water flow from the high ceiling into my waiting hands. The water was cold at first, until the on-demand water heater kicked on, releasing water so hot, it was uncomfortable on my injured hands. I dialed it down and stripped off my clothes, not caring at the moment about whatever lurked outside.

I grabbed the shampoo from the shower shelf and began scrubbing. Black dirt and grime circled the drain at my feet. Raising my arms to catch the water, the pungent onion smell almost made me gag. The dirt just kept washing away from my body. I stripped off the bandage on my ankle and the dressing from my hands and tossed them in the corner of the large bathroom.

Walking out of the shower, I stood in front of the fogged mirror and noticed that a heart had been written there from untold showers ago . . . left there for me to find, far from home, far from Tara and the baby. The way it was shaped reminded me of Tara, how she makes her hearts when she writes little notes to me. She puts little skinny hearts as dots on her *i*'s. Not quite Tara's hearts here, but the mirror still reminded me of her. I stared until the fog faded, revealing the face of a person I barely recognized.

Who was this beat-up old man with a beard standing naked in front of me, scarred from shrapnel, gunshots, and burns?

I ran my hand over my jawline, noticing a few gray hairs hidden in my beard. I looked feral, like some wild mountain man.

There was a double-edged safety razor, shaving brush, and soap, but I just couldn't bring myself to do it. Shaving flipped a switch in my head. A clean face was for when I was home, not here in the undead badlands. Out here, I was this man, not that one. Out here, I ate with my fingers from tin cans and shot dead things in the head as if they were paper targets at a shooting range in by-gone days.

I felt a lot better, though. The soap and warm water, although painful at first, were a godsend for my wounds and bruises. I didn't bother wrapping a towel around my waist, but I did sling my gun across my chest. I nonchalantly headed for the utility room, opened the washing machine, and tossed in all my dirty clothes, even the skivvies from my pack I'd been holding on to. I set a quick cycle and hit *Start*, and the damn machine worked.

I watched the cistern water fill the machine through the glass on top and the motor began to agitate the clothes, fed by the electricity generated by the turbine and whatever else this house had going for it. Upon closer inspection of the circulator in the linen closet, I found a sticker affixed to the side.

HALE GEOTHERMAL

Mark on map

Figures. I find a geothermal climate-controlled home with plenty of water, surrounded by a tall iron fence, off the beaten path and I couldn't use it. I made a note to myself to mark this place on my map.

The sun was starting to dip below the trees and my pain pushed beyond the aspirin into the realm of madness. I put on the last clean pair of skivvies from my pack and slid on my boots, not bothering to lace them up. I opened the door and was blasted by the summer heat as I limped to Goliath for the meds to help me hang on. The carbine's charging handle dug into my skin as I walked, reminding me that I was mostly naked with a black rifle machine gun slung across my chest. I'd have looked like a lunatic two years ago.

Goliath's hood was still warm and its frame still popped as the rig cooled down. I climbed up into the cab and grabbed the bag of meds, disappointed in my inability to resist. If I'm being honest with myself, these half doses were making me very uncomfortable.

After the codeine kicked in, I went around the house at sunset unplugging nonessential items that were ghost draining the local microgrid. The house was heated and cooled by geothermal, but the electricity was supplied by three wind turbines as well as an array of solar shingles situated on the southern slope of the large stronghold's roof. The generated energy supplied a battery bank situated in a small shed that was attached to the northern side of the house, away from direct sunlight. Upon inspection of the batteries via flashlight, I could see that about twenty percent of them were dead, their fluid seeping from the top of the battery and down onto the floor, corroding the bolts that held the battery rack together. I couldn't say for sure, but the battery banks probably had a year, maybe two, before they'd need replacements. Destressing the microgrid like I did would help, but wouldn't stop the eventual full degeneration of the banks.

I checked the washer and noticed that my clothes were done, so I strung them out to dry on the line in the backyard; I could have used the dryer, but I wasn't sure how much strain the home's grid could handle. Back inside the house, I flipped on the lights and went to the master bedroom on the ground level and set up temporary shop. Again I laid my pack out on the large floor and dumped it for reorganization and sorting. I recompressed my sleeping bag and put it on the bottom. My spare skivvies and socks would go next whenever they were dry, and my cooking supplies and first aid would go at the top of the bag along with a magazine that held seven rounds of subsonic ammunition. The last full mag of subs was in my carbine. I had thirty-five total rounds of subsonic remaining. Knowing how I shoot, any OPFOR of undead over thirty strong and I'd be full-time bayonet, straight-up World War I trench warfare.

At least my pack was a lot lighter than when I started this journey eighteen days ago.

I took the time to break down my gun and wipe the extreme carbon buildup off the bolt carrier assembly and bolt with paper towels and an old toothbrush I found in one of the master bath vanities. I always keep a bore snake in my kit, as they're light and have multiple uses. I ran the snake through the barrel a few times, knocking out as much carbon as I could without a full-on cleaning. A suppressor throws a lot of shit back into the receiver, filling it with gunk pretty fast. Surprised I hadn't had a malfunction yet, I reattached the upper to the lower and headed to the garage with my NOD on my head. Finding some two-cycle oil, I dabbed some into the holes on the bolt carrier, letting it seep down to the bolt, and then racked the action a few times before replacing the magazine and chambering a round.

At seven pounds, my carbine could kill twenty-eight undead at or inside a hundred meters. Thirty-five if I could get to my last magazine. Even with few rounds remaining, it was deadlier than a Spartan blade or a quiver full of bolts. Back inside, I walked every room, checking every lock on every window and door. With my rifle next to me and my boots on the floor, I climbed into the bed and grabbed the GARMR tablet I had plugged into the home's grid. I stood Checkers up and steered it around the property, looking for anything out of place. I clicked the audio on and listened to the machine walk down the path to Goliath.

After checking that the gate was secure, I turned it left to walk down the perimeter. Same corpse facedown in the dry creek, same dent on the iron fence from a lawn mower. Slewing the GARMR's sensor over to look at the house, I saw my own bedroom window glowing brightly in the machine's night vision–capable sensor array. The moonlight reflected off the low-profile solar panels, causing the machine to auto-gate its night vision and compensate for the lumen fluctuations. Satisfied the area was clear, I activated the machine's sentry mode and placed the tablet on top of my pack while it charged.

Feeling tinges of pain returning, I forced my mind to shut down before I yearned for another dose of drugs to see me through the night.

• • •

0600

Bump in the Night

At first, I wasn't certain whether it was the drugs or for real. I kept hearing a thumping sound coming from somewhere in the house. I didn't really know how long it had been going on, hidden by ambient noise. The air circulator had automatically shut off, blanketing the entire home in silence. There was no pattern to the sound; its low, methodical beat penetrated whatever barrier it passed through. I first noticed it at about midnight and immediately jumped out of my rack and began clearing rooms in my underwear with my carbine and NOD. The noise couldn't be heard in any room but the master. I flipped on the LED overhead lighting and began putting my ear to the walls to try to triangulate the source. When I was about to take my knife to the drywall, I noticed that the carpet under the corners of the bed was disturbed, as if someone had rolled the bed on caster wheels.

Reluctantly, I put my hip into the bedpost and gave it a nudge. It rolled nearly effortlessly, almost hitting the dresser. Concealed underneath the bed was a stainless steel hatch with the largest Torx hole I'd ever seen in the center of it. Must have been a T500, if they even made those before. I pushed the bed aside into the wall and pressed my ear to the cold stainless hatch. It was definitely louder. Running my fingers over the edges and contours of the large hatch, I knew it must have literally weighed a ton. Large, vault-like hinges were recessed into the two-inch-thick steel jamb, rendering the door almost impossible to attack with an angle grinder.

I sat there on top of the hatch, formulating what must be inside. The conclusion wasn't hard to come to. The house had been unlocked when I found it and music was playing. The home's local grid and water supply cistern told me that whoever owned the place had a lot of money and that they were hard-core preppers. The rhythmic pounding on the hatch door only slightly changed cadences, just enough to let me know that it was one of those things down there. If a living human was trapped inside and knew someone was above, they'd either make absolutely zero noise or they'd be pounding and screaming like crazy. The second round of long-interval thumps coming from inside was the undead.

I'd never know for certain unless I somehow found a plasma torch and another power source, but it really wasn't my place to know. Hell, any guess was as good as mine. Maybe that decomposing bag of bones I keep seeing on patrol outside, the one facedown in the riverbed, bit the owners. Maybe they didn't know what the bite would do yet. Maybe a lot of them showed up at the gate, scaring them underground with an injured kid who was already infected thanks to taunting one of the creatures through the fence. Whatever it was, they went underground; one of them turned and took out the rest of them. I imagined some vast steel cavern loaded to the ceiling with ammunition and food.

I slid the bed back over the tomb and moved all my shit into a guest room, where the sounds of the trapped undead couldn't find my ears. They'd never make it through that steel lid in a million years, thumping their arms to bloody nubs. Even so, I slept with both eyes open, my back to the wall and a chair wedged under the doorknob of the guest room.

As much as I wanted to go underground to have a peek, it would take a long damn time to break that door. Last night I dreamed of the riches below as dragons dreamed of gold.

After the unexpected discovery of the bunker, I was anxious to assess my medical situation and plan my next move. My hands were scabbed over pretty good, but the past couple days of fresh dressings and hot water had done wonders for the superficial ailments. After another hot shower, I cut bandages from clean T-shirts I'd found still folded in the drawers of the master bedroom. Hard Rock Cafe, Hong Kong, was on my right hand, Harley on my left. I rewrapped my ankle tightly with a clean bandage and got dressed. Before stepping out the door, I popped a half pill to take the edge off. Yeah, I know.

On my way out to the garage, I noticed that I was limping less than the day before—a welcome sign of recovery. Still hesitant to put much weight on my foot, I tossed the cardboard boxes around instead of stacking them neatly. No need to pay too much attention to the noise: I was surrounded by a tall fence and I had a semitruck with a mostly full tank of fuel ready anytime I needed to jet.

In the garage, I found two blue five-gallon water cans, which I promptly filled and placed in a Radio Flyer wagon. I also took some cordage sitting in a container on an industrial shelf opposite the Land Rover. I retrieved a few other odds and ends and stacked them in the wagon and wheeled that around to the front of the house under a shade tree.

Turning around to go back inside, my eye caught something out of place in the tree. I thought it might be some sort of small black climbing rope, but after following the line all the way up, I determined that it was an antenna.

Sneaky.

Some HAM radio operators like to be covert and not broadcast to the world that they have expensive radio equipment inside and likely more. Whoever owned this place was in it for the long haul. I wished they weren't walking around under the house undead. This was a fine setup and it was a damn shame that whoever earned and paid for all this wasn't alive to use it like it was intended. I couldn't be sure without a shovel and a lot of sweat, but this antenna likely led underground inside the bunker below and into the shelter's communications array. If the house was on geothermal, solar, and wind, it was a safe bet that the underground shelter was as well. If this was back when the shit first hit the fan and I didn't have Tara or the baby, I'd be taking Goliath to the nearest town and commandeering the tools I'd need to break in, just out of pure curiosity.

It was about noon when my pack was organized, my stomach was full, and I was completely hydrated. My silencer was off my gun and in a pouch on my belt. If I ran into anything a bayonet couldn't handle, I'd either crank the can on the muzzle or I'd limp away fast. I couldn't survive any Mogadishu moments with such a low ammo state.

After one final sweep, I unplugged everything that wasn't performing a vital function in the house and switched off the ceiling fans and lights, then turned the thermostat up to 72. This would ease the burden on the battery banks and wind turbine if it was set to auto shutdown when charging requirements were met. With the red Radio Flyer overflowing with food, water, and kit, Checkers and I very reluctantly left the house of plenty for Goliath and whatever road it would take us down.

OtRA

I kept Goliath moving at a comfortable speed down the abandoned highway. I'd see undead lurking in the trees and fields, but they were not concentrated in any numbers. As the miles slowly ticked by, I kept glancing at the digital clock on the stereo, waiting for enough time to pass so that I could take another half pill. My forehead would sweat, my skin would itch, and my hands would shake on the big-rig wheel, telling me it was time to partake. After about twenty minutes, the feeling of ice in my veins would overtake me as well as the pain in my ankle and hands.

Day 20t

_1300_

Full disclosure. This. Is. The. Drugs. This account will never be shared, not after what happened when I got home from Hourglass. An entire year of my life encapsulated in my private journal was ripped from my quarters by a group representing what was left of the United States government. Any and all evidence of Hourglass was REDACTED forever, relegated to my mind alone. Almost all. Even now, as I write this on paper that will never be made again, I run my lead-stained finger across the imprinted words. I must be careful to keep my pencil sharp, as a fine point makes smaller words, taking up less space on the page. Flipping through the blanks that remain, I'll need a new volume in less than a quarter inch of yellowed, water-damaged paper.

. . .

Day 21

2200

I ran the rig hard yesterday, opening the distance from the mansion. I didn't get far; I was somewhere outside of Forsyth when I nearly spit out the instant coffee I'd warmed up via the diesel engine over twenty miles ago. I'd been driving with my NOD, fully blacked out so as to not attract any kind of company, living or otherwise. Rigging tape covered the clock radio and other instruments that would white out my night vision optic. The CB was on, tuned to its original channel 19 setting. I'd never switched it to any other. With the RF spectrum clear, I hadn't noticed that I'd turned the volume up damn near full blast. All I could hear up to this point was some noise just before sunset. When the CB suddenly blared, I jerked the wheel and took a sip of coffee down the wrong hole, making me cough as I brought Goliath to a stop.

"Unknown rider, we can hear your engine. Please respond on channel 19."

I sat in the darkness listening to the first non-recorded human voice I'd heard in weeks. After another repeat of the message, I grabbed the mic and keyed the button on the side.

"I'm here. I'm on the road. Who is this?"

I was getting frustrated at the lack of response until I realized that I still had the mic keyed. I quickly released mid-transmission.

". . . trapped inside the air bridge. Just me and my two kids. Out of food; hasn't rained in two days. Can you help, please, please help? It's just me and my children."

"Where are you?" I said, this time releasing the key.

"We're on the air bridge between the two Sacred Heart Hospital buildings. Trapped on both sides. Please, mister."

The desperation in the father's voice was palpable. That feeling I'd felt long ago when I heard William's distress call was coming back, causing a lump in my throat. *I have a kid back home; what about her? What if I die saving this father's kids; what about mine?* Those questions shot back and forth through my mind a thousand times in the span of a second before I keyed the transmitter.

"How high up?" I asked.

"Uh . . . I don't know. Maybe fifty feet? I see four floors below us. Listen, we're going to die up here. Just save my kids. I don't care about myself. Just them, it's all I ask," the man said practically sobbing on the radio.

I keyed the transmitter, "Save it; just tell me where you are: streets, landmarks, anything. I have a map."

The man told me that his name was Mitch and provided detailed directions to the skybridge where he and his children were. I sketched out the directions on paper and took Goliath off the highway in the direction of Sacred Heart.

I idled down the two-lane roads until they expanded to four lanes, and I then went left, accidentally using my turn signal, illuminating the entire block through my NOD, along with the ghostly faces of dozens of reaching undead. As I left the mob of creatures, I could see lights clicking on and off on a walkway that spanned two fifteen-story buildings. The walkway was just as described, about forty feet or so off the road below. The road was thick with undead, but I wasn't sure why. Mitch and his kids were high enough up as to not be noticed by the creatures unless they intentionally made noise, attracting them. As I pulled onto the street that led to the skybridge, I understood why the undead were there.

The smell of human feces and urine was overwhelming. The smell of the living always attracted the undead. The family had to go somewhere and that meant off the skybridge into the street below. The dead now walked in human shit, looking for the living asses that dropped it. I sat at idle until the thumps on the side of the rig indicated that the creatures had found me in the darkness, attracted by the heat coming off the engine. I strung my carbine across my chest and rolled the window down on the driver's side.

"Is that you?" the CB boomed, causing the undead to moan an opera of the damned for all to enjoy. I reached down and ripped the rigging tape from the CB controls, bathing the cabin with artificial light and washing out my NOD. I turned the volume down to a 2 and replaced the tape quickly to get green eyes back.

"Yes, it's fucking me," I said angrily back over the radio.

"Sorry, I didn't mean to . . . Well, what is the plan?" Mitch responded.

"The plan is I'm going to throw a cargo strap up to you. You rig it to something up there and climb down onto the top of my rig," I said.

"Then what?" Mitch asked.

"Then we get the hell out of here, that's what," I said, obviously annoyed by the shitstorm I was currently caught in.

I pulled the rig forward to outpace the crowd that was starting to form around Goliath. Quickly exiting the cab, I ran back and released the GARMR, commanding it to the skybridge to await further instructions. Hearing the click of its synthetic feet, I barely had enough time to climb the steps back to the cabin before the undead were on me again, smelling warm flesh, growling for sustenance that wasn't.

I watched Checkers through my NOD, its LIDAR mapping terrain in real time in 270-degree swaths around the machine. The thing literally had eyes in the back of its head. After reaching its objective, it stood there below the skybridge among a crowd of undead, waiting.

I began to count the creatures under the bridge, wondering if I could take them out with the small number of rounds remaining in my carbine's magazine. I stopped counting the creatures at forty-eight, deciding my blaster would run out before they did. There would be no easy day.

I wound the yellow towing strap around my torso like a bandolier and edged Goliath closer to the skybridge, inside the detection zone of the undead that waited for meat to drop from the sky.

At about ten feet from the bridge, I keyed the mic and told Mitch to get ready to catch the steel hook from the tow strap that would be coming his way soon. I parked Goliath, leaving the engine running, and climbed through the open window, not bothering to open the door; the undead were much too close for that. Placing my carbine on the roof first, I climbed out onto the top of Goliath and surveyed my situation.

The rumble and heat from Goliath's diesel were attracting more of them from side streets and alleys. Glass shattered on either side of the skybridge and the undead spilled from high floors down onto the ground with sickening thumps. One of the corpses landed smack dab on top of the skybridge, shattering through its thick glass down into the walkway with the three survivors.

"Fuck, it's inside!" I could hear Mitch yell from above.

I couldn't respond, as the CB was bolted under the dash. If I yelled out, it would only bring everything down on top of me. I took of my rifle and slung it around the GPS antenna on the roof and unwound the tow strap from my upper body. I began to swing it in an upward arc like an old-school sling. I let the heavy steel hook go at what I thought was the perfect time to get it up to the bridge.

I missed.

My end was secured to my rigger's belt, and the other end sailed through the air under the bridge, landing smack dab in the middle of a crowd of undead. One of them curiously grasped the bright yellow strap and began to walk and tug, sending me off the roof onto the hood and then rolling off that onto the hard, piss-covered concrete. I landed square on my back, seeing stars, the sterile smell of urine coursing through my nostrils.

Stunned, all I could think to say was "Checkers, help" before the wind left my lungs.

I was gasping for air as the creatures approached. With them nearly on me, I tried to stand, still unable to recover from having the wind knocked from me moments earlier. Just before the lead creature got close enough to grab me, I heard a sound come from the GARMR's speaker. Not a horn but something else. It got my attention, but it didn't seem to be loud enough to travel much farther than the immediate area. It didn't stop the creatures from advancing but certainly slowed them down enough for the machine to get under them like a sheepdog, herding them away from me.

Checkers began its defensive algorithm, tripping the advancing undead, giving me just enough time to get to my feet and scurry back onto the hood and up to the roof.

I yanked the tow strap from the clutches of the undead and coiled it to the roof. Disconnecting my end from my rigger's belt, I attached it to the heat shield of the exhaust stack. I didn't want a repeat if I missed again.

Swinging the long tow strap once more, I let it loose, watching it sail up to the skybridge twenty-something feet above me. I was careful to account for the height of the rig and myself. The strap flew up into an opening in the glass that Mitch and family likely used to relieve themselves. One person, probably Mitch, was on the far end of the bridge, struggling with the creature that had fallen through the skybridge ceiling glass.

After verifying that one of Mitch's kids had the hook and was tying it off, I unsheathed my bayonet and stabbed the creatures that were climbing into the rig window. I flung a corpse out into the crowd, knocking over the ones standing in the immediate area. I took this chance to throw my carbine inside the truck and Duke Boys my way back through the passenger window.

"Make sure you secure your end good," I warned.

"It's good; tell us when!" Mitch said.

I put Goliath in gear and edged forward directly underneath the skybridge shit opening.

Before I could hit the brakes, I heard the first thump on the roof, then another. The undead were surrounding the truck in huge numbers with a smaller faction chasing the GARMR around the street.

Three knocks came from the roof, followed by Mitch's voice: "We're on, let's get out of here!"

I slowly pressed the accelerator, simultaneously instructing Checkers to follow the rig. Bones crunched and stomachs burst under Goliath's heavy tires as the rig rolled ahead. I hit the accelerator a little harder, tossing bodies aside like bow waves, and broke through. At thirty, I was worried I'd lose the GARMR. It remained in my rearview mirror, its LIDAR sensor coming in via my NOD. I hit the gas, bringing the rig up to forty, and the machine didn't miss a beat. At fifty, Mitch started pounding on the roof in protest and Checkers began to lag behind.

Impressive.

I slowed back down to twenty and pulled over into an electronics store parking lot, parking the rig.

"What the hell are you doing, mister? They'll be here any minute!" said Mitch.

"Relax, buddy. I'm getting my dog," I said, half smiling in the darkness.

Checkers clicked to me and stopped near the steps next to the fifth wheel, cocking its head and awaiting further instructions. I led it up the steps and secured it to its standby spot just behind the sleeper.

The NOD enhanced the infrared reflections off three sets of retinas looking at me from atop the rig, a visual trait the undead did not share with the living.

"Get in," I said sternly.

Mitch screamed at his kids to hurry up and climb down into the truck. After the kids were inside, Mitch handed two large duffel bags down from the roof to his boy. The undead were nearly to Goliath's rear tires when the doors slammed and I put the rig in gear once more.

We edged forward on a road leading back the way I'd come, in and away from the city of Forsyth. We drove for twenty minutes without anyone saying a word until the little girl broke the silence.

"Daddy, I gotta go potty."

We were driving in the dark. My passengers had no idea of the situation outside, as the moon was low on the horizon behind the trees and hills, bathing the area in darkness. Through the NOD, I didn't see any hordes or unruly masses of undead along the road ahead.

"Mister, is it safe to pull over?" said Mitch.

"Are you armed?" I asked Mitch.

"Yeah; .22 revolver with a handful of rounds is all I got," Mitch responded.

I pulled the truck over into the shoulder in front of a large billboard for a winery a couple exits up the highway. I checked both directions with night vision before letting Mitch know it was okay to open the door. The billboard had tiny fish scales, like metallic pieces on it, that shimmered in the ambient moonlight. A huge open and tipped wine bottle spilled its shimmering contents out onto the artistic canvas of the billboard for all passersby to see.

The road was still clear when the little girl climbed up into the cab in front of Mitch. The rumbling behemoth lurched forward in the direction of the vineyard. I took the exit, leaving the highway, and veered off where the vineyard sign told me to go. Why the vineyard? Why not? It was a better choice than a hospital or supermarket, I knew that much.

After two miles, I took another turn to the right, heading deeper into more rural surroundings until I came to a large wooden sign with the same metallic scales representing flowing wine. There was a swinging cattle gate closing the road off to traffic, but the bolt cutters I had in the truck took care of the flimsy lock. I pulled Goliath through the gate, closed it behind us, and reattached the chain with multiple heavy-duty zip ties. The arrow pointed out the direction I needed, so I kept on down the road until coming to a small parking lot next to a medium-sized building surrounded by rolling hills of overgrown grape vines and tall weeds.

There were half a dozen vehicles in the parking lot. Their derelict, dust-covered appearance told me that they'd been sitting there since the shit hit the fan.

Meanwhile, the rig stank from the refugees I'd taken on board. Weeks of piss, shit, sweat, and tears permeated the truck. Just as I verified the parking lot was clear, I shut down Goliath and told everyone to get the hell out before I vomited.

We headed for the vineyard building. Mitch pulled his six-gun and held it up at the ready as we got closer to the door.

"I wouldn't do that," I told him. "You don't know what's hiding in those fields, do you?"

"Yeah, I suppose you're right," Mitch said as he uncocked the hammer on his gun and put the pistol back inside his waistband.

I knew immediately that the building wasn't safe. Through the glass, I could see a few silhouettes of creatures moving around inside. I told Mitch to send his kids back to the rig and not to touch anything. We waited while I watched the kids scurry back to Goliath and climb up inside. I listened for the door to shut before I began whispering.

"Keep that wheel gun handy, but don't shoot unless you have to," I instructed Mitch.

"Okay, you're the boss," he responded.

We were headed into close quarters, so I checked the tightness of the can on the end of my gun and pulled my bayonet from its sheath. With a swift kick, the door flew inward, sending one of the corpses over a table and hard onto the concrete floor. Another took its spot in the doorway and marched out, and was met with an instant stab to the eye socket. I left the corpse on the ground inside the doorway to act as a doorstop in order to allow the others passage out. Best to neutralize them quietly, one at a time.

The third creature stepped out and tripped over the other dispatched corpses before falling forward at my feet. Looking straight down, my NOD wasn't focused enough to take a step, so I kicked it in the head like a football. Its neck broke with a sickening snap, but I could still hear its teeth scraping the concrete as its jaw opened and closed in protest. As I took care of that one, I heard a muffled gunshot from Mitch and turned to see one of the creatures falling with the barrel of Mitch's revolver still in its mouth. Good thing, as that wheel gun would be damn loud if not for Mitch using that creature's brain as a silencer. The spill noise from the gun's cylinder still snapped a bit, but nothing bad enough to call the hordes in on us.

With the last of the creatures neutralized or disabled, we dragged the bodies off to an empty parking spot and went inside to clear the vineyard building. The inside of the sprawling vineyard was full of hand-done water fountains and coliseum-style rock benches. A half-dead tree reached for the ceiling at the bottom of the stadium-style seats, just behind the massive bar lined with wine racks holding countless bottles of warm booze. I walked down the steps, kicking aside sleeping bags, blankets, purses, and other things you might find in a place where people holed up. Whoever was still surviving in there was isolated from the undead, as the gate at the road was closed and a barbed-wire fence surrounded the property along with heavy foliage. This place didn't have the luxury of power, water, and air-conditioning like my previous digs, but it was remote enough.

After checking every nook and cranny of the building, I looked over to Mitch and said, "It's safe for now. Bring 'em in."

"Listen, I can't thank you en—" he began to say.

"Don't. Just go get your kids."

I didn't have time to really let him in. I didn't want to. I know full well that children are my weak point and that I'd do anything to save them, but I couldn't let Mitch use his kids to compromise me any more than I already was. Mitch went outside while I stood at the top of the mini-coliseum, staring down at the bar and half-dead tree.

I heard Goliath's door slam and then multiple footfalls before the doorway darkened and the children cautiously entered. I clicked on my torch, revealing their dirty faces. The boy looked up and offered his thanks and I accepted without interruption.

Kids.

The little girl didn't go far from Mitch. She was a few years younger than the boy, who was about Danny's age. For a flash of a second I thought back to the day I'd met Danny and his grandmother, Dean. Hell, was it over a year ago already? I landed that aircraft at that abandoned field looking for the Davis family, but what I ended up finding was Danny and Dean. My first sight of Danny was of him pissing off the water tower onto the heads of the undead far below. I still laugh when I think about it.

I panned the torch around the interior, stopping on the upstairs balcony. I climbed the steep curved staircase to the loft area, finding another wine bar with plush sofas against the walls. Mitch followed with his chicks in tow.

"This'll be the safest place to sleep tonight," I said.

Mitch agreed and I helped him slide one of the heavy sofas over to the top of the staircase to barricade anything that might get inside. The kids began to explore this new high ground with more confidence, choosing the sofas they wanted to sleep on and leaning over the bar to see what was behind. This made me nervous for a moment, but when I didn't hear any screams I knew that nothing lay dormant, waiting for them there.

Mitch asked me if I had any water, so we both climbed over the sofa and back down the stairs, leaving the children in the loft with instructions to call out if they heard anything that wasn't us. Back at the truck, Mitch took his two large duffel bags and pulled out two empty Nalgene bottles. I filled them both. Mitch thanked me before turning back to the vineyard.

Before he got too far away, I said, "Why were you there? Why in that city in a hospital?"

"I'm a doctor. I needed supplies. You leaving tonight?" Mitch asked with a hint of optimism in his voice.

"Not anymore."

Day 22

1000

I awoke from inside Goliath's sleeper cabin at 0600 and looked outside. The window was fogged over from sleep breathing, so I used the curtain to clear a spot. Smoke climbed up from behind the building. I woke up throughout the night, noticing that the area remained clear with no signs of movement besides a lone rabbit I saw cross the parking lot. I must have shut down the rig early enough to prevent the undead in the area from triangulating our position. After lacing up my boots, I grabbed my near-empty carbine and exited the truck to a nice morning breeze. After releasing the GARMR and putting it in sentry mode, I smelled meat cooking, so I followed my nose around to the back of the building, where Mitch sat next to a fire pit.

"Summer sausage sitting on the shelves in there. Plenty to eat. Plenty to drink, as long as its wine," Mitch said with a smile.

The morning sun was coming over the tree line, illuminating the overgrown fields. I reached down to stoke the fire when Mitch noticed my bandaged hands.

"What happened there?" he asked.

"I got some cable burn coming down the side of the Florida capitol building," I said nonchalantly.

"Jesus, what . . . why?" Mitch said, flabbergasted.

"I needed some high ground. Do you think you can do anything with them?"

Mitch removed the bandages and examined my hands, noting the obvious fact that I'd lost some skin in the transaction with the metal wire. He went into one of his heavy duffel bags and pulled out some first aid implements, cleaning the wounds on my hands and applying salve to them before wrapping them with clean dressings. My hands shook from needing more codeine and I think Mitch took notice. He was kind enough not to say anything.

With my hands out of the way, he examined my ankle, performing a mobility test. Turns out it was only sprained. I was shaking worse with pain and reached inside my empty cargo pocket for meds.

"If all this wasn't going down, I'd say keep weight off it for three weeks, but you can't exactly do that, can you?" Mitch asked rhetorically. I couldn't take it any longer, so I stood up to hobble back to Goliath to retrieve a ration of drugs in order to quell the shakes and pains of post-apocalyptic survival.

"Does your dog need any first aid? I've seen them rip animals apart," Mitch asked politely.

I told Mitch that I didn't think my dog was hurt and thanked him for his concern. Mitch asked its name and if it would bite and if his kids could see it. I thought it might be time for an introduction.

"Checkers, come," I commanded into the control watch.

The titanium beast rounded the corner of the building and into Mitch's view. Mitch pulled his six-gun from somewhere and was about to ventilate the GARMR when I asked him to put his weapon away.

"That's my dog, Mitch," I told him.

"That's not a dog," Mitch said.

"It's the closest thing I've got out here."

After explaining to Mitch the circumstances around the machine's discovery, we both agreed that it was some black ops project remnant from before the world went to shit, a piece of tech designed for contingency plans in the event of a worst-case scenario. The machine settled near the far side of the fire pit as the food cooked, the smell eventually bringing the children to us.

The girl's name was Bailey and Mitch called his boy Stunt. Stunt was just old enough to hold his own, I could tell, but not little Bailey.

Mitch's story of survival was remarkable. He had escaped from Atlanta in the very beginning and was the last surviving medical doctor in the city. He'd taken refuge at the hospital in Forsyth, yielding floor after floor to the undead until he was exiled on the hospital skybridge with only his kids and the dead relentlessly beating the doors on both sides.

I asked him about Atlanta. I'd flown over it back when there was still a military and I was in it. He described it as a war zone in those early days. He was lucky to save his children. He made the decision to get them out of Atlanta instead of trying to find his wife, who'd gone missing without a trace when things really started going sideways. Mitch and his children made it out of there just before the military sealed off all the roads to all civilian vehicular and foot traffic. During the night after his escape, he'd heard automatic fire coming from the checkpoints charged with keeping people from leaving the city.

The children ate their breakfast, oblivious to the GARMR folded up ten feet away from them. Mitch and I continued our conversation. I was curious as to what his plan might be. The Keys could always use a doctor and I knew Jan would appreciate the help. After some back-and-forth, Mitch admitted that he didn't have anyplace to go. Forsyth was his last stand. After some deliberation, he admitted that island life sounded a lot better than mainland Georgia, but laughed at the prospect of making it there alive.

"I came from there. Getting back isn't impossible," I said.

"Yeah," Mitch said, laughing, "but you aren't dragging two kids around this war zone with you. Bailey was in freakin' kindergarten when those things came. We're barely makin' it as is."

I told Mitch I'd be right back and started walking to the truck for some meds and the road atlas. I wasn't three steps away when the kids started to scream.

"Shhh! It's only his dog!" Mitch said, running for Bailey to get her to quiet down.

Stunt had a walking stick raised up over his head as if about to club the GARMR.

I kept walking and Checkers followed me back to the truck. I thought it best to leave it in sentry mode overlooking the road. After popping another half dose of codeine, I promised myself I'd lower the dose to a quarter pill the next time I needed it.

It was always next time.

I grabbed the atlas and the mansion gate opener from Goliath's sun visor.

Back at the fire pit, I sat down on the stone bench near Mitch and found our current location on the maps.

"Listen, you don't need to trek all the way to the Keys with your kids. I know a place not far from here you could hole up and be a helluva lot better off than you are now," I said.

Stunt was studying the maps over his dad's shoulder. I could see him calculating the distance in his head, trying to figure out how long they'd need to be on the road to get there.

"It's got high iron gates, food, hot water, and electricity. Everything you need." I didn't think it would do any good to mention the bunker.

• • •

1500

Mitch quickly agreed to this morning's proposal. He and his kids would travel south to the stronghold I marked on my maps and wait there for evacuation. After rummaging through the pockets of the corpses we'd slain last night, we only found two sets of keys. One set belonged to a vehicle that wasn't in the parking lot and the other was a switchblade laser-cut key belonging to a black Volkswagen Jetta. We spent most of the afternoon getting the thing road worthy. After putting a spare on and scavenging another from a different vehicle, I plugged the DC air pump into Goliath's outlet and aired up the small car's tires to the spec listed inside the door. With the tires fixed, I put the car in neutral and Mitch helped me roll it closer to Goliath so the jumper cables would reach a little better.

I poured some of my stockpiled fuel into the car's tank and gave it a quick jump-start with Goliath's charged battery. After letting it run for about thirty minutes, we shut it down, leaving the jumper cables attached between the vehicles if a quick getaway was needed. Stunt and Bailey played in the parking lot, sprinting back and forth from one side of the pavement to the other. They weren't laughing and carrying on like children used to do. They knew the evil that would show up if they did. After putting Mitch's provisions in the trunk, Mitch tended to my wounds once more. Again he noticed my shaking hands and told the kids to go downstairs, but not outside.

"Listen, I know what's going on with you. I've seen it enough that you can't deny it," Mitch said.

It was difficult to hear myself admit it, but he had me dead to rights.

"Yeah, I suppose you're right."

Mitch proceeded to hand-write me a weaning-off schedule and instructed that I stick to it strictly, doctor's orders. He confiscated most of the codeine, leaving me with only enough to complete his written schedule, reassuring me that it was for my own good.

"If you can make it hundreds of miles through territory like this, you can break the spell of those damn drugs," he said confidently.

I honestly hoped that I'd see him again.

We'd go our separate ways before first light.

2340

The kids were sleeping up in the loft, and Mitch and I had brewed up some hobo tea in an empty tin can over the low fire we'd kept stoked. We couldn't risk too high of a fire, as the building was up on a hill; the fire could be seen for miles if we let it get out of control. The undead could detect heat and smell living flesh.

The folding chairs we sat in had seen better days, and the same could be said about most anything. They'd been left out in the elements since the beginning, their paint oxidizing and rubbing away onto our clothing.

After a brief pause in the conversation, Mitch stared at the fire stoically and began to speak of his wife. At first I wanted to tell him to stop; I wanted to tell him that I'd heard it all and seen it all before. I let him keep talking; his words played out like a pastor's funeral speech.

There was no dramatic story of having to shoot her in the head as she lunged for his kids, no tale of Mitch putting her down after she died on the living room couch. She just simply never came home from work. She was a cop and Mitch knew what that meant. Like so many others, she stood her watch until properly relieved, most likely by Death himself.

While Mitch spoke, he rubbed a golden lapel pin attached to his sleeve, a small police badge. Just as the first tears began to build up in his eyes, my pack began to chirp and vibrate loudly. Something on the inside was flashing. I instantaneously reached for my carbine while parting the flap on the top of my pack.

The tablet.

I pulled it up to my face and unlocked it. Instantaneously, I could see the GARMR's sentry feed displayed on the screen. The machine's sensors were tracking bipedal movement coming up the vineyard road.

"Get to the kids and have your gun ready," I whispered to Mitch, who tore off in a flash to the building.

The colors looked strange compared to the GARMR's normal feed, and it wasn't until I noticed the setting in the upper right that I understood.

THERMAL.

I was looking at heat signatures, not IR night vision mode. The movement was human.

I obsessive-compulsively checked for brass in my carbine's chamber and slipped the NOD over my right eye. I stuffed the tablet inside my waistband in the small of my back and left my pack by the pit. I needed to be fast. Although my ankle wasn't fully ready, I ninja sprinted around the far side of the building, checking the tightness of my silencer as I ran. The NOD bounced on its strap, shaking my assisted view of the dark night. Rounding the corner, I got low and pulled the tablet for another look. I could see three contacts with rifles moving toward Goliath and the building proper. I headed to the right in a wide arc to get a better view and began to low crawl about five feet from the pavement.

From what I could hear, they did not have good intentions.

"That the fuckin' truck?" I heard one say.

"Yeah, same one from Tallahassee. It's him," the other spouted off.

At first I thought they were actually dumb enough to be using a bright flashlight, but then I realized that one of them was wearing a cheap NOD. Its bright illuminator beamed like a spotlight from his head. I could see it only through my NOD, not my unassisted eye. I quickly became one with the tall grass when the IR beam swept my position and kept looking around. I hadn't been seen.

"Should we ventilate the truck?"

"Naw, we ice him and take the keys. Might need it."

Still prone, I tucked the carbine into my chest and looked down the Aimpoint. Its bright dot washed out my device, so I selected the lowest red-dot setting. The tamed glow of the dot was just enough to see via the NOD.

One of them stepped up onto Goliath to check the door and jumped down, disgusted when he found it locked. The one with the shitty NOD climbed up to look inside but soon discovered what happens when you try to use illuminators through glass. No worky very well.

The one with the NOD panned his illuminator over to the tall grass opposite my position, where the GARMR was parked in sentry mode.

"What the fuck is that?" the one with the NOD said.

"We can't see like you, idiot," said the third voice.

The NOD-equipped bad guy became curious and began to approach Checkers.

Why couldn't the machine have guns? I thought to myself as the man approached.

As he raised his gun level with the GARMR, I put the bright illuminator shining from his head inside my reticle and my finger on the trigger.

I squeezed a couple pounds of pressure into the trigger in anticipation.

"It's some sort of fucking camera!" the man said as he went to kick the machine over.

Just as the man made contact with the machine, it took itself out of sentry mode and stood up, trotting away from the attackers. The only one that could see in the dark opened fire, a round that glanced off the GARMR's frame, with bright sparks sending it stumbling off into the grass. Asshole. I lit the guy up for shooting my dog, putting a round right through the top of his head. He hit the ground mouth-first with a crunch and the other two panicked and began shooting wildly in my direction.

Unexpectedly, they returned fire with silenced guns.

I placed the dot on their heads and put their lights out, bringing my round count down to twenty-four in the magazine and one in the hole. With the threat neutralized, I let them bleed out for about ten minutes before making an approach. I made sure their brains were destroyed and went back for my pack. I could hear Checkers approach through the trees, but commanded it to wait as soon as I could see it emerge from cover. I pulled the Geiger from the bottom of my pack and slowly approached. If any rounds had pierced the machine's nuclear RTG battery, it could now be spewing lethal radiation wherever it stepped. But the Geiger stayed silent, minus the ambient background radiation coming from the cosmos, so I breathed a sigh of relief before commanding the machine to approach.

I clicked on my LED torch to give Checkers a quick physical exam. It didn't take long to notice the bright strip of bare titanium where the bullet had skidded across the frame, stripping off a micrometer or two of the gray metal. Running my finger over the machine's new shiny battle scar, I patted it on the head and scolded it for getting shot. Any onlooker would have thought I was insane and they'd be absolutely right.

I returned to Goliath with Checkers following behind and decided not to loot the bodies just yet. Pools of blood circled their heads like demonic halos, the reflected starlight glowing unholy green through my NOD. The shock of killing the men caused me to overlook a serious threat.

They came all the way from Tallahassee and didn't just walk here.

They had somehow tracked me, intercepted my CB comms with Mitch, perhaps.

I followed the winding road down the hill for a very painful two miles and positioned myself within fifty meters of the closed gate. I adjusted my NOD and swept my gun back and forth along the adjacent road.

The glint of a reflector caught my eye, so I approached the gate to get a better look.

A large tow truck was parked near the bend in the road, pointed from the direction I'd driven when coming to the vineyard. I supported my gun on the metal gate and watched the cab glow brightly in random intervals.

They were smoking cigarettes.

I quietly slinked over the metal fence, careful not to bang my gun against it and alert the probable bad guys in the tow truck. Nearly forgetting the GARMR, I pointed back up the vineyard road and gave it the command to scout. I crossed the road into the tall grass and moved up, parallel to the cracked and weathered concrete, in the direction of the truck. Starlight reflected from the large metal cross of the tow mechanism. A crude painting of Christ adorned the metal cross in direct contrast to what I'd encountered at Goliath. These were likely murderers who would kill me if they got the drop on me before I wasted them first. Still needing a fix and shaking from killing three human beings half an hour before, I could smell the cigarette smoke wafting from the cab of the tow truck as it glowed intermittently through my NOD like a large alien lightning bug.

I was only ten meters away when the door opened and a large man stepped out of the truck with a squeak of the struts. He walked to the back and unzipped his pants before watering the opposite ditch.

Zipping back up, he said over his shoulder, "Let's tear that gate off its hinges and see what the fuck is taking so long."

"You're the boss," the second voice said.

"Get the fuckin' RPK ready," the big guy ordered.

My stomach sank at the thought of killing more men, but nothing back at the vineyard could survive an RPK mag dump assault. My fears were magnified tenfold when I saw the outline of the machine gun emerge from the truck. The passenger loaded a large drum mag into the receiver and charged the weapon. The fixed bipod dangled from the gun like mantis legs. The second man placed the machine gun in the back of the tow truck between the cab and the metal cross.

My window to engage was closing rapidly when I heard the crack of a twig coming from the trees on the other side of the road.

"What the fuck was that?" the big guy said. "Spotlight it."

I raised my NOD just as the blinding 12-volt light beamed from the passenger window of the truck. I stood to look over the hood to see if I could find out what they were looking at.

A creature in a badly stained lab coat stood there, bathed in the bright spotlight, as if analyzing the men inside the tow truck. My cargo pocket began to click and vibrate, confusing the shit out of me before I remembered.

The Geiger I'd used an hour ago to scan the GARMR was going nuts.

In the span of half a second, the corpse cocked its head sideways and then charged the passenger window before cramming its upper torso inside. As the creature thrashed, one of my would-be attackers screamed in agony. I pulled up my gun and sank a round into the big guy's head as he simultaneously stood on the gas pedal. The trucked revved and jerked forward, dragging the lab coat–adorned corpse with it as the other guy continued to scream and fight for his life. The large spotlight beamed all throughout the cab and he tried to open the door, likely to get to the RPK sitting outside the truck.

It might as well be a million miles away.

The creature was vicious, tearing into the man like a starving animal. Unable to take the screaming any longer, I raised my weapon and popped a shot into the side of the thing. I listened to the round drill into its rib cage a few milliseconds after I pulled the trigger.

FWAP!

With my NOD back down I watched it pull itself out of the truck, its jowls covered with warm blood. It had a look of confusion as it scanned the darkness for who attacked it. The altered gray orbs sunken into its skull didn't reflect IR back at me like healthy retinas, but I could still see something different in there, something a few notches higher in intelligence.

The Geiger clicked with more intensity as the creature edged in my direction.

After looking around for a few more moments, it locked onto me without warning and craned its head forward before breaking out in a run. I raised my gun and placed a round into its nose, dropping the thing to the ground. Its legs kicked and spasmed for about ten seconds before the movement finally stopped.

I gave the creature a wide berth to avoid the radiation that was no doubt shooting outward in a half sphere. The corpse had endured a nuclear event, either weapon or power plant meltdown. I didn't bother to flip it over to read the words embroidered on its once-clean lab coat.

My heart began to race and then fill with dread as I approached the passenger side of the tow truck.

"Don't let it . . . don't let it eat me, okay?" the dying man begged, hyperventilating.

He was bleeding out fast; it wouldn't be long now. Warm black blood oozed from a wound on his forearm and his right cheek was gone, revealing white teeth underneath. His speech was slurred as his blood-starved brain began to shut down.

"What were you and your friend gonna do with that machine gun? Lie to me and I'll drag you out of there and fire off a few shots," I hissed, trying to stave back the lump in my throat.

I felt sorry for him.

"We were going to kill everyone, take everything. It's what we are," he responded between shallow breaths.

Another snapping of a twig caused me to turn and drop the NOD over my eye in one muscle memory movement. Here was one more creature lurking in the darkness, wearing the same type of lab coat. Light from the 12-volt spot beam shot up through the window like a Hollywood premiere beam, attracting the creature to the truck.

"Please, no!" the man screamed from the cab.

I instinctively broke contact and took a defensive position on the opposite side. The creature snapped its head to face in the direction of the man's pleas and began to charge. As the monster stepped onto the road, it tripped and slammed headfirst into the passenger door, rocking the heavy truck from side to side. I moved back around to the passenger side, unsheathing the long-knife bayonet and stabbing it deeply into the back of its skull as it attempted to stand up. The Geiger's piercing noise drove me away from the corpse. As I stepped back, I caught a glimpse of the slain creature's lab coat.

An atom was embroidered into the fabric right under the letters *Vogtle Electric*.

These were nuclear power plant workers and were obviously traveling together.

Wherever that Vogtle Electric was, I didn't want to be anywhere near it.

The passenger was gone, so I deliberated on whether or not to let him turn.

After pulling both bodies out of the truck from the driver's side and searching them, I put the vehicle into reverse and crunched over one of the creatures I'd just slain. I opened the gate and pulled the truck through it and back up the winding hill to the vineyard. I could smell the blood in the cab and heard more twigs snapping in the woods off to the left. My ankle ached from the recent strain and I needed something to calm my nerves.

The bright headlights cut through the darkness but thankfully didn't reveal any more lab coats lurking. I hadn't considered power plant fallout as a source for enhanced creatures before.

I was startled when I saw movement in my rearview mirror, but began to calm down when I saw the GARMR trotting behind the truck, trying to keep the vehicle's pace.

Just before getting to the vineyard, I turned off the lights and drove on NOD so that Mitch wouldn't shoot me. At the parking lot, I stopped the engine, revealing the sounds of gravel popping under my tires before coasting to a stop near Goliath. I got out but didn't shut the door. I could see the glint of Mitch's revolver pointed out the window and yelled up to him.

"Mitch, it's me. They're gone!" I said.

"I heard an engine rev . . . maybe a gunshot, too. Was that you?" Mitch asked.

"Yeah, that'll bring more of them. Get ready to skin out," I told him.

We loaded his supplies into the tow truck. It would be a smarter choice if Mitch had to push a wreck out of the road on his way to the prepper stronghold, but I made it from there with Goliath, so it shouldn't be a huge deal for him. I gave Mitch the bandits' guns but kept the RPK and five full magazines. He wouldn't know how to use it anyway. It wasn't that much different from the machine gun I had mounted on *Solitude*, which I hoped was still anchored just off the shore back in what was left of Pensacola.

After debriefing Mitch on what happened, I went over the route back to the house with him again and told him to monitor the CB constantly. If he found trouble, shoot first. Don't hesitate, just do it. The types of people we were dealing with were savages, and they wouldn't hesitate with him or his children. Once he got back to the stronghold, I advised him to shelter in place and not draw the attention of anyone outside the iron fence, living or otherwise. Finally mentioning the bunker, I told him not to worry too much about it, as whatever was inside was behind a few inches of hardened steel. Mitch's eyebrow rose for a moment while that sank in.

I checked the VW one last time and saw the gate control clipped to the sun visor.

Tossing it to Mitch, I said, "Might want this. It'll make it easier getting in and out."

After thanking me for remembering the opener, Mitch commented that he would be driving a tow truck and added, "Why not tow a good car behind me if the truck breaks down?"

He had an excellent idea, so we manipulated the hydraulic controls and loaded up the VW on the back of the tow truck. I shook Mitch's hand and patted his children on the back. Mitch handed me a custom IFAK (individual first aid kit), telling me that it was tailor-made for the apocalypse. We both laughed, and he reminded me to stick to my schedule with the codeine.

"The pain is in your head. Your ankle is healing fine . . . just no five-hundred-yard sprints," he said.

"Roger that, Doctor," I said.

Loaded up, they started the tow truck and pulled the VW out of the vineyard parking lot, loaded up with summer sausage and bottles of wine. I waved at Mitch and honestly hoped I'd see him and his children again one day.

I loaded Goliath with spare provisions and tied the GARMR down before I fired up the diesel and rolled down the vineyard road myself. As I left the gate, I could see a creature milling about the irradiated lab coat corpses. It was the tow truck passenger. I veered Goliath's wheel a few degrees to the right, slamming into the fucker and sending it thirty feet into the heavy foliage.

The radio crackled with Mitch's voice, "We're on the main road, hopefully headed to paradise. Probably out of range in an hour or so."

I answered, again wishing him luck. Mitch knew to check his CB at the same time every day for contact. A team was being formed back at the Keys when I left. Its mission was to extract survivors from the mainland. A no-shit doctor would be high on their priorities list. Saien was to be the captain of one of the extraction teams. They offered me the job, but a baby will change your perspective on everything. Also, I don't work very well on a team.

Ask my old unit, or the ghost of what's left of them.

• • •

Day 23

1100

Mitch made last contact at around six this morning. He got to my first map landmark, an overturned feed truck. His signal was so weak that I could barely hear anything but managed to make out *feed truck*. He was making good time.

At about 0900, I saw a bridge in the distance. Bridges are bad, especially ones that are high over the water and long enough that you can't back off them fast. I coasted to a stop and glassed the span with my binos. There were vehicles on the bridge, but I couldn't see any undead or signs of a roadblock. Confident I wasn't about to get the old okeydoke, I rolled onto the long bridge, stopping on its apex. The two-lane span was a quarter mile long. The sun was bright, so I decided to get out and have lunch on top of the cab. My fingers were soon greasy from summer sausage and my lips purple from warm red wine. I watched the river water rush under the span. The banks were littered with skeletons, both human and animal. I found it difficult to imagine what this might look like to someone from two years ago.

Panning the binos along the shore, I saw a lone figure standing on the bank a few hundred yards away. Adjusting the focus, I could see that the figure was missing an arm. The corpse stood there, waiting for something like me to come along.

Unable to resist the urge, I called out, my voice traveling over the water at the speed of a fighter jet. I looked through my binos, waiting for the sound to reach the creature. After a few dramatic seconds, it began to stir and turned its once dormant head toward the bridge. Unable to triangulate the sound, it began to walk to the bridge, searching for the source of food it had heard. I threw my empty wine bottle like a German World War II grenade, watching it arc up and then down to the large river boulders. It hit with a loud shattering sound, making the creature veer its course to where the bottle impacted. Two more emerged from the trees lining the riverbank in search of the source of the noise. I decided to pack it in before they started making their own noise, eventually causing a chain reaction of undead to appear on the banks below.

The Gates of Atlanta

<u>2200</u>

Troll

I had to make it through five different pileups and a pretty fucked-up situation to get where I am now. I spent most of the afternoon pulling cars apart so that I could squeeze Goliath through the openings. As I cleared the fifth wreck, I noted a sign peppered with shotgun blasts telling me that Atlanta was twenty-two miles ahead. Several miles behind, however, a large pillar of dust rose up above the trees. I'd seen this before and didn't like what happened after.

Swarm.

I let off the gas and let Goliath rumble down a large hill into a valley cut by a strong-flowing river. I guess I wasn't paying close enough attention: When Goliath ramped up onto the middle of the bridge, my head nearly hit the top of the cab. I slammed on the brakes, and the rig's large tires skidded to a stop ten feet before a three-foot gap in the road.

A goddamned drawbridge.

There were three cars sitting on the side of the road at the start of the bridge, so I used them to form a vehicle wall behind me so I could work the problem.

I grabbed my kit and headed to the bridge operator's box on the opposite side. Of course, it couldn't be easy. I made the jump across the steel span. The drawbridge portion was constructed of steel grates. The side I was on wasn't raised up very much, maybe a foot. It was the other side, Goliath's side, that was the problem. I began to analyze the situation, watching the dust cloud approach from the direction I'd just driven.

I hoped Mitch and his kids were doing okay, or at least better than I was right now.

I reached into my pocket and glanced at the wean-off plan Mitch had written down for me. It would be hours before I could have another quarter pill of codeine. The sadistic bastard had me on a tight schedule. With the shakes in full force, I threw open the door to the bridge operator's console room and began manipulating levers, hoping that the machine would work like the window washer lift did on the building in Tallahassee.

With the mechanical locks disengaged, Goliath's side of the bridge maybe dropped an inch before vibrating like a tuning fork and silently settling.

Reluctantly, I placed my feet on the rungs of the ladder leading from the operator's console down below the bridge. The catwalk was small, affording no room for mistakes. The waters were high and could sweep me a mile downstream before I found the shore, if I didn't get a chunk of my leg removed by the lurking dead that no doubt waited for me in the murky waters. I used my carbine as a balance pole before making it to the door leading inside the drawbridge motor room.

Cursing myself that I'd forgotten my drill, I reached down for the knob, expecting to find the steel door solidly locked. But the knob turned and then the door flew open toward me from the force of the undead that pushed behind it. Sunlight touched the face of these creatures for the first time in ages, and I nearly fell into the water along with the first one. The only thing that prevented my fall was a fire extinguisher box that jutted from the wall on my side of the door. I held it tightly with my right hand, bringing my carbine up to the ready.

Intimidated by the specter of low-ammo at the forefront of my mind, I kept myself from firing, kicking the second one off its feet and sending it tumbling into the brown waters. For a split second, I couldn't help but watch the two corpses bob and drift rapidly downstream fifty yards or so apart. They flailed and turned about unnaturally in the water. At a glance, they appeared human but drifted down the river like tsunami debris, uncoordinated and chaotic.

Then, as a third came out of the dark room, I forced open the rusted metal and glass box containing the extinguisher and pulled it from its clips. The inspection tag hung soggily from the flexible firing hose and the needle in the circle gauge pointed to green when I pulled the pin and squeezed the handle down all the way to my fingertips. I blasted the bloated, slimy creature in the face, filling its gaping mouth and eye sockets with Purple-K dust. Wildly confused by what had just happened, it stepped itself off the platform into the water as well, bobbing and flailing like the others, but surrounded by a powdery circle as it followed its friends downstream. The wind blew some of the acrid dust back into my face, causing my eyes to water. The taste in my mouth almost made me want to wash it out in the river water below. Almost.

I led with my gun blasting its 500-lumen light into the dark room, under a bridge for which I was now the resident troll. The walls of the motor room as well as the motors themselves were covered with slime. The dead had been cooking inside here for two summers, coating everything with shit. Ugh. It was a new kind of nasty. Should have brought my mask.

I worked quickly, searching for the motor that controlled Goliath's side of the bridge, eventually tracing the wires to what I thought was the correct motor. With the grid perma-down, I pulled the wires from the electrical box and scavenged the cord from a nearby work lamp that hung over the motors. With the motor wired up to a 110-volt plug, I made my way back up to the bridge. The creatures I'd put in the river had disappeared downstream, hopefully skewered forever on a fallen tree somewhere. As I climbed the ladder to bridge level, I noticed the swarm's dust cloud had gotten noticeably bigger.

I had to make a choice: cut my losses and bring the GARMR and the rest of my kit to the other side and abandon Goliath . . . or lower the bridge, keep Goliath, but potentially build a pathway for whatever evil approached.

The cumbersome generator was strapped tightly to my back as I made the three-foot skip across the bridge opening. I felt a pang in my ankle as I landed. The generator's fuel sloshed around inside its small one-gallon tank and I could smell the fumes of gasoline coming off the small 2-kilowatt Honda power plant. On Goliath's side of the bridge, I couldn't see individual corpses yet, but there was a plasma-like mirage line of mayhem at the base of the dust cloud.

I hurried down the ladder and shimmied across the catwalk to the motor room, leaving the generator outside to vent its deadly gases in the open air. I started the machine, leaving it in full-power mode, and pulled the power cord I'd rigged over to the generator. After a moment of hesitation and repositioning myself near the door, I plugged it into the generator.

Son of a bitch, it was working. The bridge motor began to run, turning the massive manhole-sized gears very slowly. The 110-volt generator was obviously having trouble supplying enough juice to the motor, but it was going anyway. I could see the large gear catch the next cog.

I inspected the gears and removed a bit of torn clothing from the teeth, not wanting to think where that came from. It took four minutes for one complete turn of the main gear. I had no idea what that might equate to the topside on the bridge. I left the generator to do its work, and climbed the ladder to check the progress. The bridge moved like the minute hand on a clock: only perceptible if you compared it to what was behind it. In my case, I watched Goliath's horizontal chrome grille sections appear one by one as the bridge slowly dropped.

I went again onto Goliath's side and my heart skipped a beat as individual corpses came into view a thousand yards distant. I ran for Goliath and tossed my kit in the passenger seat before starting the rig, positioning the front bumper over the slowly falling edge. I thought the rig's weight might ease the strain on the spinning motor below.

I left the rig running and grabbed the heavy RPK and two extra magazines. Knocking out the window glass, I set up a pillbox in the bridge operator's station with a clear field of fire to Goliath's side of the bridge.

The familiar chorus of moans rasping from undead tracheas reached my ears as the distinct but unsettling noise engulfed the bridge. This was the only artery across the river for these creatures, and they moved in unison as if they knew it. Just like water, they flowed down the path of least resistance, consuming everything with a heartbeat.

I checked my Rolex, something that used to be valuable but nowadays you could pick up anytime you wanted one. With the second hand at twelve o'clock, I began to watch the bridge. The hum of the generator competed with the penetrating barrage of undead noises.

One minute elapsed. Six inches lower on the bridge.

I'd need ten minutes to get the bridge low enough to drive Goliath across the gap.

Eight hundred yards . . . maybe. Maybe less.

The mega-horde kicked up dust and debris as it pressed forward, unstoppable. I could hear the screech of protesting metal as the river of corpses wrenched a vehicle aside somewhere under that dust cloud. That kind of force doesn't come from just hundreds.

My adrenaline began to flow as I put the RPK machine gun into battery and became acquainted with the sight picture. I didn't dare yet fire, as the sound would laser-focus the creatures to me. Right now they simply moved like a school of fish following each other down the road, reactive to one another's movements.

The road the undead traveled was covered on all sides by thick foliage. Those I could see were only the faster-moving tip of the iceberg. As I looked down the long sight picture of the machine gun, I noticed the raider's inscription in the wood stock: BITCH-KILLA.

In addition to the rifle's name, there were dozens of tick marks, no doubt representing the number of lives the poorly named weapon had taken.

I began to make out the different colors in the approaching horde, and estimated that the leading edge was at about five hundred yards and closing. The smell began to defy the winds, reaching my nostrils as more loud bellows from the mass shook the air all around me.

The bridge was nearly low enough to cross as the creatures began to reach the vehicle barricade I'd made just before. Leaving the RPK in the makeshift pillbox, I hopped over the guardrail and the narrowing gap before putting Goliath in gear and giving it the gas. The front wheels cleared the gap and I upshifted, putting the pedal to the floor. The rig's frame shuddered and creaked as it became nearly high centered on the bridge. As soon as I felt my back wheels clear, I skidded to a stop, grabbed the extra RPK mags, and sprinted to the pillbox and down into the motor room.

Working as fast as I possibly could with my multitool and electrical tape, I switched the polarity on the motor input and plugged the jerry-rigged connection back into the generator. The motor began to spin in the opposite direction, turning the massive gears slowly along with it. I hoped the generator had sufficient fuel to keep up the fight as I stepped back out onto the catwalk and up the ladder to the pillbox.

Tired of getting my ears blown out with automatic weapons, I remembered to pack some foamies in my cargo pocket. I rolled the plugs into my ears as I opened fire on the dozens of walking corpses that now managed to clear the barrier. I fired the RPK in controlled bursts, trying to do as much damage per magazine as possible. Shell casings flew around the bridge control box, bouncing off the ceiling and walls, some finding their way down my collar, of course.

The machine-gun noise caused a frenzy in the horde. I could see the mass of a hundred thousand bodies move like a stadium wave at my small barricade. I kept firing and firing as the first barricade vehicle succumbed to the immense pressure of the horde.

Crushed and pulverized bodies spilled onto the road, their still-animated replacements using them as floor mats as they advanced onto the rising metal drawbridge.

I changed mags again. I could smell burning oil and lacquer coming off the gun, and the barrel smoked underneath its hand guard. Even the left bipod arm I used as a grip was warm from the heat transfer coming off the barrel.

I just needed to keep them back for two more minutes; that was it.

Two more mags remaining.

I slapped in a new mag and laid waste to thirty more creatures with it, spraying the tops of their heads as judiciously as possible. The remaining barricade cars were being pushed inward. I'll never forget seeing all the scalps I'd shot off sitting on top of the barricade cars along with pieces of brain and skull fragments.

The swarm again surged forward, buckling the cars, using their own numbers as rams. The frontline undead were crushed to a pulp and again the ones behind them slogged forward. The creatures seemed to go on forever in the distance, and the dust in the air was starting to be a problem.

Last mag.

I squeezed the trigger, giving the advancing wave what for, arcing the weapon back and forth until the last round left a searing-hot, cherry-red barrel.

The creatures were looking at me. They approached hungrily, with their arms out front, stepping blindly until the first group came to the gap. One of them moved across the opening and actually touched my side before tumbling into the current. I pulled my Glock and pressed out to the line, waiting for one of them to make it over the void.

The next thing I knew, I was being shoved into the river side of the operator console. On my back looking up, I saw the wretched creature start to bend down to take a bite. I put two rounds of 9mm into its switch box, turning the lights out. With all the excitement on the drawbridge, I forgot one of the most important survival rules.

Look behind you.

On my side of the road, a dozen undead had wandered out of the woods, attracted by the noise of gunfire. Another creature was attempting to leg over to the walkway leading to me in the operator station. The thing was frail, nearly down to bone and tendon. I gave it a swift kick, sending it over the side into the drink to join the growing flotilla of corpses.

The drawbridge was getting high enough that the undead horde wouldn't be able to make it to the edge. With little time to spare, I cut the genny and hauled ass back up to Goliath, dodging corpses down the path to my air-conditioned biosphere. Safely inside the truck, I began running down the remaining creatures on my side of the bridge, eventually clearing it out and making another barricade. That was too close.

That night I was lulled to sleep by the pounding of undead hands on the cars up ahead and the never-ending splashes as the horde drove itself into the near wall of the bridge, spilling over the guardrails into the water. Ammo is critical. I'm gonna need to be creative.

• • •

I awoke to the sight of a few creatures on my side of the barricade. I reached for my codeine and Mitch's instructions; I was due. After taking the tiny dose, I pissed in a plastic water bottle and I stepped down out of Goliath, grenade in hand. I threw a Hail Mary at the corpse standing near the barricade and pegged it hard in the head with the full yellow bottle. The cap busted off and the bottle spun into the air, splashing urine all over the creature and the cars. It turned its head, scanning from side to side before locking onto me. As it began to march, I pulled the sheathed bayonet, revealing the glinting and still-sharp carbon steel. Stabbing the thing with a hunting knife or most tactical blades would just get me killed. A true blade for current times was the bayonet, or an ice pick. I waited for the creature to get danger-close before I leveled the blade in front of its eye, letting it walk right into its switch. Lights out.

The other two rounded the front at the same time, so I retreated behind the fifth wheel of Goliath, just a few inches from the edge of this side of the bridge. There was only enough room for single file around the back end, so I edged around and waited. I grasped Goliath's steel frame and hung half my body over the edge. The first creature fell for it and just walked off as it came directly for me. The second saw the first fall and became more cautious, hissing and clawing at me from the corner of Goliath's fifth-wheel frame. Getting braver, it stepped out toward me and I quickly climbed the truck and kicked it in the face, sending it flipping end over end into the murky waters.

With the bridge clear, I began to hook up the towing straps to the vehicles as I waited for some water to boil so I could cook the last of my powdered eggs and dehydrated meat. I tried not to draw too much attention, as I could see corpses moving about beyond my shitty barricade. They'd be alerted the moment I started the rig, so I had to get everything pre-staged.

After breakfast, I once again pulled my kit out for inventory. Laying the contents of my pack out on a blanket in front of Goliath, I began to wonder how much time I had left out here. It'd been nearly a month since I left the Keys, and I knew that I'd either be divorced or dead when Tara saw me. I just hoped she realized how important this was to . . . well, everyone, I hoped. I mean, a goddamned cure? Even a one percent chance at my daughter not having to sleep in a metal cage would be worth it all. Before the shit hit the fan, I had gone to the range all the time. I loved shooting. I supposed that would never really change, but it'd be nice to not have to sleep with a rifle someday.

I pulled the battleship-gray mag from my carbine, tracing with my finger the number Kryloned to the side: 300.

After checking the action on my pistol and topping off the 9mm mag, I began to thumb the rounds out of the gray carbine mag.

Ten rounds. Ten bolts in my quiver. Ten rocks in my sling. Ten.

The chance of finding more 300 Blackout subsonic ammo anywhere would be pretty much the same chance as me finding a fueled and maintained aircraft in the field up ahead.

I loaded the metal mag and shoved it back into the well. Staying low, I crept up to the vehicles I'd used for a barricade. The door was locked, but I had some ceramic ninja rocks on me. With a light toss, the window spiderwebbed. I used my carbine to clear enough glass to reach inside and unlock the door. I quietly swung it open and checked the backseat before I climbed in.

Never know.

Nothing in the glove box but insurance, proof of registration, and the vehicle's owner's manual. I slammed the glove box shut in frustration and pushed the trunk latch button. Nothing happened. Frustrated even more, I climbed into the back and began to pull the seatbacks to access the trunk. I shielded my eyes for a few seconds as I shined my carbine light into the dark opening. I was trying to charge the glow-in-the-dark trunk escape handle. After shutting off my torch, I climbed into the trunk and pulled the glowing T-handle, releasing the emergency latch on the trunk. Painfully, I squirmed back out into the car and out the door.

All for nothing.

The trunk only held a doughnut spare and jack, some road flares, and an emergency blanket. Full of rage, I slammed the trunk, causing one of the creatures a hundred yards on the other side of the barricade to start making its way to me. Seeing red, I slingshot the charging handle back and shouldered my carbine, putting the dot at the top of the advancing creature's head. The tip of my finger pulled half a millimeter of slack into the trigger. Just an RCH more and the thing will be toast and I'll feel better.

Squeeze.

Nothing.

Fucking safety. I stepped back and took a deep breath, staring out into the flowing water to the opposite bank before letting it out.

"Breathe," I said aloud to myself.

I just stared, watching the water churn. Probably a hundred wet corpses milled about on the opposite bank a few hundred meters downstream. They'd have to find another fucking way across; this bridge was mine.

I rolled Goliath slowly through the makeshift barricade leading off the bridge. The vehicles creaked but gave way, their nearly flat muddy rubber tires squelching across the asphalt.

A few miles farther down the road, I came upon a convenience store. I rolled to a stop about a hundred yards out and jumped down out of the truck with my carbine. I released the GARMR and felt comforted by its clicking sound on the pavement as it trailed behind at its programmed rad-mitigating distance. I moved forward, casual at first, but my stance became more defensive as I approached the derelict storefront. The glass in front of the barred windows was smashed out in the front and the automatic door was propped open. Whatever was inside would come out and vice versa. At the door, I nudged the cinder block out of the way and told Checkers to stay as I went inside the darkened building. The automatic door sprung closed behind me with a *thunk*.

I wasn't here for supplies, just one specific thing. The shelves were bare, with only air fresheners, windshield cleaner, and a pack of atrocious black licorice. I took the candy and shoved it in my cargo pants. Maybe the undead would smell it and leave me alone. I hopped over the counter and checked underneath.

Bingo. Phone book.

It was a few years old, but it would do just fine.

I thumbed through it until I found the listings for all gunsmiths in the area. As I ripped the pages I needed, I could hear the GARMR moving around outside the door.

I told it to wait, I thought.

Looming shadows crossed the bottom of the door.

"Checkers, go to the door," I commanded into the Simon.

The machine trotted over to the door.

"Checkers, stay until I call," I said.

I wasn't sure if the machine understood complex commands, but I didn't have time to think about that. I made for the back door and pressed the horizontal bar that warned me that this was an emergency exit only and that an alarm would sound. Doubting that, I pushed it anyway and was bathed in bright light and the smell of a long-full green dumpster. A half-decomposed corpse lay on its back near the dumpster; the only thing still moving was its eyes. Everything else had shut down from advanced decomposition, likely severing critical nerve endings to the extremities.

I quickly but carefully jogged the hundred yards back to Goliath, calling for the GARMR as I escaped.

Strapping the machine back to the rig, I was back up inside and watching the creatures try to open the door, disinterested in Checkers, as it left them moments before. When the rig fired up, they immediately turned and began their approach, signaling my departure from the area.

I was now on my way to Larry's Guns, Class 3 & More.

Class 3 SOT dealers were a strange breed. They sold machine guns, silencers, and short-barreled rifles, among other interesting things. The one I'd found in the phone book was on the outskirts of a residential area a few miles from Atlanta. Whoever Larry was, he lived in a small, nondescript house surrounded by a five-foot chain-link fence with an external building. The building was his gun store, evident by the business hours posted to the door and the dark neon sign that two years ago would have indicated "open."

I tried the door: no luck. Thumping on it from the outside, I could tell it was a solid hurricane type, with two bolt locks as well as a knob lock. What else might I expect from a business that sells machine guns and silencers?

The small gun store was coated with dried residue from eye level all the way to the ground. Paying closer attention to my surroundings, I'd noticed that everything was. A horde had been here, cleared everything out. This explained the dented S10 pickup on the street outside. It was beat up on one entire side as if an elephant had used it as a back scratcher.

I decided to take more drastic measures with the door, as I didn't want to be here any longer than absolutely necessary. I attached the tow strap securely to the window bars of Larry's store and pulled the damn thing out of its frame. Nothing about this was quiet. The sun was positioned to shine bright beams into the gaping hole of the tiny gun store. A corpse sat on a cashier's stool, held in place by the counter in front of it. It wore blue jeans, a plaid shirt, blue blockers, and a ball cap, complete with the exit hole of a large-caliber round from the pistol still in its bony grasp.

I quickly untied my makeshift breacher straps and climbed through the jagged hole into the store. I looked around but immediately fixated on the M4 in the display case. The handwritten paper placard below the gun said:

TRANSFERABLE 1967 COLT M-16 COMMANDO,
CARRIED IN VIETNAM BY USAF PJS,
REGISTERED DURING NFA AMNESTY, 1968.

The price tag attached to the trigger guard demanded a shocking $37,500. Movement from the corner of my eye caused me to get low behind the jagged opening near the suicide corpse. Four creatures came into view, scanning their surroundings, their decaying brains reduced to only primordial-level calculations. They were using what little cerebral capacity they had remaining to find me.

I waited for them to pass before moving Larry's rolling stool out of the way to get to the display case. It was of course locked, so I reached for the keys on the corpse's belt, realizing they were attached via a small retractable cable. I pulled the cable down to the lock, inadvertently pulling the body down on top of me. Pushing it off, my hands sank into its soft gut, penetrating its bloated skin and organs inside. Dry heaving, I rolled over, removing my slime-coated hand and wiping it all over Larry's clothing.

After regaining my composure, I looked outside again and discovered only one creature remaining in the streets. I pulled the keys and went through them one by one until I found the key that would open the display case. After sliding the door over, I reached in and recovered the weapon that was literally worth its weight in gold both before and after the dead walked.

I checked the action on the relic, noting that it functioned just like my modern carbine with the same auto sear holes and other mechanical markings. The only difference was that this was a 5.56-caliber gun and Larry's shelves were full of that ammunition. After loading up the Commando, I brought my gun to the back and cranked off the silencer, removing the upper receiver. After torquing the upper receiver tightly in a vise on Larry's gunsmithing bench, I removed the silencer's proprietary quick-detach muzzle device. After taking off the Commando's oversized moderator muzzle device, I went to twist on my device, when the whole thing fell down onto the collar of the Colt's barrel.

Wrong thread diameter.

The damn threads on the Colt were smaller than my gun, so my eyes quickly shifted to the other glass display case full of silencer boxes. With the keys, I finally got the second display case open and began rummaging until I found what I was looking for: a direct-thread silencer. After hand-tightening the new silencer down on the Colt Commando, my anxiety began to drop and I knew I could once again kill those creatures without bringing all of Atlanta down on top of me. The antiquated markings on the Colt were of another age that I couldn't connect with, but I knew some would. I was now downgraded to iron sights but, hey, at least I got a carry handle.

I loaded everything I deemed valuable from Larry's store into Goliath's passenger seat and closed the door, revealing a corpse snarling at me from three feet away. It must have turned the corner around the front of the truck. I had a thousand rounds of ammunition, so I decided to test the antique. I stepped back as the creature lunged forward. I pulled the charging handle back, checking that I had remembered to chamber a round and clicked the receiver from safe into semi mode. Shouldering the gun, I peered just over the top of the carry handle through the sight aperture of those old-school irons that probably pointed to Vietcong long ago. As the creature went to lunge again, I kicked the selector switch back another position to auto and pulled the trigger.

The gun proceeded to empty the entire mag, walking up the torso of the corpse so fast that I nearly needed to reload. The last three shots of the thirty-round mag tore through the creature's head, sending skull and brains flying when the bolt locked back. The sound was uncomfortably loud, even with the silencer attached. My ears were on the verge of ringing as smoke billowed from the end of the silencer and out the receiver's open dust cover. I pulled the empty mag, replacing it quickly with a new one from my back pocket. Twenty-eight rounds of 5.56 was clearly not the best way to kill one of those things, so I made sure to leave the Commando in semiauto unless I really needed to get it on.

Ingress

After Hourglass, there were still remnants of the United States government remaining. I know because I sent the tech we recovered to a classified site. I wasn't told where it went, but I knew it went to some type of research facility. That node went dark a few months ago, along with the last remaining A-10 Thunderbolt squadron. Our base in the Keys did not have the resources to find out what had happened, and no one was going to volunteer for that shit show "rescue." I was asked, but my response was *What is the point?* Without a distress call, I'd get all the way to the coast of Texas looking for what was left of an air base and probably get killed myself. If I were those Warthog pilots, I'd probably get airborne and land in the pasture closest to my home of record at the first sign my base was getting overrun. As far as the facility where we sent the Hourglass tech, all I knew was that it was hundreds of miles inland and that the facility had gone dark. No one liked to give locations for covert facilities over the radio. The raider element was very much out there and they were listening 24/7. Any indication of a viable government facility with power, water, and even limited infrastructure and you could bet that they'd be headed that way to wreak havoc, just like those fucks in Tallahassee tried to do to me.

I will forever have the scars to show for it.

Right now I am on board Goliath, tracing my path on the map to the Wachovia Tower somewhere south of downtown Atlanta. It's my best assumption based on the radio recordings that the CDC has set up their site B there. If the transmissions are true and there is a cure or even a vaccine for this, well, my adrenaline kicks up every time I think about it.

• • •

Day 25

2300

I'm up on a billboard sign, watching them pass through my NOD. They smell food but don't know I'm here. If I make a sound, they'll never leave and neither will I.

I'll die up here of exposure, as the nine magazines full of 5.56 won't be enough to push them back to offer me an escape route through the masses. Not quite a horde, but not quite a baker's dozen, either. The torn and faded billboard represented some law firm, but I can only see the letters *nnarah*. The rest of the name was torn off long ago. Underneath the peeling law firm's banner was a car dealership advertising zero percent interest. The GARMR is dormant in the ditch a hundred yards away. If it comes to it, I'll use Checkers to help me get back down.

The moon is reflecting the sun's light, casting a glow over the whole area. The blue halo around it is unnerving but beautiful. Looking up, I think about the American flag there and how the living dead will never disturb its majestic flight. I find some comfort that man created something beyond the undead's reach. This thought brings my spirits up a bit.

Rolling toward south Atlanta this morning, I encountered lines of traffic headed out of the city in both lanes. For the first time, no amount of pulling cars out of the way would let me get Goliath through the impasse, bookended by a giant wall closing off access to Atlanta. I thought back to those days when this first started, using the robotic arm in my mind to recover my own personal memory tapes, to somehow recount what I did in the aircraft. Fighting through the fog of PTSD, addiction, and other terrible things, I remembered flying over Atlanta in an EP-3, an FBI agent on board. I picked up CDC comms. Atlanta wasn't City Zero, but it was City One in the U.S. The anomaly spread from here quickly, after they brought the patient back from China to Maryland and eventually moved patients nearby to the Atlanta CDC.

As I pulled Goliath up to the wall of cars, I knew it was time to walk. I found a place to hide the rig just off the road and marked a nearby tree with a can of orange spray paint. Goliath had well over a quarter tank of diesel and was in good mechanical condition. I really hated to leave the rig, my source of air-conditioning, safety, and transportation (emphasis on air-conditioning). The sinking feeling in my stomach increased as I stepped down out of the rig into the southern U.S. heat with my cumbersome ruck and ear-piercing Vietnam-era Commando carbine. The beast was ten times louder than my 300 BLK gun and packed a wallop on my hearing, even with the can cranked on. I suppose the only use it had was preventing fast location of the shooter. The supersonic crack of the 5.56 round let out an omnidirectional boom that made it tough to know the shooter's location, as the muzzle blast was heavily attenuated. At least I'd found this titanium silencer at Larry's that made the muzzle sweep a little faster than my heavy Stellite alloy can.

The little things.

The mosquitoes were bad in the immediate area, but I handled it long enough to chop some branches and cover the rig in such a way that any passersby wouldn't pay too much attention. I hid the keys underneath the rig and released the GARMR. It ran its familiar diagnostic and cocked its head at me as it's done a hundred times before. I didn't think it would ever be possible, but I actually liked the damn thing. It was loyal, reliable, and just shut up and did its job. Before heading out, I went back through the tablet, again familiarizing myself with the machine's capabilities, being careful to stay away from some of the menus marked with a skull-and-crossbones and fingerprint icon.

After consulting the tablet map, I plugged the device into the GARMR's micro power grid and dropped it in its saddlebag. The tablet was down to ten percent and I needed it to be at full capability so I could use it to get to the tower where the cure and Phoenix were holing up. At least, that's what the recordings said.

After making a quick sweep of the immediate area, I pulled out the radio and tuned up the HF freq again. I was close enough to nearly see the Atlanta skyline, but the freq was dark. I tuned up the Morse channel and it was also dark. Nothing but silence intermittently interrupted by solar activity beaming in from ninety-three million miles away. It had been twenty-two days since I first picked up the Phoenix signal, and now nothing. This gave me pause for a few moments, questioning whether or not I needed to take another step in the direction of south Atlanta, to the Wachovia Tower.

After a long deliberation, I slung my Colt Commando across my chest and began to walk. The clicking of the machine's feet behind me pushed me forward. I wasn't alone, and that meant a helluva lot out here in the badlands. My pack was heavy, having been replenished with food and drink with Mitch.

Based on the last Wachovia Tower transmission, the facility was being swarmed by the undead. I had one full mag in my gun, two on my belt, and the rest stuffed into Checkers' saddlebag. Two hundred and fifty-two rounds of ear-piercing 5.56 millimeter were at my disposal, but the now dark radio call told me it wasn't enough.

The sight in front of me was incredible. Both interstate lanes were packed with cars trying to leave. Consulting my maps, I knew that I was about eight miles from the building. As the sun began to set, I climbed up onto this billboard sign and began to plot out my next move. I wrapped my pack straps around my legs and also around a pole on the platform to avoid falling in my sleep. As I drifted off, I smelled them first, then heard them rage through the area like a herd of cattle. They're starting to thin out; I just hope they're gone by morning. I had no choice but to take the high ground. Sleeping low is suicide this close to the city. Too many dead things lurk.

I woke up to a morning rain, dousing me to the bone and sentencing me to violent shivers. The mass of creatures was gone, leaving only three in the area. I tried to wring out my sleeping bag and dry off a bit before packing my shit and moving carefully down the ladder. As I went, my Commando clanged against the railing. I cringed before looking over my shoulder. I'd been made.

They began to converge on the ladder as I reached the last rung and went the rest of the way down with my arms as the ladder didn't reach all the way to the ground. I'd put a nearby car into neutral and pushed it under the ladder yesterday. As soon as my foot touched down on the vehicle roof, I slid down the back window and across the trunk onto the wet grass. Falling head over heels, I went down the hill and into a small stream that had formed with the rain. The creatures gave chase and tumbled down the hill in pursuit. As they came at me, I pulled myself up and began running upstream, hitting the follow button on the GARMR control beacon as I went. Over my shoulder, I could see the creatures stand up and begin their never-ending pursuit of flesh. They'd chase me for years if I let them. I didn't want to get into a shootout this early in the day.

It wasn't gentlemanly.

Besides, loud noises after a night of sleeping in the rain on a metal platform thirty feet above the ground was just not something I wanted to deal with. I began to run, not yet fully trusting my ankle. I'd been following Mitch's instructions and only craved the codeine a little at this point. I headed toward what looked like a suburban neighborhood from the back side. The GARMR was close behind when I pulled two boards from the neighborhood's privacy fence and ducked through. The machine came in behind, entering the tall grass of what used to be an American backyard. I saw a rusted barbecue grill, propane tanks, covered hot tub, and a tattered awning waving in the morning breeze. The homes here didn't have individual privacy fences but one seemed to cordon off the neighborhood as far as I could see in both directions. I stayed as low as I could, grazing the tops of the tall grass as I moved. I could sense the GARMR behind me, but it was sneaking along pretty well and not making much noise. At the very least, hopefully we threw our pursuers off the trail.

Rounding the house out onto the street, I froze in terror. Forcing myself to act, I got really low. Twenty-seven creatures standing there, completely still, frozen in time. They waited patiently for a stray dog, deer, or foolish human like myself to cross their path, turning their primordial bio-machine switches to kill mode. I low crawled backward and decided to slog through the thick foliage from backyard to backyard until I could circumvent the deadly mob.

I led, Checkers followed; we parted the foliage into the clearing of the next backyard. I saw a trampoline with a small tree growing through it, a long-dead armadillo, and some week-old drag marks that bent the grass, leading off into the woods toward the privacy fence. The house I was hiding behind had no curtains; I could see the undead in the street as I looked through both the back and front windows of the house. I stood there watching one of them twitch, as if it would wake up any minute and crash through the place to get to me. I was fixated on the creature, its chin touching its chest, its head twitching from side to side, distantly resembling a human in REM sleep.

My trance was interrupted by movement inside the house. A skeletal creature wearing a police uniform stepped in front, blocking my view to the front windows. It began to slam its arms against the back sliding-glass door. My heart began to race as the street beyond came alive with movement, and a chorus of moans erupted and echoed throughout the neighborhood.

I followed the drag marks into the trees, chased by the horrible noises of doors splintering and glass shattering. At the fence, I began pulling on boards. None of them were loose enough. I had no choice.

I tossed my pack over the eight-foot fence and climbed, leaving the GARMR to fend for itself in a neighborhood suddenly gone mad.

After flinging myself over the fence, I grabbed my pack and ran along the neighborhood's drainage canal. The fence boards on my right moved by rapidly as I ran, giving me moving picture glimpses into the hell beyond. The undead were tearing through the houses and spaces between. The sound of glass and fence boards creaking was so damn loud. In the time before, these types of sounds never happened without being accompanied by large demolition equipment and revving diesel engines.

The whole quarter-mile-long privacy fence buckled and strained, funneling me into a kill box from which there was no escape. I attempted to dive into a drainage opening but couldn't fit with my pack. The manhole cover was seated tightly and I didn't have a key. I cursed to myself on this one as I distinctly remembered telling myself to carry a large bolt with a piece of paracord tied to it. This combination made a wonderful manhole remover, but that didn't matter at all when I almost broke my finger trying to remove the heavy manhole cover. The bold words on the cover, MADE IN INDIA, were etched into my eyes as I slung my pack off and shimmied down into the concrete drainage catacombs with nothing but my M4 Commando and spare mags.

The fence splintered and collapsed and the undead spilled forth like a tsunami from the neighborhood. What I'd estimated to be twenty-five was more like two hundred and fifty, or higher. I stayed quiet, slowly reaching out of the opening to reposition my pack to cover the rectangular spillway opening. The full pack covered all but a few inches of the opening, so I rotated the pack to expose the zipper to my side and brought out my NOD.

Switching it on, I checked the cistern surroundings and noticed four-foot-diameter openings heading in two directions. Water trickled from one of the openings, but not much. I felt like the target of a monkey trap, with my pack being the fruit and the opening only large enough for my hand. I couldn't get my pack through the opening; it was too full and the undead began to close in on my position.

I tried to look through the small opening for Checkers. It was too risky to recover the tablet and even more risky to set off the GARMR's sound beacon. It could be nearby and I definitely didn't want to draw them to this drainage cavern.

"Checkers, stay," I commanded into the control watch.

Better to have it folded up into itself, awaiting my command, than to risk it giving away my position.

Night 26

The empty cistern began to cool down as night approached. The undead remained heavy in the area, but the cover of darkness was to my advantage. There was no way I'd escape the same way I entered. They'd detect my heat signature and overwhelm me, ripping me to pieces before I left the drainage ditch. There was moonlight; I could see it through my NOD spilling through the small opening into the room. Every now and again, I could see the shadow of a creature break the moonbeam, reminding me of my situation. I was trapped, separated from all of my gear.

As I pissed into the trickling runoff, I thought about the monkey trap again. My pack wouldn't fit through the opening as it was, and I couldn't leave my kit behind. Dehydration and exhaustion were to blame for my ignorance. All I needed to do was carefully and quietly open the top of the pack and bring my kit down with me into the cistern piece by piece before pulling the empty pack through the hole and then reorganizing my kit.

I moved slowly, as if trying to thwart a motion detector, unclipping the top of my bag. Thank God there was no Velcro. With the top unclipped, I began to roll the waterproof shell open, exposing the inside of the bloodstained pack. I took out the first items, spare mags. Carefully, I sat them down on the floor of my subterranean abode. If I dropped them, the room would act like an amplifier, drawing the miserable sacks of shit to the opening. Pulling out my maps, the paper crinkled some as I took it through the concrete spillway opening.

In the magnified green moonlight, I could see one of the nearby creatures cock its head sideways and begin to shuffle toward the opening. I stepped away, sinking farther back into the cool cistern, not wanting the creature's rudimentary thermal sight to pick up any of my 98-degree heat from the opening. I watched as the moon shadow shifted with the creature's approach. Through the slit, I could see an ankle and then a knee as the thing lowered its undead body to the ground. I pulled my bayonet half out of its scabbard, green moonlight glinting off its venerable blade.

Time seemed to slow down and I began to move when I saw a skeletal hand reach down. Just as its chin began to be visible in the spillway opening, I thrust the bayonet forward into the roof of the creature's mouth, up into its head. The blade stopped on the inside surface of the creature's skull.

The room was now in total darkness as the impaled head of the corpse blocked the remaining moonlight. My NOD adjusted and I pulled my blade from the gaping mouth of the corpse, careful not to cut my fingers on its jagged and broken teeth. I ran the knife through the trickling runoff water and wiped it off on a piece of wooden pallet from some large storm that happened who knew when.

I kept working until my pack was empty enough to bring it through the opening. I dragged it at sloth speed, just enough to not register with the creatures still lurking outside. Eventually, I had the pack inside the cavern with me and I began to hastily fill it once more for my trip through this foreboding Morlock realm.

As I entered the north pipe, I wondered where Checkers was and if it was okay. Was it folded up in plain sight for approaching raiders to destroy? Was it deactivated in some pool of water somewhere, its RTG battery arcing and sparking to oblivion?

I was worrying about something made of metal and composite, not a flesh-and-blood thing. Damn that: I didn't care. It was still valuable to me and I wasn't leaving it. It was mine and it could be trusted; it didn't betray or die and walk.

The light began to fade as I opened distance from where I started. I was faced with numerous turns and decisions until I arrived at another cistern with another spillway opening filled with debris, more so than the last.

I carefully navigated the debris but stopped when I heard something move inside. I stepped off the pile and used the Commando's suppressor to peel away the layers of pine needles, trash, and other refuse until I came to the source: A severed head and attached meaty spinal column lay in the trash, ripped apart somehow and sent down the drainage system. The muscles and other biologics on the spine moved, resembling a snake along with the snapping jaws. These things would never give up, not as long as their brains remained even halfway in one piece.

The creature looked up at me with its one remaining eye sunk deep into its exposed skull, and you could see it lock onto new food. Its spine disgustingly and violently wagged and its jaws snapped like a mousetrap. Its brain sent its non-body the signal to attack, but the synapses fired into dead-end nerves. I dispatched it with the bayonet, making sure no other surprises were in the cistern with me before looking through the spillway opening.

There were no undead in the area, so I tried to remember how long I'd moved through he pipe. Thirty minutes? Maybe forty-five— no more. Satisfied the area was clear, I stepped up onto the center concrete platform and put my back into the manhole cover.

The damn thing didn't budge. I pulled my composite cleaning

rod from my pack frame and pushed it up into the manhole key opening. It went about eighteen inches before stopping against something metal.

A fucking car was parked on the lid.

Cursing, I stepped back into the northwest tunnel, checking my wrist compass often, using its bright tritium lamp as a lantern in conjunction with my NOD. I went for two or three hundred meters based on my steps, when the tunnel ahead got so bright that my NOD had to once again compensate and adjust to the beaming moonlight. I kept moving slowly, my back aching from being hunched over. I approached the source of the light and hit *Follow* on the command watch as I saw where the moonlight was coming from.

The drain was washed out completely up ahead and the whole road above it had collapsed into a sinkhole. An overturned cement truck lay far down into the ditch, its intense weight probably responsible for the spillway damage. I felt like Andy Dufresne, crawling out of that nasty sewer pipe outside of Shawshank Prison. The air, although laden with flesh rot, was fresh. I climbed upon the overturned cement truck and waited. Consulting my maps, I knew I was only a few short miles to my objective at the tower.

The game was afoot.

The Path of Charon

The GARMR didn't show up. I hysterically rummaged through my pack from atop the concrete mixer truck. Rushing to turn the tablet on, I unlocked it and attempted to connect with the machine's video feed. I went through every single menu realizing that *find my mechanical dog* wasn't an available option. Panicking, I kept switching spectrums on the machine's optics and was continually greeted with *attempting connection* each time. I impatiently waited for two hours, watching the moon rise up over the trees before making a decision. I held my wrist up high, pressing the follow button multiple times in the hopes that Checkers would receive my signal and come to me.

Through my NOD, I could see figures moving in the distance and moans were carried on the wind, reminding me of the danger I was walking into on my way to the distress signal. Reluctantly, I slid down the side of the overturned concrete mixer truck into the tall grass and disappeared north into the thick foliage adjacent to the gridlocked road.

The wind shifted out of the west, bringing their smell to me. The pungent odor of forty thousand dead washed over my body, coating every cilium inside my nostrils. I pulled the shemagh up over my mouth and nose in a bid to somehow abate the rancid stench of death. I walked into the wind, all the while listening for the bellows of an army of dead as well as hopefully the clicking of synthetic GARMR feet. With the shift of the wind once more, the smell intensified to a level I didn't think was possible, and the moans I expected to hear based on the radio transmissions were carried to me in that rhythmic way in which they travel, infecting the dark fear recesses of the living mind. I imagined that the creatures were speaking telepathically to each other and what they might have to say.

Come to us, let us embrace
Like old friends meet face-to-face
What's living is bad and what's dead is good
Give us the chance to be understood . . .

The creatures' moans were infecting my logical thought, their smell driving me mad. I wanted nothing more in the moment than to raise my gun up into the sky. *Come and get it, motherfuckers, come on!*

My anger at the undead grew as I stomped forward without my metal companion. At about four in the morning, I crested a hill and was met with the terrible sight of a tall building. Writing it like that may not seem terrifying to whoever may pull this journal from my bony (un)dead hands, but the building had a companion, a great cancerous growth that rose from the base, rising to an apex near the roof itself. It was too dark to see the grisly details, but it was great stacks of corpses. Thousands and thousands of them had been dispatched, forming a massive pile. I studied the scene in disbelief, realizing that the corpses had formed a giant biological ramp. *This is impossible,* I thought. My epiphany arrived simultaneously with the great flamethrower blast that shot from the building's roof down to the top of the advancing creatures.

The massive stream of flames sent corpses tumbling down over thousands of arms, legs, heads, and torsos. The undead slowly but deliberately kept driving forward, unable to be concerned with their own attrition. Every one of them that was fried and fell upon the charred pile of corpses below added to the foundation that would slowly but eventually give the creatures passage to the roof, inevitably overtaking the entire building like ants on a dropped ice cream cone. Judging by the raw numbers of burned and dismembered bodies, it appeared that this giant formation of corpses had been slowly constructed over some time; the undead being the bricks and the men with flamethrowers the masons.

I sat there watching the flamethrower deliver hell on the undead and wondered how the survivors kept from burning the building down. The creatures aflame had to be touching the building's exterior. Whoever was firing that from the rooftop was using their last option: Do not pass Go; flame or death. I slung my pack to the ground, lying prone over it with my binos. I could see only two men on the roof. I also saw a balloon hovering above the roof access structure. It was just like the dead soldier's antenna balloon from when I found the GARMR. I was too far away to make out fine details. Eyes down in the binoculars, I lost situational awareness.

As I stared at the flames attacking the ramp with extreme prejudice, the wind was suddenly knocked out of me by a growling mass of fur. Some sort of wild dog had grabbed my shemagh at the nape of my neck and begun to shake back and forth, making breathing impossible. I saw stars and began to flail and punch blindly against my attacker. I now had the large dog in a bear hug, and it still had a death grip on my shemagh; I had to rotate it to the front of my neck.

With my shemagh locked tightly in the dog's jaws, I went forward with it, tumbling into a culvert and hitting my shoulder against the concrete. I could make out the dog's white fangs in the light of the bright flamethrower. The dog was heavily scarred, missing an ear, the outline of undead jaws in its place. I pulled my bayonet but it was too late; the feral dog jumped. I tried to stab it through the neck but it was all I could do to keep it at bay, keep it from biting through my jugular, spilling my blood everywhere. It would then wait for me to bleed out and go unconscious before eating me half alive as my brain shut down in the darkness. If the dog left my brain in one piece, I'd wake up and try to join the great undead ramp that was being built over there, fire-hardened by the most badass flamethrower I'd ever seen.

I felt the wet muzzle of the animal under my chin just before the loud yelp. The feral beast was tossed several feet away by the charging GARMR. After hitting the beast so hard I thought I heard ribs crack, Checkers took a defensive posture between the wild dog and me. The GARMR cocked its head to the side as it always does, and so did the dog. Sizing one another up, the dog didn't like what it was looking at, so it turned and ran off into the tall grass.

I was scratched up from its claws and I thought it might have nicked my forearm on its fangs, but I'd be okay for now. I didn't stop to notice if its mouth was foaming, but I was quadruple-digit miles from the nearest possible rabies shot; I just had to make things work.

I patted the GARMR on its titanium head and thanked it out loud for its performance. Would it understand me? I don't know, but it seemed like the right thing to do. I really hope that some special ops team on the ground in Afghanistan had one of these before everything went to shit. It would have been a valuable thing to have around.

I checked the saddlebags on the machine, confirming that my extra 5.56 mags were still inside. Removing those and placing them in my cargo pockets, I slung my pack and my M4 and looked for some high ground to set up shop.

The first hint of sunlight was beginning to peek over the trees. I needed to hurry. I had no shelter and was surrounded by undead near enough that I couldn't escape if detected. I had a loud gun, suppressed or not.

I broke through some foliage and arrived at an opening in the trees. Just up ahead, I could see a large playground with a fort and a tunnel slide. I slowly crept to it, keeping aware of my surroundings. The large wooden fort had two ways up—three if you counted going up the corkscrew tunnel slide.

Ladder or steps?

I stepped up onto the fort and climbed on the roof, giving me a view of the top floor of the building as well as the immediate playground area. The GARMR negotiated the first step and went into standby mode within ten feet of where I was at the mouth of the corkscrew slide. I was about fifteen feet off the ground, with multiple ways down if too many creatures showed up and cornered me.

I unslung my pack and pulled out my small handset radio. I dialed up the Morse freq—nothing—and then the voice recording freq—nothing. Switching frequencies to the UHF band, I began to spin and grin, looking for anything that sounded like communications. After finding nothing, I went out on the common Motorola two-way freqs I had written down in my notebook and began to broadcast in the blind. You'd be surprised how many survivors had small Motorola radios.

"Wachovia Tower, I've received your distress call. Is anyone out there?" I keyed, sending my voice at the speed of light out into the rotting wind.

Day 27

The sun peeked up over the horizon, revealing the ant-like movements of the mass of corpses piled up the side of the building. As soon as my watch said 0600, another burst of flames erupted from the roof down onto the apex of the mass. It wouldn't be long now. My radio crackled.

"Station calling Wachovia Tower; please come in," a voice I recognized from the recording said.

Fishing for my handset, I keyed a response, identifying myself by my name, rank, and home area.

"Commander? Of Hourglass?" the voice on the radio said.

I rogered up to the affirmative and could hear hoots and hollers from atop the building hundreds of meters distant.

"How many with you, sir?" the man asked.

"Just me, I'm afraid," I responded.

There was a long silence before the defeat-stricken voice responded.

"Commander, might as well turn back. Don't know if you can see, but we're surrounded on all sides. A hundred thousand dead, maybe. The bottom half of the building is compromised; we did everything we could, but they just kept coming, piling up, and smashing through the floors as the corpses stack higher."

"What about the goddamned cure?" I said, annoyed that they'd written off their chances of getting out.

"We have it, but there's only two canisters of chemical coolant remaining. We lost generator power a week ago, and without chemical coolant the RF-shielded container needs to be plugged in to 110 soon to keep the cure viable," the voice said.

"Who am I talking to?" I asked.

After a short pause, the radio beeped before the response: "Doc, Task Force Phoenix."

"Damn good to hear your voice, Doc. Can you toss the transport container off the building?"

"No, the tech says the coolant unit wouldn't survive the impact. We've got three parachutes from the Hotel 23 drop with us. We thought about BASE jumping off the roof and catching a lucky breeze, but there are just too many fucking zombies down there. We'd land on top of them, Commander," Doc responded.

"First off, I'm Kil. Neither of us has been paid in two years, so let's lose the formalities. How much ammo?" I asked.

"We're dry. All we got are homemade flamethrowers. We still have our M4s, but the bolts are locked back, dry as fuck," Doc said.

"Roger," I said flatly.

"Me and Billy don't blame you if you skin out. There ain't no way up here unless you got a helicopter we don't know about."

"I'm not leaving you up there. How many you got in the building with you?"

"We're overrun two floors below, all the way to the ground. They climbed in the windows and took most of us out. We've got me, Billy Boy, and a CDC researcher, bit yesterday when we lost the sixteenth floor. He knows he's not gonna make it," said Doc.

"Thought you guys had the cure up there."

"We were briefed that it doesn't work like that," Doc said, annoyed by my question.

"How much longer before they pile up to the roof?" I asked.

"I don't know, Kil. Tonight? Tomorrow, maybe. We only have one can of fuel left for the flamethrowers. They keep clawing their way up here, and pretty soon we'll be fighting them at eye level, hand to hand."

"Sit tight, Doc, I'm coming for you."

"You're fucking crazy."

Nova

My pockets were jammed with 5.56 mags and the M4 Commando was slung across my chest. I had the bayonet crudely duct-taped to my silencer, jutting out in front of the muzzle. The GARMR tablet was stuffed down the back of my pants and my pack lay hidden under the corkscrew slide. The GARMR looked at me curiously as I stepped off the fort onto the shredded-tire-covered ground. Reluctantly, I left my pack and pressed toward the building with only the minimum essentials.

The cure was getting off the roof of that fucking building today.

I slowly worked my way through the thick growth, stopping just short of the Wachovia Tower's south parking lot. The massive corpse pile had formed on the west side of the building, with only "small" ten-foot piles of writhing bodies on the south side where I was accompanied by a mob of a hundred or so.

I keyed the radio.

"Doc, Kil," I said.

"Doc can't come to the phone right now: He's on vacation in Tahiti" was the response.

"Cute. Toss a line down, center south," I said.

"Aye," said Doc.

After a couple of minutes, a green rope fell to the corpse pile and unraveled onto the ground at the feet of the undead. They took no interest in it. There was no heat signature; it didn't smell like meat.

"*Gracias.* Can you pull me up? Probably two hundred pounds with my kit," I said.

"Yeah, we got you, fat-ass," Doc replied as laughter echoed from the top, further taunting the hungry corpses on the ground in front of me.

Gallows humor.

I approached the GARMR, patting it on the head.

"Good boy."

The words escaped my lips faster than I could stop them from leaving.

Using the tablet, I sent the machine to the south side, just far enough away from the horde to give it maneuverability.

I looked down at the miniature Simon replica on my wrist and wedged my index finger into the protected red button.

The GARMR's ear-piercing klaxon blared, sending visible shock waves through the undead. The new stimulus polarized the horde in one direction, sending them grasping for Checkers. As the south-side parking lot began to clear out, I used the tablet and dragged the GARMR position a half mile west of the building, drawing the creatures away. I stuffed the tablet back down the back of my cargo pants and sprinted for the building. A hundred meters before, a creature stepped out in front and got the bayonet. My ankle began to ache a little but I wasn't due for another dose yet, according to Mitch's schedule.

It was a clear shot to the ten-foot corpse pile. I began to carefully climb the horrible Twister game gone mad, careful to avoid the gaping maws that seemed to flash at me every step of the way up the hill of corpses, all with head-shot wounds. My left hand had reached the rope and I quickly tied it off to my rigger's belt.

"Ready," I said into the radio.

The rope took slack and began to pull my pants up higher, squeezing the tablet to the small of my back. The rope tugged again, but my pant leg was snagged on something. I shook my foot back and forth, unable to release it from the snag, when I realized that a bony hand was clutching my pant leg, unwilling to let go. The rest of the corpse was buried somewhere underneath.

"Let me back down: I'm stuck!"

I pulled my blade and cut my pants, releasing the buried creature's relentless grip on me.

"I'm good. Let's go."

I ascended slowly up the side of the building, using my legs to offset some of the weight as the men tugged. Halfway up the side, I again felt a grip, this time on my right leg. I kicked off with my left, swinging off the side of the building, dragging a skinny corpse with me through the air. The thing wasn't letting go, so I had no choice but to blast it in the face with the Commando, sending echoes reverberating off the building.

I couldn't hear the GARMR klaxon any longer. Either it was too far away or dogpiled by a thousand undead. Absent the klaxon, the loudest noise in the neighborhood was my Commando, but it was too late. The unholy new tenants of the Wachovia Tower were awake and hyperaware that something alive was nearby. My 140-decibel suppressed rifle blast made sure of that. My ears weren't ringing, but it wasn't a comfortable feeling. The concussion blast from the short-barreled 5.56 slapped me in the face when I was forced to make a second shot. The creature released its grip and tumbled end over end, joining the piles of face-shot bodies below.

"Oh, fuck, you went and did it," Doc said over the radio.

I could feel the rope surge faster. I tried to use my legs to help ease their effort and was making good headway until a dozen corpses started jutting out of every broken window, grabbing for anything they could get a grip on. I was left with no choice. I kicked hard, swinging my body out, away from the building, and opened up on the creatures that threatened my safety.

Ten shots left the barrel in short order, wasting creatures, leaving their torsos hanging half out of the broken windows.

"Pull!" I screamed to the rooftops.

The rope surged upward five feet in the span of two seconds, revealing another dozen undead hands shooting out of the building to grasp warm flesh. I kicked out again but was too close to the top, my hang time cut short. I still managed to pop some instigators in the face, buying me another five-foot surge.

Breathless and shaken from gunfighting my way up the side of the building, my gloved hand finally reached the top ledge. I reached up to grab it, but a huge, powerful hand reached down and gripped my forearm. My body launched up and onto the roof as if weightless. I lay there for a moment, catching my breath, brought back to the here and now by the intense heat and distinctive jet of a flamethrower.

. . .

After catching my breath, I finally shook hands with Doc and Billy for the first time. Doc was about five foot nine, probably about two hundred and thirty pounds, built like a brick shithouse. His beard was singed, likely by the flamethrower. Billy had blond hair and appeared to be nearly a foot taller than Doc but was skinny like a college basketball player. Doc fished around in his pockets before pulling out a peeled and scratched ID card. He handed it over and I looked down at my younger, clean-shaven face. I felt a wave of nostalgia.

"Thank you," I said, fixated on the photo.

"Don't mention it. Now, why don't you tell me and Billy Boy why you came all the way up here?" Doc said.

"To give you these," I said, pulling full 5.56 mags out of my cargo pockets.

"Hot damn," Billy said, snatching two from my hands, eagerly feeding the mag well on his M4. I heard his bolt go home with a *whack* and a broad smile crossed his face from ear to ear.

"You couldn't have made it down. The rope wouldn't hold more than one person at a time, and that'd take too long," I said.

"Agreed," Doc replied. "What the hell was that noise?"

"It was my dog—long story. I have a big rig a few miles from here. Let's get our parachutes on, grab the cure, and get the hell off this building," I said with as much authority as I could muster.

"That's a good plan, but the coolant canister for the transport container is going to run out soon. The last spare is two floors down. First, the undead are thick down there again, thanks to your gunfire, and second, if we managed to get off the building alive, the cure would dissipate by tomorrow without another coolant canister or an electric outlet," Doc said.

"I'll go," said a lab coat from the roof access doorway. "I'm the one that knows exactly where it is."

"You wouldn't make it ten steps before you were torn apart," Billy said to him.

"That may be true, but I'm dead already. Gimme the Pig. I wanna get this over with. If we don't do this, what was the whole fucking point?"

Billy said a few words to the already-dead man he called Feel Good before strapping the flamethrower to the man's back and cinching it down. The heavy tank on the researcher's back was painted with the image of a large pig breathing fire. Doc and Billy asked the lab coat if he was sure, and the man nodded before lighting the pilot on the Pig and disappearing down into the stairwell.

"I'm going to the door with him. Someone's gotta make sure it gets closed behind him," Billy said to Doc.

Doc nodded and Billy disappeared down below after the lab coat. We spent the next few minutes listening for signs of trouble and checking our chutes. The best side to jump was going to be east, opposite the massive pile of corpses. Curious, I walked over to the west side of the building to peek over and was greeted by a grinning corpse just below the edge, its finger nearly touching the lip of the rooftop. More were making the climb and would soon reach the apex. The last working flamethrower was two floors below, and any gun fired here would speed the advance of the undead up to us.

I checked the bayonet, noticing the blistered and melted duct tape that held the knife to the can. Satisfied it would hold, I jabbed downward, killing the creature, sending it backward into the pile and constructing yet another step by which the undead would advance.

My west-side field trip was interrupted by a three-round burst of gunfire coming from inside the building. A scream echoed from the stairwell and also from the broken windows. Even more undead gathered around the building. Doc and I put on our parachutes and took defensive positions in front of the roof access opening. I dreaded unleashing the Commando again, but the jet of the flamethrower and more gunshots from below were about to make it necessary.

Billy exploded from the opening covered in blood, wide-eyed, with a chunk of his left hand missing from an obvious bite. Blood covered his carbine hand guard but he paid no attention to it as he spun to face the opening alongside us. The researcher, on fire, fell through the opening with what looked like a can of shaving cream in his hand. He fell face-first, dropping the canister. It rolled forward, stopping at Doc's feet. Doc quickly snatched it up and secured it in his cargo pocket.

The burning man came to and began to scream in agony, *"They're coming! They're coming!"*

Billy stamped the fire out with his hands, leaving a charred screaming mess in the doorway.

The undead began their assault on the roof and Billy's gun barked loudly, holding back the tide. They'd taken the building. Some of them stopped to take a bite out of the charred man. Paying little attention to the inevitable, Billy's carefully placed shots bought us a few seconds of preparation. I pulled the tablet from my pants and manually called in the GARMR. I flipped on its camera and watched it negotiate through a sea of undead legs and thighs. Through a break in the creatures, I could see our rooftop and the gunfire flashes from Billy's carbine. The moans of the undead were growing loud in response to the weapons fire, and every creature for miles seemed to converge on us.

I reengaged Checkers' klaxon with the press of the red button on my wrist, but nothing happened. I thought the machine must have been too far away, but when I got a visual on it and still couldn't hear its blaring klaxon, I knew something was wrong.

Glancing west, I could see hands reaching up over the lip of the edge. More undead erupted from the access stairs, but Billy's carbine kept cutting them down. It wasn't long after this that Billy ran dry and dropped his gun. I was about to toss him another mag when he reached down to his waist, pulling out an axe of some sort. Maybe a tomahawk. He began cutting into the dead with well-placed hacks and slices, sending them back down the stairs on top of the creatures behind them.

"We stay, we're dead. We jump, we're dead!" Doc screamed over the sound of the screeching horde below.

I had no choice. I had to make the call. Placing the GARMR in a position I thought would do the most good, I navigated through the skull-and-crossbones–adorned menus to the machine's RTG self-destruct protocol. After ignoring three warning menus, I entered my thumbprint and set the delay for thirty seconds.

"Get low!" I screamed.

Billy ignored my words and kept slashing at the undead coming up the stairs.

Doc and I huddled close as the thud of Billy's tomahawk cracking skulls could be heard over the chorus of the creatures.

I closed my eyes tightly, trusting Billy to keep them off us while I waited for my mechanical friend to sacrifice itself for the greater good.

Then the bright flash came, followed by the deafening crack of an unholy thunderclap. The flash temporarily blinded me, even through my eyelids, just before the blast wave hit the building, collapsing half of it in a matter of seconds. Looking over, I saw that the storage container containing the cure was carabinered securely to Doc's chest harness. Debris filled the air and I pulled my shemagh up over my nose and teary face, attempting to hold my breath.

The building was going over.

My last sight from the roof of the Wachovia Tower was Billy still slashing the undead, even while the building tilted and turned uncontrollably.

"Jump!" I screamed loudly as we tossed our chutes out into the air in front of us.

Then we were airborne, hanging from our risers when the building fell out from under us, pushing an updraft of thick dust and debris into our chutes.

"Guns out!" Doc screamed over the sound of the collapsed building's wrenching metal and crumbling concrete.

Doc's gun blasted, popping heads long before his boots hit the scorched earth.

I followed suit, picking out targets through the iron sights of the ancient Commando carbine. I hit the ground first in a dust storm, unable to see five feet ahead of me; I just ran forward blindly, following my wrist compass to our planned rally point at the playground, shooting everything that looked fucked-up. Somewhere between the crumbling building, second-order explosions, and raining rocks and dust, I could hear Doc behind me.

"My optic's dead; what the fuck was that?" he asked from somewhere over my right shoulder.

"Small nuke!" I yelled over the background noise.

"Small, my ass!"

Doc had the cure and the coolant; now all we had to do was fight our way south, to Goliath and eventually the seaborne safety of *Solitude*.

We cut our chutes and disappeared into the tree line, leaving Atlanta forever as I held back the tears of the day's incredible loss and monumental gain.

Solitude

Day 35

The sea is unforgiving but a welcome reprieve from the dead mainland. The trip from Atlanta to *Solitude* was not filled with conversation. Doc didn't speak a mention of Billy. Our silence was sometimes punctuated by gunfire as we fought, making our best speed south with the cure container plugged into Goliath's inverter. Doc did reminisce about BUD/S Class 199, Hell Week, OEF, Afghanistan, and his miraculous escape across Pakistan when the shit hit the fan. I suppose he was just looking for a way to deal with the tragic loss of his friend. I never saw him break down, but I never followed him topside, either. Although I'd only had Checkers for a month, I did miss the loyal machine and felt that it should have been on board *Solitude*, along with Billy.

We'll make landfall in the Keys in two days. I didn't know Billy in person, but his sacrifice on that rooftop was nothing short of heroic. I feel extreme guilt for what he did to save our lives and get us off that building. Reeling from the loss of Billy and Checkers, I haven't craved meds since the rooftop. Thank you, Mitch.

I've already spoken to Tara and Bug. She was pissed! I can't say whether or not I'll be sleeping in *Solitude*'s stateroom for a week after I get back, but news of our cargo may soften the blow. John says that the excitement in the Keys is palpable and celebration planning is already under way. All the kids in the Keys are cutting up paper dollars for a ticker-tape parade.

Phoenix and Hourglass are coming home.

Day 55

KEY WEST TELEGRAPH STATION #001

DISPATCH TO KIL FROM MITCH
FRIEND OF YOURS SHOWED UP AT THE GATE TODAY.
FOUR LEGS, METAL.
COME GET YOUR DOG.
ALL THE BEST
MITCH SENDS

Acknowledgments

Ghost Run is yours. I'd like to thank each and every one of you who wanted the saga to continue. This was the last Day by Day Armageddon novel written on active duty. As I end that twenty-two-year military chapter, I begin what's next.

Would you like to come along?